KATHRYN FOXFIELD

IT'S
BEHIND
YOU

SCHOLASTIC

You know who you are.

Published in the UK by Scholastic, 2021
Euston House, 24 Eversholt Street, London, NW1 1DB
Scholastic Ireland, 89E Lagan Road, Dublin Industrial Estate,
Glasnevin, Dublin, D11 HP5F

SCHOLASTIC and associated logos are trademarks and/or
registered trademarks of Scholastic Inc.

ISBN 978 0702 30277 0

A CIP catalogue record for this book is available from the British Library.

Printed by CPI Group (UK) Ltd, Croydon, CR0 4YY
Papers used by Scholastic Children's Books are made
from wood grown in sustainable forests.

3 5 7 9 10 8 6 4 2

This is a work of fiction. Names, characters, places, incidents
and dialogues are products of the author's imagination or are used
fictitiously. Any resemblance to actual people, living or dead,
events or locales is entirely coincidental.

www.scholastic.co.uk

ONE

Extract from the transcript of the T-minus-one-day final interview with Lex Hazelton [LH], contestant 1/5 *It's Behind You: Season 3, Episode 10 (Umber Gorge Caves)*. Interviewed by Jackie Stone [JS], producer of *It's Behind You*.

JS: Tell us why you've volunteered to spend the night in a haunted cave, Lex.

LH: I don't believe in the supernatural, so it's a night in a cave and ten grand at the end.

JS: But you must be aware Umber Gorge has quite some history – strange disappearances, ghost sightings, the legend of the Puckered Maiden?

LH: The heart-eating ghost? Yeah, that's a good one.

JS: It doesn't scare you?

LH: Look, can I level with you, Jackie? We both know you've got a team of special effects nerds working behind the scenes.

JS: Actually, Lex, *It's Behind You* doesn't use tricks like other reality TV shows. Other than the challenges, everything you'll encounter in the caves will be real.

LH: My arse it will.

JS: [Sighing] I don't think you understand the purpose of this video. You want the viewers at home to root for you—

LH: No, I don't.

JS: Lex. The show has a format we have to adhere to. So if you want to take part, you need to play along.

LH: Fine. Yeah. I'm puckering up in anticipation.

JS: Maybe try to be less . . . never mind. Let's try again. We need a few sound bites we can splice in with the other contestants' videos. It's how we'll introduce you to the audience. You could tell the viewer why you're here, perhaps?

LH: All right, all right. My name's Lex and, um, do I look at the camera or at you when I talk?

JS: Stare straight into the lens and pretend you're

speaking to the people at home. Try to connect with them. Get their attention.

LH: Got it. [Sound of chair dragging as LH moves closer to the camera] I'm here because I'm ... can I swear?

JS: No.

LH: But I can get my heart eaten on TV? You're OK with cannibalism?

JS: In this instance, yes.

LH: Good to know. I'm here because I'm pucking bored. That's it.

JS: [Growling noise] You're bored?

LH: I thought the show sounded like it might be an adventure. But this interview isn't filling me with much hope.

JS: Lex, this isn't working. Let's try a different angle. [Sound of papers shuffling] All right. What does your mum think about you being here?

LH: Er, what does my mum have to do with anything?

JS: I'm just surprised she's OK with it. All things considered.

LH: All things ... ahh, I see what you're trying to do. You're trying to manipulate me into breaking down or losing my temper. But it's not going to happen.

JS: We'll see how you feel when you're locked in the caves. I've filmed a lot of contestants who are confident they'll hold it together. They never do, and it makes for some brilliant television. Why do you think I picked you?

LH: Because no one watches your show any more and you're desperate for contestants?

JS: It's a slight dip in ratings, that's all. And I am not desperate.

LH: You look desperate.

JS: Change of subject. What's your greatest fear?

LH: Bad hair days. Is the ten grand prize fund cash or cheque?

JS: Bank transfer. So you're not – I don't know – terrified of losing a loved one? You're not here because you want to know if there's more to this life than what we can see?

LH: Nope. Just the money.

JS: [Sighing] Fine. Last question. Do you think you can win?

LH: [Laughing] What kind of stupid question is that?

TWO

The evening smells like candyfloss and blood.

There's a procession making its way up the high street, towards Umber caves. The townsfolk are lit by glowing lanterns; their heads are bowed. The moon watches on from a clear sky as the rocky gorge reverently spills over with greenery. It's a beautiful scene, if you can get past the platters of pigs' hearts carried by a troupe of solemn schoolchildren.

"I think I love this town," I say.

"It's a cesspit." Veronica jiggles from foot to foot. "Seriously, Lex, we should go. If we get caught, I'll lose this gig. And you'll be disqualified. I'm meant to be keeping you out of trouble."

"Where's the fun in that?"

"I have some books on the geology of the caves back at the B & B. They're much more interesting than this nonsense."

I ignore my cowardly chaperone. All five of us contestants have someone like Veronica specifically tasked with keeping us in our respective hotels for the entirety of the annual Umber Heart Festival, so we don't meet each other or get in trouble. But the way I see it, some rules are made for breaking, and some are an all-out invitation to make mischief. This? Definitely the latter.

I peek out from the shadows of a shopfront as the locals crowd around the children. They each take a heart and toss it on to the pavement with quiet plopping sounds. Someone throws theirs a little too hard and it slaps against the cliff face, then slides slowly down into the dirt. Everyone has blood on their hands.

I laugh in horrified wonder. "Run this past me again. The hearts are . . ."

Veronica sighs dramatically, rolling her eyes so hard her little skeleton earrings dance a jig. Veronica is all skeletons, from her jewellery to the pattern on her clunky boots. It's a look that clashes with her red cheeks and golden hair. She looks like a cherub disguised as a Satan worshipper.

"The hearts are offerings to the Puckered Maiden. So she won't come out of the caves and kill any of us this year." She shifts anxiously. "Lex, please. Someone will see us."

"Why hearts?"

"Because that's what the Puckered Maiden eats. She hates people with hearts."

I'll be OK then.

"Two hundred years ago," Veronica continues, "a local woman was jilted by her fiancé and took her revenge by cutting out his heart. Before she could be brought to justice, she escaped into the caves and was never seen again. The end."

"You missed out the exciting bit where she drowns in a lake and comes back as a vengeful ghost. Love that part."

She smiles wryly. "Of course you do."

The locals abandon the cliff face and follow a path lit by lanterns and fairy lights over to the market square, where a number of long tables are set up with pot luck dishes. Everyone tucks into pies and fruit crumble as red as the splashes of blood on concrete. Someone produces a crate of unlabelled bottles. The gathering soon resembles a big family reunion, with all its bitter gossip and drunken elderly relatives.

The hearts lie forgotten in the road. "Do you locals seriously believe this nonsense?"

Veronica takes her time to answer. Her jaw is grinding as she stares across the road at the festival. When she finally speaks, her voice is oddly quiet and serious. "Lots of people have been killed in those caves."

"Were they all eaten by the Puckered Maiden?"

She pushes herself off the wall and trundles up the hill. "It's not a joke. I'll show you."

I go after her. We pick our way through the abandoned hearts and sneak around the perimeter of the party, avoiding the lights. The cave entrance stands set back from the road across the market square. Once a gaping maw in an expanse of towering rock, it's now boarded up and closed off with a metal gate for good measure. Dozens of TV vans are parked up, ready for tomorrow. I get the impression the caves are holding their stale breath in anticipation.

Next to the gate, there's a large brass plaque set into the cliff face. I use my phone as a torch to read the words. It's a memorial list of names and dates, with plenty of empty space for more to be added. The dates range all the way from the nineteenth century to just two years ago, when someone called Laurie Cox died.

"What happened to them all?"

"Cave-ins, mostly. Some got lost and never found their way out." She takes off a pair of huge glasses and cleans them on her dungaree dress. "Those caves can't be trusted, you know? They're full of secret passageways and freezing lakes."

I tap my finger on the plaque. "All of the deaths stopped in the nineties. Except for this Laurie Cox."

"The caves were closed off about thirty years ago, but teenagers still used to sneak in at night. Until a rockfall trapped three people. Two of them found their way out. Laurie Cox wasn't so lucky. She was buried under tonnes of rubble."

"Huh. Did you know her?"

8

"Everyone knows everyone in this town." Veronica crosses her arms. "Why are you asking me all these questions?"

"Trying to get an idea of what I'm dealing with."

She jabs a finger towards the party. "That's what you're dealing with."

I follow her line of sight. Producer Jackie, lit up by a thousand fairy lights and looking expensive in a tight purple dress. She's blonde, beautiful and squeaky clean, like a movie star. I'm not sure she understands not all of us want to be like her. We met in person for the first time this morning, when we recorded my "Who is Lex?" sound bites. To say we hit it off would be a lie of the highest order. I didn't even have to try to piss her off.

Jackie is accompanied by a cameraman and a large microphone like a fluffy rat on a stick. Filming local reactions for the show, I presume, and footage of all those scattered hearts. They'll use it to set the scene when they edit the show together.

Veronica and I duck behind one of the TV vehicles, even though we're mostly hidden in the shadows of the cliffs. I lean against the side of the van. "Way I see it, Jackie expected me to sneak out tonight," I say. "She *wants* me to see all of this and be freaked out. Except, I'm not."

Veronica grimaces. "You're not?"

"Nope. Lex Hazelton is scared of nothing."

Nearby, something hisses loudly and I jump. But it's only the brakes on a bus. Its windows reflect the lights of the party as its doors swing open and someone climbs out. A boy, slouching as he walks, like he's not used to the length of his own limbs. A black hoodie obscures his face. His tight black jeans have rips at the knee. His black boots are only half-laced.

The party stalls. Everyone stares at this boy dressed in black. People point and whisper, then fall silent. Someone who was in the middle of spooning out a bowl of crumble loses concentration and lets the mushy fruit plop on to the road. I glance at Veronica and see that she's frozen to the spot. Like her soul's flown straight out of her nose and left an empty body standing in the street.

The boy nervously glances around at his rapt audience, then shoulders his bag. But before he can move, two of the TV production company's security team hustle him into a blacked-out four-by-four. Jackie jumps in the other side and the car immediately accelerates away. It takes ten slow breaths for the party to stutter back into life. Drinks are raised once again; locals pour cream over stewed rhubarb.

"He changed his mind," Veronica whispers.

"Who was that?" I say.

"What?" She jerks, like she's waking up. "No one. Look, I've remembered I have to meet someone. You can find your own way back, right?"

She hurries away without waiting for my reply. I watch as she weaves through the street party and approaches a boy with movie-style muscles. He's wearing a tight T-shirt that digs into his biceps and he keeps smoothing the fabric over his belly, like he's checking his eight-pack is still there.

The pair of them step away from the party, heads close together. Veronica keeps gesturing in the direction of the four-by-four. Interesting. One thing about me: I'm impossibly nosy. It's a strength and curse all rolled into one. But life would be unbearable if I didn't fill it to the brim with conflict and adventure.

So it goes without saying that I'm going to follow Veronica and get in on those local secrets.

"Lex," my mum's voice warns in my head. I try to ignore her, but she's incorrigible. "Remember what happened last time?"

She's referring to my dad's affair. But come on, the way he took to obsessively trimming his eyebrow hairs was too big a red flag to ignore. I simply followed the stench of lies and musk and – bam! – there's my dad, kissing another woman in his car. That was something I didn't want to see.

Of course, when he realized I knew, he came clean to Mum and they patched things up. I lost a lot of respect for both of them after that. Some would expect me to have learned a valuable lesson from the whole experience. Except I'm immune to learning lessons. So I shush my mum's voice and go after Veronica and Mr Muscles.

Only, as I cross the road, I'm nearly run over by Jackie's four-by-four. I duck behind the van again as they park up and Jackie emerges, minus the boy in black. Clicky heels

11

approach my hiding place and I make the remarkably adult decision to cut my losses and get out of here.

Besides, there's no time for drama. I need to get my head in the game. It's less than twenty-four hours until they shut us inside the caves and switch on the cameras.

I can't wait.

THREE

The sounds of merriment fade as I wander down through the town. I have to admit that, in the low light, Umber is pretty, with its ornate lamp posts and cobbled pavements. There's a quaint little tea room with dolls in the window and a watermill like something off a postcard. There are less than a dozen shops, all with old-fashioned swinging signs and frilly curtains.

My mum would call it "chocolate box", and she'd buy a watercolour print for the house. I can imagine it hanging on top of the flowery wallpaper in our living room, in a frame that's dusted daily. "That's Umber Gorge," Mum would say. "The most delightful little town we discovered on our holidays."

The thing is, when you look more closely, you start to notice the rot.

The shopfronts are a collage of mouldy wood and cracking paint. A stagnant aroma drifts up from the water. The main road on which I'm walking cuts the town in half and provides a straight run to places elsewhere. It's as if the builders had expected visitors to think "no way" and keep on going as fast as possible.

And the Puckered Maiden and her taste-for-human-hearts thing? Well, that's just freaky.

I stop walking. Glance over my shoulder. I'm sure I heard something, only the road is empty. In the distance, I can see the party, but my part of town is deserted. Affecting a swagger, I walk on. Like a spy, I keep looking for suspicious reflections in the shop windows, but I'm alone.

I pause outside the butcher's shop. There's a tray of shrivelling pigs' hearts sitting in a poorly lit bay window. Next to them rests a doll wearing a filthy wedding dress. She's as pale as one-dip tea, with peeling skin three sizes too large for her skeleton and a split-faced grin full of teeth. A sign propped up next to her reads: THE PUCKERED MAIDEN WELCOMES YOU TO UMBER GORGE. I'm not sure if this is a greeting or a threat.

"Good to meet you," I say, pretending to lift a hat as I bow.

I walk closer to the window, so my reflection stands next to the Puckered Maiden. In my dark suit over a T-shirt,

I could be the groom to her bride. My complexion isn't much healthier than hers but at least my skin fits. My hair is going flat, though. I fuss with my quiff, making it stand up straighter. The damp air is turning it floppy, as if the town's ennui is catching.

The reflections shift. A shadow peels itself out of the darkness and straightens up into a figure. I freeze with my hands still styling my hair. The figure drifts closer as if floating an inch above the ground. Its arms stretch towards me. Crap, now I'm in trouble. Think, Lex, think. I jump around into a fighting stance, with my fists raised.

It's no ghost or monster or whatever.

Instead, it's an extremely old lady with a lace skullcap on that makes it look like her brains are exposed. She's literally the oldest person I've ever seen. Like, *has a hundred and four great-grandchildren and hates them all* old. *Eats smoked fish and enjoys it* old. I lower my hands with a roll of my eyes. The woman spits a glob of saliva on to the road. Gross.

"Your kind aren't welcome here," she snarls.

"My kind?" I'm not sure what she's referring to. Outsiders in general or people who still have a pulse?

"They're my caves and your sleazy little show needs to go back where it came from."

Ah. TV people. She has a point. I'm presuming she's met Producer Jackie.

Oldie McOldFace, as I shall now call her, bares her gums at me. Literally no teeth in that mouth of hers. "Or else," she adds.

I bite my fist in fake terror. "I'm so scared. What you gonna do?"

"Last time a bunch of teenagers went into them caves, one never came back out." She smiles wickedly. "Maybe the Puckered Maiden got them. Maybe she'll get you too."

Then she's off, scuttling up the road with surprising sprightliness, looking pleased with herself. You'd think the locals would be happy to have a production company bringing some revenue into this toenail of a town. Clearly not. And what was Oldie McOldFace talking about when she said "my caves"?

I continue down the hill towards my B & B. Simply Gorgeous, as it's called, is run by Veronica's mother, a woman who has rules for how many sheets of loo roll her guests are allowed to use. She's filled her entire house – and I mean the entire thing – with china dolls she never dusts.

I sneak in through the dining room window, expecting it to be empty. Only it's not. One of my fellow inmates is sitting in the dark, drinking from one of the unlabelled bottles I saw at the party. The air smells like the school science lab. A single spark could turn us all into Guy Fawkes Night.

The man glances at me, one of my legs through the sash window and my other still outside. It's Cameraman Carl – a bleary-eyed man in his thirties, whose beard reminds me of a bird's nest. He's the only other human joining us in the caves. Most of the action will be picked up by the static cameras, but he needs to be there to capture the close-ups of our snotty, sobbing faces.

He grunts and goes back to the bottle. I take this as agreement he won't tell Jackie about my evening out if I don't annoy him by trying to strike up conversation. I salute him and commando roll out of the room. The wooden floorboards make a worrying cracking noise, as does my hip. Won't be doing that again. I dust myself off. A hallway of creepy dolls stare at me in disapproval.

"You're all jealous," I say, sneaking up the creaky stairs.

The landing leads on to a dark corridor with low beams and a carpet that's peeling up from the corners. There are four rooms on this floor. Three guest bedrooms – occupied by me, Cameraman Carl and some guy from Sound – as well as a shared bathroom. Veronica and her mum sleep in the converted attic, up another flight of stairs.

My room is number three, although someone has recently tried to glue a one in front to make an unlucky thirteen. Jackie, probably. I unlock the door and shove it open. The room is tiny, making me feel like I'm living in a child's playhouse. There are dolls on every grimy surface. Some are sitting there; others languish in old prams rammed into the spaces between the bed and a single chest of drawers and the wash sink.

I weave through the junk and flop down on the bed. I should sleep, but I'm too wired. So, instead, I revisit a top ten *It's Behind You* moments video on my phone. The show is a simple format. Five strangers locked in a supposedly haunted location overnight. The production company throw in a few challenges but mostly leave the contestants to freak themselves out in the dark. A reality TV version of those haunted location shows that were popular way back. Anyone who lasts until morning gets a share of ten grand, boom.

"Number ten," the annoying voice-over declares. *"Edinburgh tunnels."*

A group of people are huddled together in the darkness, their terrified faces green in the night-vision video. Someone points at a shadow as it flits past the end of the tunnel. The group scream, clambering over each other to escape. The video rewinds and freezes to show us a zoomed-in close-up of the shadow. It's vaguely person-shaped with glowing white eyes. If you squint.

"Could it be the ghost of a PLAGUE victim, bricked up beneath the city for ALL eternity?" the commentary asks.

"Unlikely," I mutter.

I remember this episode. Not because I watched it, but because it's the one that got everyone talking about *It's Behind You*. The creature in the tunnels was on the news, in the paper and even got its own meme. Even today, people still post the frozen image captioned with: "Oh hellooo there!"

I scroll through the comments. There are tens of thousands. *It's Behind You* still has a considerable fan base despite plummeting viewing figures. Some comments are arguing about the order of top ten, while others are sharing

18

banal scary experiences. There are in-jokes, too. People keeping commenting "BABES!" for some reason.

"*Number nine. Redmire Pool, and one of the CREEPIEST moments from season two.*"

The contestants are sitting by a lake. One of them films the others playing a game of Never Have I Ever on a handheld camera. Suddenly, a girl starts to scream. She leaps to her feet, swatting at her arms and legs and tearing at her clothes. The others soon join her and the soundtrack becomes a cacophony of cries. The person with the camera drops it and it falls into the lake.

"*Later,*" the commentary whispers, "*the contestants would find themselves COVERED in scratches. Whatever presence lurks beneath the still surface of the water, it did NOT want them there.*"

"Ants," I say. "It was ants."

I've already watched this episode. It came at the end of season two, when the novelty of the show's format had begun to wear off and the producers started picking increasingly irritating contestants in an effort to keep things fresh and interesting. The show's become a joke, if you ask me. Like most reality TV once you get past the initial season.

Yes, I realize entering a show I don't like is kind of dumb, but I am literally only in it for the money. And to piss off my parents.

I've been on TV once before. Some antiques programme my mum watches religiously came to town, so my friend

19

and I went down to interfere with the filming. All the onlookers had clustered around one table where an antique carriage clock was getting its five minutes of fame with the presenters. If you watch the episode closely, you'll spot me in the background of the shot, tweaking the nipple of a marble Aphrodite statue.

My normally unflappable mum didn't talk to me for three days. It took a while for me to get to the bottom of her distress. I'd embarrassed her in front of her friends. Didn't I care about appearances? Ha! It's those same *appearances* I'm running from by taking part in *It's Behind You*.

See, caring about appearances is a slippery slope that ends with spending your weekends cutting the front lawn so the neighbours won't judge you, and scrubbing the toilets on your hands and knees in case the Tesco delivery driver randomly needs a wee. It's hiding your husband's affair and sticking around in a loveless marriage because you don't want people thinking you've failed. Hell, it's marrying my dad in the first place because you were thirty years old and worried you'd end up alone.

Me, though? I'm going to be alone for ever. No one's going to drag me down but myself.

"*If there's one thing MORE exciting than ghosts*," the video says, "*it's lurve.*"

"Bleugh," I say, pretending to gag.

"*Number eight is Sudsbury Hall, where it wasn't only the spirits going BUMP in the night.*"

The video plays a night-vision clip of two contestants

fumbling in a cupboard. The commentary debates whether their hands remain above clothes or if they ventured below. I suspect this is the reason the show is still running into its third season. Viewers might have given up on seeing a ghost irrefutably disembowel someone, but there's still a possibility two or more contestants will have sex.

I leave the video playing and go over to the window. The quiet streets are eerie in the moonlight. I hear whispers of the street party, but my view is of the housing development hiding behind the main road. The fences make a complicated jigsaw of small back gardens, reminding me of where I live. All squeaking trampoline springs and BBQ smoke.

I think about my competitors, somewhere out there in crappy B & Bs of their own. I try to imagine who they are and what their weaknesses will be, but the TV people have done a good job of keeping us in the dark. So I think about that boy dressed in black, and try to decide if he's a contestant or a local or both. I make a mental note to question Veronica relentlessly when I see her tomorrow. I'll irritate the truth out of her if I have to.

I'm about to turn away when I catch sight of movement in the shadows. Down in the concreted yard behind the B & B, hiding behind the overflowing wheelie bins. A curve of a hunched shoulder. A strip of dirty fabric that's trailed through several puddles and who knows what else. The strip of fabric flaps, then it's pulled out of sight by what looks like a pale, skeletal hand.

I jump back. Shit, I've got my bedroom light on. Rookie error. I'm glowing in the dark like a human–meat vending machine. On the bed, my phone continues to play the top ten video. "*I can feel it watching us*," a girl sobs. "*It knows my name.*"

I straighten up. I'm not in the caves yet and this show is already getting the better of me. I'm imagining things, just like all those dozens of crying contestants. I eye my reflection in the mirror. "Go and look if you don't believe me," I tell myself. "Yeah? Maybe I will."

I sneak out of my room and down the stairs. Each step groans like I'm trampling on a sleeping monster. I tiptoe into the dining room. Cameraman Carl is still there, now with his forehead resting on the table. His snores are making ripples in the half-empty bottle.

I slide open the window with a loud juddering sound. The night air rushes in to greet me. I climb down on to the pavement and pad slowly around to the back of the guesthouse. Wind whistles through the rooftops, rattling the guttering and banging the lids of bins. There's my bedroom window, a bright beacon overhead.

And there are the bins where the *thing* that doesn't exist is definitely not hiding. There's no such thing as monsters: no such thing as hunched figures with long, thin fingers watching me from the shadows. I tell myself all this, but still my heart is hammering.

Something stinks. It has to be the bins: a combination of old food and rain and fox piss. But I can't help thinking about the Puckered Maiden, all rotting flesh and peeling skin. Veronica reluctantly told me she was a jilted local woman who got lost in the caves and, hundreds of years later, preys on loving couples by tearing out their hearts and eating them.

I take another step. My eyes are starting to adjust to the darkness. I can make out the hunched shape now. The dirty fabric flapping in the breeze.

I breathe out heavily. "Thank fuck for that."

It's a bin bag and a ripped strip of white plastic. The whole thing was my mind playing tricks on me.

I glance up at my bedroom window, the light beckoning me upstairs into the warmth. I climb back into the dining room, finding it silent and empty; Cameraman Carl must have dragged himself up to bed. I take the bad-tempered stairs two at a time.

A warm sense of relief hits me as I close the door into my bedroom. And then I see it.

On the bed, where I was sitting five minutes ago, there's now a doll. It's the one from the butcher's shop, with tangled hair, wrinkled skin and filthy wedding dress. I think of the scrap of dirty white fabric I saw out of the window.

Someone – something – has been in my room.

I pick the doll up. It's cold. Like, fridge cold. Like, possessed by evil cold. I quickly open my bedroom window and chuck it outside. It floats down to the ground weightlessly, as though sinking in water. I slam the window and rip the curtains closed.

From the bed, my phone is still playing videos. But not *It's Behind You* clips. It's changed. The soundtrack is now a child's nursery rhyme, sung slightly out of tune. The image is a slow-motion shot descending down a dark tunnel. The camera moves deeper and deeper into the cave. A pool of water comes into sight. The surface is still.

"Here she comes with skin so white,

Through the water, through the night.

A taste of love, then torn apart,

Here she comes to eat your heart."

I hurriedly snatch up the phone and turn off the video. I hurl it back on to the bed. I half expect it to switch itself back on, but the screen remains black. Out of the corner of my eye I catch sight of my face in the tarnished mirror over my wash sink. I'm a mess. Hollow eyes, flaring nostrils, narrow lips. I've become one of the contestants on *It's Behind You*, right after one of Jackie's tricks catches them unawares.

Jackie's tricks. My expression cracks into a grin and I laugh out loud.

"Well played, Jackie." I smooth my hair in case she's planted a camera in my room. "But it's going to take more than that to break Lex Hazelton."

Bring it on, I say. I'm scared of nothing.

FOUR

Last night, I dreamt I was drowning.

I was swimming through a narrow tunnel. My breath was running out. I clawed at the rocky walls, pulling myself through faster and faster, fighting the urge to inhale. But then skeletal fingers wrapped themselves around my ankle, and no matter how hard I kicked, I couldn't free myself.

Even now, in this bright, soulless dressing room, I can still feel the burning suffocation as I held my breath to buy another minute of life. And, with it, a crushing weight. The weight of all the things I never did. The Puckered Maiden dragged me down into death, but wasting my life was all me.

I rub my chest at the memory, then reach for another

crisp from a platter of party snacks. I have eaten far too much beige food, but I can't stop. It's not like there's anything else to do. I've been confined to a dressing room in the town hall for six hours, waiting for my turn to go through orientation, and I swear Jackie's leaving me to last on purpose.

We're meant to be accompanied by our chaperones. It's their job to ferry us between locations, filling us in on all the Umber Gorge legends and keeping us entertained slash out of trouble. Presumably hiring locals and injecting some money into the town makes up for any disruption caused by the filming. I have to admit that it's nice having someone to talk to who isn't one of the jaded and overworked producers.

Only my chaperone, Veronica, has gone AWOL. When I got up this morning, Cameraman Carl and the sound guy were finishing breakfast, but Veronica had already gone out. "Trying to impress her boss, no doubt," her mum clucked, sounding proud. Only, Veronica's not turned up for work yet. I can't help but think this has something to do with that boy in black.

I'm stuffing a chicken dipper into my mouth when Jackie barges in. I raise my eyebrows at her and gesture to the food. "Wanna neg samidge?" I ask through my mouthful.

"I'm on a juice cleanse. I've lost three stone since I was your age and it's not been easy." She laughs hysterically. "Even my own grandmother doesn't recognize me these days."

26

"Sounds like a miserable way to live," I say.

She smiles tightly. "I wish I was the sort of girl who doesn't need to worry about her appearance."

She does *not* mean this as a compliment. Holding her stare, I stuff a sausage roll into my mouth with the flat of my palm. It's a large sausage roll so it barely fits and I'm forced to chew with my mouth wide open.

"Where's Veronica?" she barks, looking disgusted.

Veronica picks this moment to poke her head around the door. She's bright red, like she's been running. She spots Jackie and winces, then ducks back out of sight.

"Still in the toilet," I say, fighting a smile. Now I know Veronica is OK, my determination to discover what she's been up to has intensified.

"Still?"

"Dodgy rhubarb crumble. It's like Mount Vesuvius in there. Lava, only it's—"

"Yes, thank you, Lex." She checks her watch. "I'll have to dock her pay."

"I'm here, I'm here," Veronica says, bursting in. She smiles and pretends like she's not trying to catch her breath. "I feel much better now."

Jackie stares between us. "Something's going on. Cut it out." She swishes out of the door with her heels clicking on the linoleum.

Veronica falls into step at my side as I follow Jackie. "Thanks for covering for me in the most disgusting way possible."

"I may still drop you in it. Where've you been? I thought you were meant to keep me company."

"Nuh-uh. I'm meant to keep you out of trouble. There's a big difference."

"I could have done with some backup when Jackie, mistress of the devil, started trying to neg me." I smooth down my jacket. "Unfortunately for her, I'm un-neggable."

I think back to my first week at sixth form college, and Charlie Henshaw. Charlie is one of these people who should be hot but, thanks to a shocking deficit of personality, are about as attractive as a horse's butthole. On day four, Charlie cornered me in the common room and told me how he usually only dated model-pretty girls, but my sense of humour was good. Then he flicked his hair and glanced back at his mates, smirking.

I guess I was meant to be simultaneously so flattered and ashamed that I'd agree to blow him. Instead, I ended up with a two-day suspension and he was still walking funny when I returned.

"I suspect she's trying to find your weakness, so she can exploit it for the show," Veronica says.

"I have no weaknesses. Except for chicken dippers." I rub my belly and pull a face. "I should have stopped at twenty."

Jackie takes us into the main room of the town hall. It's been set up as a hub for the production crew. The last people to rent the space must have used it for a kid's birthday party; there are still balloon strings tied to the light fittings. We plonk ourselves into plastic chairs for my health and safety orientation. Mr Health and Mr Safety – I didn't listen to their real names – clearly take their job very seriously.

"It's our job to keep you safe," the two men say in unison.

"Caves are dangerous places, even when all the rules are followed," Mr Safety continues.

"With that in mind, we need to brief you on the exit strategy and what will happen in the event of an emergency. If you'd please turn your attention to this slide show." Mr Health takes out a laser pointer.

I sigh inwardly as the two men take me through a map of the cave system, on which they've marked all the potential hazards.

"There are more than twenty known caverns arranged across more than a square mile horizontally and half a mile vertically. Many are connected by tunnels excavated in the nineteenth century, which in itself presents challenges from a health and safety perspective."

When Mr Health pauses to take a breath, Mr Safety continues where he left off. "As you can see on the map, many of the deeper caves were rendered impassable by a recent cave-in that resulted in one fatality. Filming will be confined to the six caves closest to the entrance, which have recently been subjected to a thorough survey."

Mr Health flicks through the papers on his clipboard. "Jackie has the survey paperwork, but if you wanted to view the results you could speak to her."

"I will definitely do that," I say. "Love a thorough survey."

"This isn't a joke. I also have some forms that you will need to sign agreeing that you will not venture out of the approved caves." Mr Safety produces a thick folder of paperwork specifying dozens of don'ts. Don't climb the lighting scaffolds, don't go in the water, don't lick the walls. Don't, don't, don't.

Finally, the two men switch on a pre-recorded video about what to do in the event of a fire and leave us to watch it. I lean over to whisper to Veronica. "I didn't save your ass for purely altruistic reasons."

She stills. "Oh?"

I wait a beat before I answer. "I need you to help me sneak some contraband into the cave. Jackie took my phone this morning, so I'll need a torch. And a multitool penknife just in case and, most importantly, there's a bag on my bed if you can get it into the car."

She relaxes slightly. "Depends what's in the bag?"

"My Jackie-approved outfit blends into the background a little more than I would like. But there'll be nothing they can do if I change right before filming starts."

"I don't know. I'm not big on rule-breaking."

"I won't mention your name. Promise."

"OK. But I better not get fired. I'm getting a hundred quid for this job and I'm saving up for some new textbooks."

"Wow, a whole one hundred pounds? You're clearly in it for the money!"

Her gaze drops out of focus and she goes quiet for a moment, then she blinks and comes back. "My mum fixed it for me. It's something to do."

The fire video finishes. "Any final questions?" Mr Health asks, switching the monitor off at the plug.

"Yeah," I say. "What if a ghost attacks me? A real one, I mean."

The two men walk off without answering. Jackie bustles over, smiling like a shark wearing lipstick.

"Before we get you over to Sound, are you all set on your in-cave persona?" she asks.

"My what-what?"

She sighs. "We discussed this on the phone, Lex. We encourage contestants to come up with a few set pieces that showcase their personalities. A calling card."

"That thing about me being the comedic relief? I thought it was a joke."

"Are you worried you're not funny enough?" she says innocently.

"You suggested I run into some walls, Jackie. Walls."

Veronica snorts, then tries to disguise it as a cough.

"I thought that would be very funny," Jackie sniffs. "But hey-ho. Listen, I have a favour to ask. There's going to be a couple of contestants who I am sure will hit it off. It would be amazing if you could act as a sounding board for them. You could even do a bit of matchmaking."

Is she serious? I lean in close. "*I'm* the one who gets the boys and girls. I'm nobody's sidekick."

Jackie grumbles something under her breath, then pointedly looks me up and down. "There are some big characters in this episode, with camera-friendly ... personalities."

"Just say pretty people if that's what you mean."

"Their stories are stronger than yours. You're here to make up numbers, if I'm being honest, and I doubt the final cut will include much of your footage."

"We'll see about that." I fold my arms and stare her down.

"You know what," Veronica interjects. "Why don't Lex and I discuss this on our way to Sound?"

Jackie checks her watch. "Yeah. Fine, I have to visit some, um, locals. And you have to be over the road in exactly twelve minutes."

I wait until we're out of the room to raise an eyebrow at Veronica. "You're sucking up to the boss."

"She knows I skipped work this morning, I can see it in her evil little eyes. Come on, if we're quick there'll be time for ice cream."

FIVE

We walk up the high street towards the caves. The locals are all out shopping, with their wheelie trollies and their upside-down smiles. As they trot in and out of the butcher's and the greengrocer's, they glare at me. I spot Oldie McOldFace from a distance. She's blocking the road and waving a placard that reads GET LOST. A crew lorry is holding down its horn but she refuses to get out of its way.

Veronica spots the woman and rapidly changes direction, crossing the road to avoid her. The woman notices Veronica and turns a full circle to stare at us.

"Who's the old lady?" I say.

"Sally-Ann Kingston," Veronica replies. "She's trouble."

"I take it she's not happy about the show."

"And other things." She stops at the ice cream hatch on the side of the cafe and rings a countertop bell. "Sally-Ann's family – the Kingstons – were the ones who excavated the caves back in the nineteenth century. The caves stayed in the family until thirty years ago, when Sally-Ann lost them in a bet."

"Thirty years is a long time to hold a grudge."

"She claims the caves still belong to her family. The man who won them from her – Mortimer Monk – tried to turn them into a tourist attraction in the nineties. He called it the Puckered Maiden Experience and was kitting it out like a museum-cum-haunted-house. Sally-Ann's interference was part of the reason he walked away from the project."

"Part of the reason?"

She fights a smile. "That, and the contractors all quit because they claimed the Puckered Maiden was smashing up the exhibits and stalking them from the shadows. What flavour ice cream do you want?"

We take our ice creams up to the caves to find the audio truck, so I can be fitted with a mic and shown how to use it. The caves are open now and the gate lies in a nearby skip. A few workmen are fitting a new door that will be used to seal us in. It's a reinforced metal monstrosity, more for appearances than anything. If we want out, we only have to knock and shout: "It's behind me!"

There are dozens of crew members carrying box after box of equipment into the caves. Cameras and lighting rigs and microphones. Everything will be powered by one of several large, greasy generators. They're juddering away behind a couple of vans, with wires snaking off in every direction, held down by plastic mats muddy with boot prints. An oil-smeared woman is bashing one of the generators with a torque wrench. I'm not sure if she's trying to repair it or if she's had enough of its nonsense.

We're intercepted by an official-looking man with a clipboard and walkie-talkie, who hustles me away, complaining about schedules. The man knocks on the door of the Sound lorry but we're refused entry for having ice cream with us. Instead, we sit on a bench and watch the caves.

I spot a familiar figure carrying a metal case with wheels and a handle. The muscly boy who I saw Veronica speaking to last night. He should be pulling the case, not carrying it; I can see some of the more weathered crew members shaking their heads at him. He's oblivious. Or showing off.

"Who's the Neanderthal?" I say.

Veronica frowns mid-lick. She plays with a skeleton earring. Then she sighs softly. "Ben."

"Do you have a *thing* for him?"

She turns to me in surprise. "What's wrong with him?"

"Oh, nothing. If you like boys who look like prize bulls dressed in human clothes." I make a low mooing noise.

Veronica laughs. "I don't have a thing for him. We're friends, that's all."

I put on a sympathetic, syrupy voice. "You sure? Because I could play matchmaker?"

35

She grins. "I can't believe Jackie thought she could cast you as the supportive friend. No offence."

"What Jackie fails to understand is that I'm the star of this show, not a secondary character."

"I'm sure she'll edit the footage to make you look how she wants. Once someone makes up their mind about you, it's hard to make them see you any differently." She's watching Ben as she speaks. I don't think she's talking about Jackie any more.

"You should go for it," I tell her. "And if he rejects you, we kill him. Make it look like the Puckered Maiden got him."

Her eyes widen. "Lex!"

"Veronica!"

"You can't say things like that round here. And I already said there's nothing between us." She crunches a bite out of her cone. It breaks and a dribble of melted sorbet runs down her chin.

"So you'll be totally fine that he's walking over right now," I say.

Veronica panics and wipes her mouth on her sleeve. "Hey," she says, but her voice comes out as a deep growl. She clears her throat and goes red.

"What's up?" Ben says. "Didn't expect to bump into you, Ronnie."

She opens her mouth but doesn't speak.

"I'm Lex," I say, leaning across Veronica. "The winner of this show."

Ben barely notices me, which is a first. He continues to stare at Veronica. "You didn't mention working for the TV show last night. I'm wracking my brains trying to understand why you'd even want to be here."

"You're here too," she says weakly.

"I need the money now Ma can't work any more. I told you weeks ago and *you* had a go at me for selling out."

She nods and keeps nodding like she's forgotten how to stop. Nod, nod, nod. He glares at her, like the hamster wheel in his head has jammed. The tension between them is as thick as tar.

This incredibly awkward moment feels like the perfect time to ask about the mystery boy from last night.

"While I have the two of you together," I say. "Who was that boy dressed in black who arrived on the last bus? He seemed to create quite a stir."

They both slowly turn to me. Veronica's cheeks flush even redder and Ben's nostrils flare. I grin at them and eagerly lick the side of my ice cream cone to catch a drip.

"He's no one," Veronica says.

"Someone who we went to school with," Ben adds. "He moved away a year ago."

"Is he here because of the show?" I ask.

"I don't know why he's here." Ben's a terrible liar. He runs a hand across his face and glances over his shoulder at the caves. He's lost in thought for a few moments, then he shakes it off. "I have to get back to work. We'll talk later, Ronnie."

He walks away. We finish our ice creams in silence.

Veronica keeps eyeing me when she thinks I'm not looking. She's trying to work me out. Trying to understand why I've been sticking my nose into her small-town secrets. I pretend I haven't noticed as I crunch through the last of the cone and wipe my mouth.

"Thanks for the ice cream," I say.

"It's all really boring," Veronica says. "I know you think there's some drama here, but it's nothing."

"Sure," I say, smiling at her.

"The three of us were friends, years ago." I note the *were*. "But I suppose we grew apart. No dark secrets. Sorry to disappoint."

"OK." I shrug like I don't care.

She sighs deeply. "Liam told us he'd changed his mind about coming to visit this weekend. That's why we were surprised."

As stories go, it's not exactly convincing. Then, as we head over to the Sound truck, she nudges me in the ribs. "I'm going to dedicate the whole afternoon to making sure you have everything you need for the show. Whatever you want."

I nudge her back, grinning. No one tries this hard unless they have something to hide.

SIX

It's the final countdown.

Us five contestants are waiting in separate blacked-out hearses, still hidden away from each other. Out of one window, Veronica and I can see four cars parked up in front of mine. Out of the other, there's a decent view of the cave entrance and all the final preparations. It's a military operation involving close to a hundred people.

Huge spotlights the size of small cars bathe the evening in blinding white light. A winding path of lanterns is arranged to mark the route we'll take from the cars to the caves. There are cameras everywhere to catch our entrances from every possible angle, as well as a roving cameraman who pushes his camera on a wheeled trolley.

Sound engineers shout into walkie-talkies; crew point and scribble on their clipboards.

Something slams against my window. I recoil in surprise and Veronica screams. A face comes into view. Sally-Ann! She's remade her sign and it now reads FUCK OFF, painted in what looks like blood. Nice touch. She's baring her teeth in a way that makes her look rabid. She's accompanied by a large group of bedraggled townsfolk, also with unfriendly signs.

"She's rounded up some more protestors." Veronica anxiously smooths her dress. It's a 1950s-style number with a tight top section and a big swingy skirt that comes down to her knees. There are little skulls all over it, to match her earrings.

"We don't want your money," someone screams.

"Our caves aren't for you," someone else yells. "The Puckered Maiden is not a joke."

"Do you think they'll stop the filming?" Veronica asks. "Jackie won't risk going ahead, will she?"

I eye the security guards, lazily leaning up against the barriers, chatting and laughing. Then I peer across at the HQ truck. Jackie is standing on the steps in an hourglass green dress and fuchsia-pink spike boots. She's directing crew members to film the protest.

"You serious?" I say. "I'm surprised Jackie isn't providing the locals with burning torches and pitchforks for dramatic effect."

Veronica sighs heavily. "I'm surprised they didn't bring

their own. I hate this town. As soon as I'm done with school, I'm gone. I'm going to apply for uni somewhere no one knows me. I'm going to civil engineer my way to a new life."

"Civil engineering," I say. "You know how to live."

"Working with what I got. You?"

"Go travelling with the money I get from winning this thing."

She purses her lips in amusement but doesn't say anything.

The lights outside the caves switch on, then flicker off. Jackie is summoned over to one of the generators. My watch ticks closer and closer to eight p.m. Not long now. Veronica twitchily plays with her earrings.

"I'm going to check there's not a problem with those generators," she finally says. "I'll be right back."

The time alone gives me a chance to get my head in the game.

Obviously, I have a plan. The way I see it, the worst-case scenario will be if all five of us contestants make it through the night. Two grand isn't going to cover my travel expenses. I need all ten. So I have to ensure the others are so terrified they'll be hammering on that door to get out before the sun comes up. I check the driver in the rear-view mirror. He's watching TV on his phone. I quickly grab the bag Veronica stashed in her footwell and tuck the torch and penknife into my bra.

Then I wrestle my old clothes off and put on my new

41

outfit. My tailor-made suit is modelled on one of the ones worn by Blake Lively in that film *A Simple Favour*. God, she's hot in that film, and I'm hot in this suit, which is probably why one of Jackie's minions vetoed it earlier. It's cream with a fine grey pinstripe, paired with leather brogues. Let's see Jackie try to edit me into a supporting role. I rub my hands together. Everything is perfect.

Ten minutes later, Veronica breathlessly climbs back into the taxi and slams the door behind her. "They're still going ahead. You're going in first. You ready?"

"I'm always ready."

She looks me up and down again, and pulls a face. "Jackie will not be pleased."

"Jackie can do one. I'm not letting her cast me as the unpretty girl who's only good for comedy moments." I point at myself with both thumbs. "All of this is epic and Lex Hazelton refuses to blend into the background."

A runner taps on the window of the car. He holds up his fingers to tell me two minutes. The protestors yell insults at him, and he rolls his eyes. Excitement bubbles up inside me. Time to get this show on the road.

"You sure you want to go in there?" Veronica whispers, suddenly sounding unsure. "It could be dangerous."

"I hope so," I laugh.

"You're so weird. Just ... be careful, all right?"

"It's almost like you're worried about me."

"I'm gonna bribe the video dudes with some popcorn

42

so I can watch what you get up to. Stick to the main caves. Don't go rogue."

"Can't make any promises."

The runner opens the car door. "You're a go in ten, nine . . ."

"Lex," Veronica says, gripping my arm too tightly. "There's something I should—"

"And it's go, go, go," the runner interrupts.

Veronica releases me. There's no time to think too hard about what she was about to tell me. I swing myself out of the car and strut down the path towards the caves.

There are cameras on me from every angle, which is fine as all my angles are my best angles in this outfit. The crowd of protestors boo and hiss. I spread my arms wide, tilt my head back and soak up their attention. Call me a fame hound, but I could get used to this.

Then someone throws something at me. It slaps against my face with a burst of wet and sticky that trickles down my neck and arms. I lift my hands. Blood. Actual blood.

Someone's thrown a balloon full of blood at me. Animal, I guess, but who knows in a town like this one. In retrospect, a cream suit was an error, but maybe it will play in my favour. Security guards wrestle the balloon thrower away from the barrier. I'm amused to see it's Sally-Ann again. I hope that, when I'm a hundred and ten, I'll still be causing trouble wherever I go.

Raising a middle finger at the crowd, I spin around and continue on my way along the path. I stare down each

43

camera as I pass. The roving cameraman gets in my face, so I shove the lens away, growling in anger. It's hard to be serious though; I'm having too much fun.

Let's see Jackie try to edit this to make me look like I'm here to make up numbers. Like a *sidekick*. If I'm going to play any part in this show, it's going to be the badass troublemaker who doesn't give a damn.

SEVEN

I pose outside the caves and count to ten. Like Jackie told me to. I make the sign of the horns and stick my tongue out while the cameraman circles me. Then I throw my head back and roar, before strolling through the open door like I own the place.

The cave is instantly cold and the light drops to near-darkness. Even though my eyes haven't adjusted yet, I keep on walking. I've seen enough episodes to know how our entrances will be edited. They'll cut shots of us exiting the hearses and walking towards the door with snippets of our interviews and our nervous little faces surveying the caves for the first time. I'm not giving them anything to work with.

I take in what I can see of the tunnel. It's encircled by hundreds of bulbs that once must have hummed with electricity. Now they're all dusty and half of them are smashed like someone took a bat to them. There are old neon signs, too: big arrows put up by Mortimer Monk as part of his Puckered Maiden Experience. I imagine that, lit up, it would have had a fairground aesthetic, all tacky colours and flickering light.

I step out into the first cavern and hide my surprise with a low whistle. It's huge – as vast and as cold as a cathedral, with a tall ceiling of fang-like stalactites and what looks like a waterfall of melted ice cream running down one wall. I touch it. Solid rock, with the slightest feeling of damp to its smooth surface. The production company have lit the walls with red and purple floodlights, giving a vague sense of threat and highlighting the dark nooks and crannies. Beyond, I know, are a dozen death-trap tunnels, most of which lead nowhere.

I don't believe in ghosts but, if I did, this would totally be the sort of place they'd call home.

As my eyes adjust, I see there are shapes jutting out of the ground like rows of wonky teeth. I walk closer. They're tombstones. Simple crosses, large slabs, weeping angels, even a couple of mausoleums like creepy little houses. It's an underground graveyard. In the low light, I can't tell how far it goes on for, but there must be dozens of graves.

Something rustles behind me. It's only Cameraman Carl, extending his waist-mounted camera rig to get his close-ups. We're not allowed to talk to Cameraman Carl; we're not even meant to acknowledge his presence. He's a bit of a cult hero among *It's Behind You* fans. Back when I was researching the show, I found entire vlogs dedicated to all the times his bored, unkempt reflection sneaks into one of the episodes.

I saunter over to one of the tombstones – a tall cross – and take a closer look at the inscription. Victoria Carlisle. The name seems familiar. It takes a second to remember where I've seen it before – on the brass plaque outside.

"These are all graves of people who've died in the caves," I say.

But there's something weird about the tombstone. I tap on it with my knuckles. It's made of fibreglass, like the kind of prop you'd find in a carnival funhouse. This graveyard is part of the Puckered Maiden Experience built in the nineties. The tackiness of the props is completely at odds with the natural beauty of the cave and I'm beginning to understand why Sally-Ann disapproved of Mortimer Monk's plans.

I lean back against a tombstone and wink at Cameraman Carl. He continues to film me, most of his bearded face hidden by the bulky camera. We wait for something to happen, but nothing does. I suppose they'll make it snappy when they edit the footage. Music, multiple angles, views of the caves. Usually, they include interviews with locals about all the terrible things we might encounter. I presume Jackie will use some shots of the demonstration, too.

Finally, a projector stutters into life and a dozen images of the outside appear on the wall, distorted and shifting. Nice touch. There's a countdown in the top right corner, presumably marking the seconds until the second contestant emerges. I step closer and Cameraman Carl follows me.

The countdown hits zero. Suddenly, half of the screens are filled with movement as the next contestant erupts from his hearse. He's dressed in leopard-print leggings and a leather jacket over a sleeveless vest, like something off one of my dad's 1980s rock CDs. He's even got long dyed blonde hair, black eyeliner and pasty white skin. He looks like the sort of person who always has to be centre of everything.

"What a tosser," I say.

But I have to give it to him – he knows how to work the unimpressed audience. He's strutting and air thrusting like his life depends on it. He stares down the cameras with a perpetual grin, pointing and winking, and shaking his ass all about the place. He blows a kiss at the silent locals, basking in applause that never comes. Then he literally dances up to the door and limbos inside.

I stare open-mouthed. It was so horrible. And I have to spend the next twenty-four hours with this attention-seeking idiot. I duck behind some rocks as he rounds the corner.

"Holy fricking heck," he screams.

I remain hidden. This way, I can scope out my competition before they get to meet me. Cameraman Carl, to his credit, doesn't give me away. He keeps the camera trained on the newcomer.

"Hello?" the boy says, sounding less confident. "I saw someone come in already?"

I chuckle and press myself further into the darkness.

"Hello?" he whispers, biting his thumbnail. "Are you there?"

The projector flickers. On the wall, a third contestant is already about to enter. She steps out of her hearse. Even projected on to the bumpy wall of the cave, this girl is strikingly beautiful. She also has a picture of contestant number two on her T-shirt. I raise an eyebrow. Either they know each other or this strutting peacock of a boy is some sort of minor celebrity I've never heard of. I guess this is the romance angle Jackie's pushing. Gross.

"She's a fan, she's a fan," the boy says, jumping up and down so his bleached hair bounces with him. "I love you, *It's Behind You*. You guys are AWESOME."

The girl sashays up to the cave, making eyes at the cameras. The roving cameraman zooms in on her face. She has to be a model. No one else is that aware of how to present themselves on film. Shiny brown hair, flawless olive skin, a cute little gap between her front teeth. And then she's inside.

"BABES!" the boy screams.

The girl stops dead. "Python! Oh my gosh, what a surprise."

I peer around, thinking maybe the producers have

49

chucked in some snakes. Then I realize she's talking to the boy. A boy called . . . Python?

"I am SO happy to meet you," Python says, hugging her tightly. "I thought there'd be someone else here, but it's only us."

She smooths down the cute little cape she's wearing over that horrible T-shirt. "I'm sure there was another contestant who went in first."

"Maybe they chickened out." He glances over at Cameraman Carl but receives nothing but a stony expression in reply. "Anyhoo, we're both here and that's what matters. So, introductions. I'm Python."

"Um, I'm Marla. And I know who you are, silly! I've watched all your vlogs."

So the boy is a YouTuber. Interesting. I wonder what his thing is. Make-up tutorials, maybe. Or that weird ASMR shit where people chew food in your ear in the name of relaxation. Actually, no, he's too loud. I'm putting my money on him having some kind of fashion and lifestyle channel. I couldn't hate him more.

"And who ARE you, Marla?" he says. "Tell me everything."

"Well, I'm an actress—"

"Oh my GOSH, I knew it! You've got this creative energy I'm totally vibing off."

Scrub my previous comment. I *can* hate him more.

I'm saved from having to watch these two idiots fall in love by the arrival of the third contestant. The door opens on her hearse. It's a girl with a tight ponytail, light brown skin and a massive rucksack. Jackie told me we weren't allowed to bring anything in with us. The big lying liar.

This girl looks like she's taken full advantage of the closing-down sale of an outdoor clothing shop. She's wearing a waterproof jacket, trousers and walking boots with thick socks folded over the top. Nothing matches. The jacket's mustard yellow. The trousers are an unpleasant turquoise. The boots are pink.

She strides into the caves like she has something to prove and flips on a brief smile. "I'm Abbie," she says, already rooting through her rucksack.

"BABES!" Python screams, spreading his arms wide.

Abbie drops the bag and recoils, her eyes widening. "Whoa. Python, isn't it? I've seen your show."

"Another fan!"

Abbie hesitates, then removes a strange device from the bag. She waves it around in the air. "We have overlapping interests in the supernatural."

Python grins like this is the best day of his life. "Please tell me you're a ghost hunter?"

"Paranormal investigator," she says.

"Like, one of the ghostbusters?" Marla says, sounding unsure.

"Definitely not," Abbie says. "I'd say I am ninety per cent historian, eight per cent cynic and one per cent ghost hunter, as Python calls it."

"That's only ninety-nine," Marla says.

Abbie's lips twitch into a small smile. "Is it? You sure about that?"

Marla frowns and I can see her adding the numbers up in her head. She shakes her head. "I saw a ghost once. I woke up in the night and there was this woman on my ceiling, with all her hair dangling down over her face. When I got up in the morning, my grandmother had died. I think she came to say goodbye."

"Couldn't she have sent a nice fruit basket instead?" Python says, shuddering.

"That's interesting," Abbie says. "I've never encountered an actual ghost. Every sighting I've investigated has always had a scientific explanation."

"A ghost hunter who doesn't believe in ghosts?" Marla says.

"Paranormal investigator. And I do believe. That's the problem."

"Why's it a problem?"

Abbie doesn't answer. "If I'm going to find evidence of the spirit realm anywhere, these caves are a good bet. Did you know they've been here for millions of years? Ice Age meltwaters created these caverns by gradually wearing down the limestone into the formations we see today."

Python's face slowly cracks into a broad grin. "Some would say this place . . . rocks."

"You're so funny," Marla says, and she starts laughing like a choking donkey. She glances quickly over at Cameraman

Carl. Making sure he's catching her performance on camera.

I turn my attention back to the projected image, but there's still no sign of the final contestant. Maybe they're not coming. It doesn't matter to me. Three people will be easier to destroy than four.

I burst out of my hiding place, bellowing inhumanly and flailing my arms. Python and Marla scream and leap towards each other. Abbie throws her handheld ghost device at my head. It smacks into my forehead and I go arse over tit.

Fuck. Am I the clumsy sidekick after all?

EIGHT

"So that's definitely not real blood?" Marla says for the third time.

Marla, Python and Abbie stare down at me as I sit on the floor, next to a grave. Cameraman Carl silently films me, the unfeeling bastard.

"It's real, but it's not mine," I say, poking at the painful bump on my head.

"You look like something out of an abattoir," Python says, clutching his chest.

"There's so much blood," Marla says, her voice still shaking.

Without a mirror, I can't see the full impact of Sally-Ann's blood balloon, but I suspect it's made me look more striking than ever. Even if it has wrecked my favourite suit in the process. The shirt is sticking clammily to my skin and there's no way this fabric isn't going to stain.

"I drained a whole local pig to look like this," I say. "Fresh from the field."

Marla laughs nervously. "You're kidding."

"Am I?" I incline my head creepily as Cameraman Carl's lens circles me.

"A protestor threw it at her," Abbie says, without looking up from her ghost-hunting equipment. "Your forehead has scrambled my EMF detector."

"I have a hard head. And your reflexes are impressive."

"I work out," she murmurs. The girl has hidden depths. And the overarm throw of a professional cricketer.

I hold out a hand so Python can pull me to my feet. I wipe my palm on my thigh and he does the same. His grip is unpleasantly moist, mine bloody. "Who were you again?" I say.

"You know exactly who he is. It didn't hit you that hard," Abbie mutters.

"It's Python?" Python says, like he's talking to a three-year-old.

"A one-word name, like Pink, or Malaria?" I ask.

"Python's a YouTuber," Marla says. "He has a channel on *It's Behind You* and has reviewed every episode to date."

"I'm surprised you've not heard of me." Python winks at me. "I'm kind of famous."

"Riiighhtt," I say.

55

Now I think about it, though, I *have* heard of him. He narrated the top ten video I watched last night. I look at him more closely. He's accessorized his leggings and vest top with a star-print neckerchief, like the sort an air hostess or a rich Labrador might wear. He's wearing emo black eyeliner, which suits him, if I'm honest. But he's not my type. Too loud.

"You been on this show before?" I ask.

He laughs. "No way. I made my name mocking previous contestants. I'm going to be eaten alive in the comments."

"So why are you here now?" Abbie says, looking up from mending her EMF device. "Are you being paid to appear?"

"No," he says quickly. "*It's Behind You* never pays its contestants or uses plants. It's one of the few reality shows that doesn't script anything. Everything's real once the cameras start rolling."

I look around at the fibreglass graveyard. "Real. Right. And you avoided her question."

He shuffles uncomfortably. "I thought it might be fun, you know? To be on the other side for once."

Liar. There's a story there, I can sense it.

What about the others? Abbie's motivations are clear, but I haven't worked Marla out yet. As I watch her, I notice how every time Cameraman Carl catches her in his shot, she dips her chin and lets her long hair fall across her face. It must be exhausting to care so much about what others think of you.

"So, why are you here, Marla-the-actress?" I say.

A brief flash of panic crosses her face. "Normal reasons. The usual reasons."

"Have you acted in anything we might have seen?" Python says.

"Urgh, no," she sighs. "One could say my acting ambitions are still in the planning stage."

"So what you're saying is you're a waitress?" I say.

Abbie glances up at me again. "Is that a problem if she is? My mum's a waitress. One of her two jobs."

I raise both hands in surrender. "Just playing."

"I work in a supermarket, actually," Marla says. "But this show is going to be my big break. Jackie says she'll make me famous if I ... if I be myself."

"That's nice of her," I say. No way has Jackie told Marla to be herself. It goes against everything Jackie stands for.

"I had this audition for a cool independent horror the other week, only I lost out to some girl who already made her name on some TV talent show."

I think of the way she screamed when I jumped out at her. "I can imagine you in a horror," I say.

"Really? Wow, thanks. The casting director said I was too classically pretty to make it as the last girl," she says, matter-of-factly.

"You could TOTALLY be the last girl," Python exclaims.

"Because you think she's ugly?" I say sweetly.

"The last girl has to be a girl-next-door type who lacks

confidence," Abbie says. "Heterosexual, obviously, but mostly chaste. Not too girly. She has to be able to defeat the monsters using typically masculine skills."

"Girl next door? You're dying first, then," Python says, patting me sympathetically on the shoulder.

"I don't know about that," I say. "I think I'd stick around long enough for the audience to fall in love with me and believe I might make it. Then I'd die memorably and with style."

"You're thinking of the feisty secondary character who deserves a bigger part," Marla says. "Like Tatum Riley in *Scream*."

Abbie is still watching me. "Those character types are defined by their likability. You're defined by something else."

"Ohhh, b-URN," Python says. "Someone fetch the fire brigade, because there is a fire."

"Ha ha. But talking of *sparks* – pun totally intended – can we talk about Marla's T-shirt?" Time to move the conversation away from ripping into yours truly. "You must really love Python to have worn that thing."

Marla flushes. "Jackie got it for me after I mentioned being such a huge fan of Python's show. I'm not sure I would have worn it if I'd known he would be here. It's kind of embarrassing."

"You're rocking it, babes," he says.

"You're too sweet. It really is a dream come true meeting you."

"You two should definitely fall in love. Doesn't the Puckered Maiden eat hearts?" I say.

The moment I speak her name, the lights in the cave all flicker. A shadow flashes across the ceiling.

The lights dim, then brighten, then return to normal. I glance over at Cameraman Carl, but he has the ultimate poker face and doesn't react. The rest of us look at each other, eyes wide. Rationally, I know it's a stunt. That, or the dodgy generators. It's still kind of creepy.

Footsteps patter in the shadows, followed by a burst of laughter. I instantly imagine a child's doll: the sort with a cracked smile and staring eyes. Marla gasps.

"They're just pissing around with us," I say, forcing myself to be brave.

Python shakes his head. "They don't fake the ghost sightings on the show or even use props of their own unless it's for one of the challenges."

For someone who's obsessed with reality TV, he's extremely naive. I click my fingers at Abbie. "Give me that camera."

Sure, I have a torch, but I don't want anyone to know what a cheat I am just yet. I make sure the camera flash is switched on and advance towards the source of the noise. The others stand in a tight group, watching like the cowards they are.

I weave through the tombstones, stepping over loose rocks that once marked out the edge of a path for visitors. The cemetery feels unfinished. Some of the tombstones lie on the ground; others are still in bubble wrap. I remember Veronica telling me that the caves never opened to the public. I can see why Jackie wanted to film here. The abandoned props from the old haunted attraction are doing her job for her.

There's hardly any light at the far end of the cavern. I reach a cluster of three mausoleums arranged in a row. I don't think they're meant to be next to each other as they're all identical, down to the inscriptions above the doors that read R.I.P. HOPE. I glance back. Python gestures for me to keep moving.

I take a step into the first mausoleum and press the shutter release. The flash lights up all the dirt and grime that the empty darkness hides. The inside of the mausoleum is as fake as it gets. The walls are uneven and unpainted. It's carved from fine styrofoam propped up by a flimsy wooden frame. I move on to the second. I take another photo. There are a few cardboard boxes full of polystyrene, and an empty crisp packet.

In the third, the light flares and I spot a pale face watching me from the corner of the room.

I jump back, then compose myself. I check the photo on the camera's bright screen. It's only a doll, like the one I tossed out my bedroom window. Jackie must have bought a job lot of them. Unless it's the same doll . . .

I hurry back to the others, back to the light. "I found a creepy doll," I say. "No sign of anyone else."

"But I heard something," Marla says.

"And it heard you too," I stage-whisper. "Now it knows your name. Marla, Marla, Marla."

"Stop that," Marla says.

"She's winding you up," says Abbie.

I carry on – I can't resist. "How do you even know I'm one of the contestants? None of you saw me arrive in the caves. Maybe I've killed the real Lex and her body is lying metres away, hidden by the darkness."

Python stares at me with his mouth lolling open. Then he throws back his head in laughter and claps his hands together. "This is going to be so much FUN! Arggghh! I mean, I'm totally going to shit myself, but it will be EPIC."

Not the response I was aiming for, but at least I've unsettled Marla. Getting rid of her will be easy; I give her an hour before she's hammering on the door to get out. By then, I'll have worked out Python's and Abbie's weaknesses. The ten thousand will be mine before midnight.

At this happy thought, I can't help but laugh out loud. It comes out more supervillain than I'd anticipated and the others exchange worried looks.

"Aren't there meant to be five of us in here?" I say, clearing my throat.

I walk over to the projected images of outside on the walls. The hearses are still parked up near the local protestors. No one else has emerged yet, and it's been a long time. I think I see something darting from behind the generators and disappearing underneath the Sound truck. It moves too quickly to tell if it's human or something else.

I keep staring, but nothing moves. Maybe I imagined it. The only signs of life are the protestors waving their placards.

"I can sense a presence here," Marla whispers.

"I'm not picking up any EMF fluctuations," Abbie says, glancing at her equipment. "But that doesn't mean we're alone."

"You got any holy water in that bag?" Python asks. "Or some stakes?"

Abbie wrinkles her nose. "That's vampires. Which most definitely don't exist, at least not in the blood-sucking man-bat form."

"You're very cynical for a *paranormal investigator*," I say. "Do you even believe in ghosts?"

She doesn't blink. "Of course I do, otherwise he . . . Yes. I believe. But I need to get proof."

I narrow my eyes. "What for? Why's it so important to you?"

She doesn't answer me. Instead, she takes out a leather notebook and leafs through the pages.

"How DOES one even become a ghost hunter?" Python says.

"My dad was one. He dedicated his whole life to investigating the supernatural."

"He *was*?" Marla says quietly. "Is he dead?"

"Yes. He is." She tosses her notebook back into the bag and zips it up. "Is this show ever going to start?"

Outside, it's still quiet. The cameras all record nothing

but the empty square and silent hearses. "There was a problem with the power earlier," Marla says. "When I was down for my mic orientation, the generator kept packing up. Maybe that's why there's a delay."

I look up at the scaffolding with all its cameras and colourful lights, thinking how we're one dodgy generator away from pitch blackness. I didn't get it before, when I watched those top ten moments, with people screaming and sobbing and begging to leave. Don't get me wrong: I won't be doing those things. But now I understand why some people do.

Finally, I spot movement. A person, pushing through the small crowd of protestors. They're intercepted by Jackie. Then the security guards open a gap in the fence to let them through and they make their way down the path towards the caves.

They're not bothering to perform for the cameras, but they don't have to. Just the way they walk is menacing.

It's a boy, dressed in ripped black jeans and a black hoodie. The boy from the bus.

My face breaks into a grin. I can't wait for this show to begin.

NINE

Extract from the transcript of the T–minus–one–day final interview with Liam West [LW], contestant 2/5 *It's Behind You: Season 3, Episode 10 (Umber Gorge Caves)*. Interviewed by Jackie Stone [JS], producer of *It's Behind You*.

JS: Welcome to *It's Behind You*, Liam. I wasn't sure you were going to turn up. Is there anything you want to tell me about before we start recording your sound bites?

LW: No. Sorry. I got caught up with a family thing.

JS: Nothing to do with the show, then? Or Umber Gorge caves?

LW: No. I've never been here before.

JS: Who'd want to! Oh, let me move that light before it falls and crushes you flat as a pancake. [Laughing]

LW: Yeah. Thanks. That would be the opposite of great.

JS: It would be, all things considered. Well then. Let's get started with an easy question. What's your biggest fear?

LW: Um, I've not been a big fan of clowns since I watched *IT* as a kid ... You're totally going to use this against me, aren't you? I should have said kittens. It's kittens. I'm terrified of kittens.

JS: There are scarier things in those caves than clowns. Or kittens. Have you heard the story of the Puckered Maiden?

LW: Um. No. Who's she?

JS: Really? Well, she's a local ghost said to eat the heart of anyone who gets lost in the caves.

LW: Man, that's gnarly. I'm in so much trouble.

JS: Are you a fan of scary things, Liam?

LW: My friends rip me 'cause I always hide behind a cushion when there's a horror on. But I love it. It's all fun, right?

JS: Let's talk about heroes, Liam. In the films, there's always a character who rises to the challenge of being a hero. Would you say that's you?

LW: Ha, no. I'm more a run away screaming kind of guy.

65

JS: What if one of the other contestants gets into trouble in the caves? Would you run away then, or would you try to help them?

LW: . . .

JS: Liam?

LW: Sorry, I was thinking about something. Um, I couldn't leave someone behind, so I'd have to try to help.

JS: Has something upset you, Liam?

LW: Nah, I'm good. Still thinking about that Puckered Maiden thing and wondering if I've made a terrible, terrible mistake applying. [Laughing]

JS: Why did you apply?

LW: The money. And the glory.

JS: All right, well, I think we've got some great material here, Liam. Before we finish, there is one more thing you should be aware of. A couple of years ago, a local girl disappeared in those caves and her body was never found.

LW: Um, OK?

JS: Some believe she was crushed to death. Others say the Puckered Maiden took her. I just wondered if you believe in ghosts, Liam?

LW: When people die, that's it. They're gone. So no, I don't believe in ghosts. We done now?

TEN

The reinforced doors close behind the new boy and the electromagnetic lock clunks, sealing us inside. I rub my hands together. The game is afoot.

Cameraman Carl scurries over to the entry tunnel to film our latest addition as he walks in. The boy rounds the corner and spots the rest of us eagerly awaiting his arrival like groupies outside the stage door. He stops. I can't make out his face, as it's hidden by his hood and all the shadows, but I'm imagining Brooding and Scowling and Bad Boy.

He drops the hood. And he is *not* what I was expecting.

The boy is tall, with warm brown skin, spiky curls and thick-rimmed glasses. He's got this smart geeky guy look going on. He grins at us and it's the brightest thing I've seen this side of a toothpaste advert. I feel my cheeks flush.

The smile falters when he spots me. "What's with the bloodbath?"

"We don't talk about that," Marla mutters. "It will only encourage her."

"So who ARE you?" says Python. "You can call me Python, because that's my name."

"Liam." He shakes Python's hand and pulls him into a one-armed hug.

"A HUGGER! You're late to the party, but we're going to forgive you," Python says.

"I like to make an entrance," Liam laughs.

Marla air hugs and air kisses him. It's a complex ballet that involves getting very close but not touching. "I'm Marla. This is Abbie. And I think that's Lex over there."

"The one and only." I salute him and lean back against the wall. "What brings you here, Liam?"

He stuffs his hands in his pockets. "Nothing better to do than get myself eaten by a local monster. All of you?"

"I have a YouTube channel all about *It's Behind You*," Python says. "I'm here to experience it first-hand. The lovely Marla is an actress who is going to be a NAME after this. Abbie's a paranormal investigator, looking for ACTUAL ghosts and Lex is a . . . something."

"You from round here?" I ask.

Liam frowns at me, then glances at Cameraman Carl. "Nah. I'm from the other side of the country," he says.

Interesting. Veronica's already told me that Liam grew

68

up in Umber. So why is he lying and who is he lying to – us or the cameras?

He flashes me that thousand-watt smile. "There a reason you're soaked in blood?"

"Why not?"

"No judgement here. So ... any guesses what the first task's going to be? And which of us is going to publicly humiliate themselves by crying on TV?"

At this, Cameraman Carl snorts quietly. It's the first time I've seen the smallest sign of him being human.

"It's totally going to be me," Python says.

There's a crackling noise, like an old film starting up. We all turn towards the sound. The projected images on the wall are going out. They flare into white brightness, one by one, as if an explosion of light has washed away the whole set, the way a nuclear bomb goes off in a movie. The ground rumbles beneath my feet and something slams against the reinforced door hard enough that the noise echoes through the whole cave.

We're all left staring at crackling static and then a blank wall.

"Er, what happened?" Python asks.

"That felt like an earthquake or something," Marla says.

"The vibrations are off the scale," says Abbie, checking her device.

"It's got to be part of the show, right?" Marla says. We all turn to Cameraman Carl. He continues to film us, his face expressionless.

The cave lights sputter out, then swell back to life. They flicker on and off like dying moths. We all stay still, as if that's going to stop us from being plunged into absolute darkness. After a few tense seconds, the lights return to normal.

"Uh-oh, we're in trouble," Python sings tunelessly.

"Maybe the generators have exploded and we're going to be locked in here for ever," I say.

It's a joke, but maybe something really has gone wrong. Maybe the whole set is burning – the trucks, the hearses, Jackie – and we'll know nothing of it until twenty-four hours comes and goes, and no one appears to release us.

No, I think. The whole point of this show is they try to scare us. And they're doing just that.

There's a knot of nervous anticipation in my belly. It's like the butterflies I get when something bad happens. A while back, a neighbour's house was struck by lightning, and it wasn't like I wanted anyone to be hurt, but part of me was excited.

I remember telling my mum all about the searing brightness and the stench of burning. I couldn't keep the waver out of my voice. She thought I was upset, but it wasn't that, not exactly. It had made me feel alive, knowing how close someone else had been to death. Screwed up, right? Of course, when someone I care about is in danger, the feeling's different. But I don't want to think about that.

"They're messing with us," Liam says, pretending to

wipe his brow and flick the sweat away. "See, the lights are fine now."

At this, the lights go out completely. This time, they don't come back on.

"Ahh, shit," Liam sighs.

Someone screams. I'm not sure if it's Marla or Python. Amateurs. Once you let that first scream out, there's no going back. That's why, whenever something remotely troubling enters my mind, I shut it down. Pretend it isn't happening and distract myself by going for a run, making a joke, or entering a stupid TV show.

So now, instead of panicking, I let the darkness swallow me up and I tell myself I'm absolutely fine. I dig out the torch I smuggled into the cave and creep up behind the nearest heavy breather. They're on the verge of hyperventilating. I wait until they stop turning in nervous little circles and then I roar like a monster.

Whoever it is loses. Their. Shit. Think flailing and falling and shrieking. I flick on the torch and point it down at Marla, curled up in a foetal position at my feet.

"Some horror fan you are," I say. "You wouldn't make it out of the first act."

She unfurls herself like one of those acting exercises where you pretend to be an acorn growing into a mighty tree. Except Marla grows into a demon, with her hair tangled over her face and her chest heaving in ragged gasps.

"Don't . . . you . . . say . . . that," she wheezes. "You total, utter BITCH!"

71

She screams the last part and it's enough to make me recoil. I laugh nervously. "Wow, that was unexpected."

She squashes the demon back down. "That was mean, Lex," she growls, and I can hear the threat in her voice.

"I'm picking up some serious vibrations now." Abbie squints at the illuminated screen on one of her devices. She doesn't seem remotely bothered by the power cut. If anything, she sounds excited.

It's going to be hard to break her.

I head for the tunnel through into the next cavern. Everyone has to follow me or stand around in the darkness. Mwah ha ha. I am the queen of the torch.

"What if something's gone wrong?" Marla pleads.

"Knock on the door if you're worried."

Marla makes an exasperated noise, like she's not used to not getting her own way. She continues to follow me.

I weave through the tombstones until they abruptly end. The last one belongs to a man who died in 1991. Ted Kingston. Another of the names from the plaque. The only tombstone missing is Laurie Cox's, but I suppose she died long after these fake graves were installed.

The tunnel is blocked off by a metal gate with an old-fashioned lock.

"This is the first challenge! There'll be a key somewhere," Python says, jiggling on the spot.

I hold the torch in my mouth. There's a piece of paper tied to the thick bars. I turn it around to read the words on one side. "The first victim."

"The first grave!" Python sets off across the cave at a run. There's an "oof" as he collides with one of the tombstones. "I'm good. Come on, Torchbearer of the Light."

I stroll after him and helpfully prop my torch up on a neighbouring tombstone so he can examine the first. It's for a woman called Sophia Kingston, who died in the mid-nineteenth century. There's nothing on the fake cross or around the grave that could hold a key, though, and the ground looks way too hard to dig.

"Maybe it's buried," I say.

"You're right!" He starts scrabbling at the ground with his bare hands.

While Python futilely scratches at the hard ground, trying to dig a hole, I lean back against the neighbouring tombstone. Victoria Carlisle again. There's a dead rat curled up round the back, semi-preserved by the cool temperature of the caves.

I spot something. Hanging on one corner of Victoria's tombstone is a thin piece of string. And there's a key on the end. An idea takes root. Checking no one is looking, I kick the rat out of its hiding place. It's flat on one side and its fur is matted.

"People, are we sure this Sophia was the first victim?" I say.

"Sophia Kingston wasn't a victim," Abbie says. "She was the local woman who disappeared into these caves after murdering the man who rejected her."

"The Puckered Maiden," Marla whispers.

No way. Kingston. That means Sally-Ann is a living descendant of the Puckered Maiden. No wonder she's so eccentric.

"So who was the first victim?" Python stops digging. The hole he's made is less than a millimetre deep. He glances over at Victoria's grave. Then his eyes fall on to the rat.

"I think the key's hidden inside the rat," I whisper.

Python shuffles closer and reaches out a finger to tentatively poke the corpse. "It's REAL!" he squeals.

"Here." I take the penknife out of my bra and open the scissor tool. "Cut its head off."

Cameraman Carl shifts position and follows Python's shaking hand as he lowers the scissors towards the rat. I try to fight a smile but it's impossible. Across the torchlit space, Liam is staring at me with his mouth hanging open.

"Stop that," Abbie says, reaching down to pluck the scissors from Python's hand. "The key's hanging on the tombstone behind Lex."

"Oh, is it?" I say, taking back my penknife. "I didn't see that there."

I whistle cheerily and swing the key as I make my way back to the gate. *Hi ho, hi ho*. Behind me, the others are grumbling about how evil I am, and it's music to my ears.

I unlock the gate and duck into the narrow tunnel. The bobbing torch lights up slashes of the imposing walls that surround us on every side. There are bundles of wires hanging from the ceiling where the neon lights were never hooked up.

There isn't much room. Sharp rocks protrude towards us and, in places, we have to duck low when the roof suddenly dips. My feet splash in puddles. My arms brush against wet stone. When I manage to trip on a large stalagmite growing in a bulbous mound on the floor, Abbie tells me it is hundreds of thousands of years old.

We emerge into a cave. It feels gigantic, with an airy sense of openness and a fresh, earthy scent. There's a tapping noise, like a wind chime but less melodic. I sweep the torch light around in a circle. On the way past, it briefly catches something flapping like washing on a line. Dirty white fabric and matted hair.

The Puckered Maiden.

ELEVEN

My heart hurls itself into my throat, like it's offering itself up to the Puckered Maiden. I wildly flick the torch around, but I can't find the *thing*. I know it's there, metres away, no doubt getting closer and closer. But all the torch illuminates is cold stone and dusty air that sparkles in the light. Shit, shit, shit.

Then the beam finds the flapping thing and I stumble back into Liam. There's a woman in a white dress crawling on the low ceiling, her head lolling back to stare at us. She's surrounded by bones, strung up into macabre mobiles. Femurs and tibias tap together like the wind chimes I thought I heard.

Marla screams again, but the woman isn't real, and

neither are the bones. The bones are painted styrofoam and the woman's face is moulded latex, as far as I can tell. Like the smaller doll I keep seeing, she has wrinkled skin so white it's bloodless, same as the pads of my toes if I stay in the bath too long. Her hair is long and knotted. Her mouth is open to reveal pointed teeth.

"What the hell is that?" Marla says, recovering herself.

"The Puckered Maiden herself," Abbie says.

I shine my torch past the dummy and across the cave, but it doesn't reach far enough to see much more than a whole lot of rock. Just then, the lights suddenly surge back into life, blindingly bright after so long in darkness. I'm standing in front of what looks like a street of quarter-size houses that slope down steeply away from us. An underground town hidden away from the sunlight.

I feel both tiny in comparison with the vastness of the cavern, and god-like, surveying an entire world from above. Then the lights go off once again. The world shrinks back to a torchlit bubble that surrounds us contestants and Cameraman Carl, plus the Puckered Maiden dummy. The thought of all the things I can't see makes me shiver.

"What is this nightmare?" Python says.

"That was a reproduction of Umber," Liam replies. "The main street leading up to the caves."

"I thought you'd never been to this town before?" I tease.

"I haven't," he says quickly, glancing at Cameraman Carl. "I recognized it, that's all."

77

The lights flicker again. On, off, on, off. Jackie is having fun with us. Each time the lights come on, I expect to see a malevolent figure, jerkily moving closer and closer. But the underground town remains empty. Python squeals every time the lights go out. I consider killing him under the cover of darkness.

The boom of speakers powering up accompanies the lights coming on yet again. And this time, they stay on. We all hold our breath, waiting for the darkness to return. It doesn't. The lights fade through several colour schemes and settle on dull reds and oranges, bathing the town in artificial sunset. I click off my torch to conserve the battery.

With Cameraman Carl angling the camera towards me, I venture along the street. Like the real version, this fake Umber looks pretty from a distance. Like the real version, it's a dump when you get close. The houses are all the size of small sheds and fronted with wooden facades like something from a pantomime set. There's empty boxes and bubble wrap everywhere.

I stop at the butcher's, like I did last night. The window is painted like the real thing. The hearts are daubs of purple. A tiny Puckered Maiden sits next to them, two blobs of beige paint with grey arms and legs. There's something else there, too. I don't know if it's a discoloured patch or if it was deliberately painted on, but it looks person-shaped, like a reflection in the window. I can't help but think it looks a lot like me, standing there, checking out my hair.

"Lex, what are you doing?" Marla says. "I don't think you're meant to go there yet."

I straighten up. "It's going to be a boring episode if we all sit around doing nothing."

She stares nervously at the butcher's shop window. "I think we should wait."

Ignoring Marla's cowardice, I continue through the model town. Doors into the shops and houses are all dark holes. I imagine actors would have been employed to jump out from inside, if the Puckered Maiden Experience had ever opened. Instead, it's like everyone downed tools and walked away before the building work was finished.

We reach the end of the street. I stop next to a replica of the open square outside the entrance into the caves. In the square are two full-sized coffins. The plaques read *Tommy Brook* and *Victoria Carlisle*. A dummy version of Tommy lies in his coffin with a noose around his neck. I can see a steel mechanism that would have once made him reach out of the coffin and grab at unsuspecting passers-by. Only Tommy won't be doing anything ever again. He looks like someone has tried to destroy him with an axe. His latex skin has been hacked through to reveal the expanding foam and wire mesh beneath.

The second coffin is empty, but Victoria's dummy is lying nearby, half-hidden by a watermill. She's in nineteenth-century dress, with a hole in her chest where her heart should be. But like Tommy, she's been mutilated, great gashes across her face. As though someone attacked them both in a fit of rage.

"Who were Tommy and Victoria, I wonder?" Marla says. She speaks woodenly, like she's rehearsing a script.

"Two of the Puckered Maiden's victims?" I say. "We definitely saw Victoria's grave earlier but I don't remember a Tommy."

"Who cut them up like that?" says Python. "What if it was the Puckered Maiden?" He starts wheezing and goes a worrying shade of purple.

"For goodness' sake, breathe normally," Abbie says.

Python takes a deep, rasping breath and fans his face with a hand. "Thanks, babes, I needed that reminder."

"Don't call me babes," she replies.

"Sorry, love."

"Abbie."

"Ab-Abs?"

"Are you trying to be annoying?"

At that moment, a projector mounted on the cheese shop flares into life and colours swirl across the walls, forming themselves into the silhouettes of running figures. A soundtrack booms out of hidden speakers. It's the hum of a crowd talking. There's a sharp, rapping sound, and the voices stop.

"*Thomas Brook, thou art brought here today to answer to the charge of murder. Did thou or did thou not kill Victoria Carlisle in yonder caves, and dispose of her body so that none might know what thou hath done?*"

The language sounds like it was written by a person who was aiming for nineteenth-century speech patterns but didn't really have a clue. I'm not sure if it's the original recording from the Puckered Maiden Experience, or something Jackie has cobbled together to provide us with the caves' backstory and terror inspiration. I'm guessing it's from the museum. *It's Behind You* seems to pride itself on sending contestants into "real" haunted locations and too much obvious fakery would annoy the loyal fans.

The colours on the wall swirl again, becoming streaks of light that dart over the cavern's uneven walls. It's a trippy effect that makes it appear like the rocks are moving around us, breaking apart and re-forming into something new. The colours coalesce into two abstract people standing by the mouth of the caves. Their silhouettes waver like flames.

Another voice speaks: *"The year is 1857 and a young couple – Victoria and Tommy – are much in love. But their families have forbidden them from seeing each other."*

"So romantic," Python says, clutching a hand to his chest. "Like Romeo and Juliet, but with farmers."

"Victoria and Tommy need somewhere to meet where they won't be discovered. Somewhere quiet; somewhere secret."

Marla rolls her eyes. "And obviously they're going to choose the caves of fricking nightmares. Then they die, the end."

The images swirl apart again. They re-form on another part of the wall, this time surrounded by the outline of a cavern. They take each other's hands and embrace, then drift away like smoke.

"The couple vanish," the recording continues. *"Days go by*

and there's no sign of them. Everyone believes they've run away together."

"You know what, I think I've heard enough," Marla says. "I know it's going to be horrible."

"Never leave a ghost story half told," Abbie says. "That's a sure-fire way to get yourself haunted."

More images form on the wall. These ones are cast in reds and purples, and their edges are sharper and jerkier. The caves are suddenly chilly and full of threat. "*Six days later, Tommy is found. He's covered in dried blood from head to toe and he won't tell anyone what happened to Victoria.*"

"He totally killed her," I say. "It's always the boyfriend."

"*He's charged with Victoria's murder. He refuses to defend himself at the trial and he's sentenced to hang.*"

"See?" I say.

The projected images become a scaffold with a swinging rope, and a slow procession of people circling the cavern. The chattering voices start up again. Jeers and shouts; the cry of a judge as he passes sentence and slams down the gavel.

"*On the morning he's due to die,*" the narrator says, "*Tommy tells a priest he was with Victoria in a cavern called Montgomery's Auditorium when he heard laughter.*"

At this, laughter echoes around us from all directions. I know it's clever speaker positioning, but it's still disconcerting. I glance around the cavern. The spiky stalactites cast long, teeth-like shadows on the walls. I imagine it would have been terrifying for Victoria and Tommy, hearing that laughter in a place like this.

"*There's a lake in Montgomery's Auditorium. The surface is always still; so still the mirror image in the water is identical to reality. Except, that night, Tommy and Victoria saw a ripple. It spread towards them, distorting the reflections. They stepped closer.*"

"Why would they do that?" Marla says.

"*Something broke the surface. A slender hand, reaching out of the water. Then an arm, and a face, with knotted hair obscuring their features. Skin hanging from their bones in wrinkled flaps.*"

"This is the point when my ninja fighting skills would be put to good use," I say.

"*Slowly, a woman with jerky limbs crawled out of the water on all fours and crept towards them.*"

"Oh my god," Marla says.

"*Tommy tells the priest that the woman, as quick as lightning, plunged her hand into Victoria's chest and ripped out her heart.*"

"This is so gross," Python says, rubbing his hands together.

"*Tommy was sure he was about to die, too. He closed his eyes and felt the woman's claws scratching at his chest, searching for his heart. But for some reason, she released him and vanished.*"

The images on the wall act out Tommy's hanging. His feet twitch and the crowd erupts with cheers. His body is cut down from the scaffold and drops into a coffin. A horse and cart drags it off.

"*One more thing,*" the narrator says. "*Tommy's body is given to the local doctor for dissection. When they remove his heart, they discover the mark of a handprint on its surface. Like someone squeezed his heart while it was still inside his body.*"

Cackling laughter echoes once again, and the recording ends with the image of a pulsating heart that fills the entire wall.

I find myself unconsciously rubbing my own chest. It aches with dread. I know it's a story, but in the darkness of the cave, with its endless tunnels and all that impenetrable rock surrounding us, it feels like it could be real.

There's a brief moment of nervous silence. Then Python takes out a small hip flask. "Don't tell anyone, but I brought vodka." He offers the flask around. Marla and Liam take a sip, but Abbie and I decline. Cameraman Carl has brought his own, and he swigs like a parched man in the desert.

The others chatter among themselves, laughing at the story and how it's left us all surprisingly terrified. I don't join in. Instead, I'm fighting this sense of uneasiness that refuses to dissipate. I keep thinking about corpses, running on all fours, with their mouths unhinged and blood dripping from splintered teeth. What can I say? I have a good imagination.

I'm trying to reassure myself I won't be falling in love with any of this lot. The Puckered Maiden preys on couples, right? So I'll be safe from any heart-eating nonsense.

Then I hear it. Quiet laughter.

Something is in the cave with us.

TWELVE

The laughter stops abruptly. Pattering footsteps fade away into the darkness of a nearby tunnel. Once again, I'm painfully aware of how much darkness there is down here, and how tenuous our little bubble of sunset is. As if confirming my thoughts, the lights flicker. Python clamps a hand over his mouth and makes a long keening noise. He sounds like a slowly deflating balloon.

I'm drawn into a memory of my twelfth birthday, when I had three friends around for a sleepover in a tent. My mum pitched it at the end of the garden, so less than four metres from the backdoor. Even still, as the day faded into quiet darkness, it brought with it an eeriness that turned passing cars into growling wolves.

We'd barely fallen asleep when something dragged against the side of the tent. Not a branch in the wind; we didn't have trees, only a low fence separating us from the neighbours' gardens. The four of us in the tent huddled together as the dragging, scratching noise came again, followed by laughter. Whatever it was outside was delighting in our muffled sobs.

Turns out, it was Leo and Harry from next door, trying to scare us. My mum was outside like a shot, threatening them with all manner of torments if they came near us again. I smile at the memory. Mum always seemed invincible back then, like she could take on the whole world and still have time to make us hot chocolate afterwards. My smile fades. She's not coming to rescue us this time. We're on our own.

I force myself to march in the direction of the footsteps, even though my legs are wobbly beneath me. *There's no such thing as ghosts, there's no such things as ghosts*, I tell myself. It's all a trick. A creepy soundtrack designed to scare us. And I'm going to prove it to myself.

The cavern twists off to the left, sloping steeply towards a tunnel. The entrance is surrounded by a painted chipboard face – the Puckered Maiden, silently screaming at us, her peeling face screwed up in fury. I hesitate.

Python jogs up beside me. "So you know, in no episode of *It's Behind You* have they ever used actors. It's their number one rule. Sound and lighting only."

"I ain't scared of no ghost." I flick up my collar. The blood is still sticky.

"Laughter is the Puckered Maiden's MO," Abbie says, catching up with us. She's already recording, her video camera in one hand and some device emitting clicking noises in the other. She's slung her open rucksack on one shoulder. "I know it's most likely recorded. But imagine if it's really her?"

"Seriously?" Marla says, her mouth hanging open.

"Stay here with Liam," I say. "Just don't fall in love with him. The Puckered Maiden will definitely want to eat your heart if you do."

"Might be hard," Liam calls after me. "I'm adorable."

Yes. Yes, he is.

The three of us creep towards the tunnel. Or four, if you count Cameraman Carl. We duck under the Puckered Maiden's rotting teeth and step inside her mouth. I sweep my torch across the walls.

It looks like an old mining tunnel, with large wooden beams making square archways and holding up horizontal planks that line the walls. There are framed pictures and portraits hung everywhere. I recognize some of the names. "The Puckered Maiden's victims," I say.

Most of them are men wearing old-fashioned clothes. Unfortunate explorers who went looking for new and exciting caverns to name after themselves and never came back. There are only a few women, so Victoria's portrait stands out. A young woman in nineteenth-century garb, with a haughty expression, stares back at me. Only her eyes are wrong. There are holes cut in the canvas so someone can spy on us from the opposite side. I shine my torch through the holes. There's a narrow space back there, big enough for a person.

Footsteps approach, but it's only Marla. Liam is skulking a short distance behind her.

"You can't leave me alone with him. I don't want anyone at home thinking there's something going on," Marla hisses, gesturing back to the cave. She doesn't know Liam has followed her.

Liam makes a "what the hell?" face. He creeps closer to her. "Boo!"

Marla leaps into the air in shock, knocking into one of the frames. She hurriedly loops her arm through Python's, pressing herself tight up against him. We walk on. Cameraman Carl swears as he struggles to manoeuvre his camera through the uneven space.

I sweep my torch between the portraits, expecting to see one blinking at me, but we're alone. And then Python screams. He launches himself across the tunnel, tripping in the process, grabbing at my shirt as he falls, and sending both of us crashing back against the wall.

"You're not my type, mate," I say.

"Something TOUCHED me," he cries, drawing out the words into terrified squeals. "Something grabbed my leg."

"Like, a rat?" Marla whispers. "I didn't sign up for rats."

"Like a HAND. A demon zombie HAND." He stops squealing and curls a lip at me. "Also, don't flatter yourself, Lex."

I return his sneer. "You grabbed my tit. What was I meant to think?"

"Eww, someone fetch an AXE, my arm has to go."

I snort in amusement, then turn my attention to the wall. My torch finds a curtained hole at ankle height. Liam stoops down and lifts the curtain; I shine the torch into the hidden space. There's nothing in there.

"I definitely felt something," Python says. "I don't think I could live with myself if I'd touched Lex for no good reason."

I pat him on the back. "It's nothing to be ashamed of. I am hard to resist."

He mimes being sick. "My type is nice people."

"But I thought you liked Marla?"

"You can do this, Marla," Marla whispers. "Just act your way through this and it will be over soon."

We continue down the tunnel, checking for grabbing hands as we go, but there's no sign of anyone else here. The torch shines on more framed portraits. They're arranged in a timeline, with the decades marked off on the beams. The portraits become photographs. The last picture is from thirty years ago – or so I think.

But then I notice a more recent photograph nailed to one of the beams. This one isn't framed; it's just a tattered six-by-four snap. It's not part of the original museum, rather something that the TV people must have deliberately added to the wall. Which surprises me as I thought the show was usually careful to leave the supposedly haunted locations as they stand in real life.

The photo's of a smiling teenage girl with bright blue locs, half-hidden by a monster face bobble hat. Liam's noticed it too. He's staring at it the same way Veronica stared at him when he turned up in town.

"Who's that?" I say.

"Um, I don't know," he says quickly, forcing a smile. He's lying.

"That's Laurie Cox," Abbie says.

"Who?" he says.

"She's the girl who died in that cave-in everyone talks about," I say. "She was with some other kids but they got out. Surprised you've not heard of her. Didn't your local chaperone tell you anything?"

"I knew about the cave-in but that's all," he says, his voice raspy like he's struggling to get the lie out.

"How come you recognized her?" Python asks Abbie.

She eyes Cameraman Carl's lens, her jaw twitching. "I've done my research."

I take the picture with me, then lead the group into the next cavern. Like the previous one, it's full of tacky scares. A couple of large spiders mounted on articulated metal arms. Several plastic hands stuck to the wall like they're reaching through the rock. A severed head is hanging overhead with an unlit bulb in its mouth. Without mood lighting and a creepy soundtrack, everything feels cheap and fake, like a joke shop at night-time. Comical rather than terrifying.

Abbie reaches up and rests a camera in an alcove. She

hooks it up to a long wire and a small box that she places on the floor.

"Vibration sensor," she says. "I'm going to see what it picks up."

"What else do you have in that bag of yours?" I ask.

"Static electricity gauges, a temperature gun, voice recorder, a *broken* EMF reader." She takes out another camera and cradles it reverently. "And this. A motion-activated thermal camera. It cost an absolute fortune, but it was totally worth it."

Cameraman Carl nods like he's agreeing and films her as she places it in another alcove. She flips over the screen and adjusts the angle. I peer over her shoulder. It shows the cave in shades of blue, and us in yellows, oranges and reds. One area shows up black, like a spreading stain on the wall.

"What's that?" I ask, tapping on the screen and earning myself a slapped wrist.

"Never touch my stuff," says Abbie. She peers closer. "Interesting. It looks like a cold spot. That's promising in terms of supernatural activity."

I shine my torch over into the corner. And of course there's a Puckered Maiden doll, sitting on a rock in her ruined dress, with her skin like a screwed up ball of damp paper.

We approach slowly. Abbie takes out a temperature laser and points it at the doll. The numbers go down. It's like the doll is surrounded by a freezing aura, chilling the wall and the rock on which it sits. I remember the doll that

91

appeared on my bed. It didn't just feel cold; it was more like an absence of warmth.

I take a slow breath. Remind myself of that ten grand I'm going home with. Bolstered by my greed, I march up to the doll and pick her up. Her body is lumpy with old stuffing. She has wooden arms and legs. Just a doll, cooled to cave temperatures.

"Lex, noooo," Python cries. "You can't touch haunted objects. Now you're going to die."

But the doll doesn't look haunted to me, just old and stinky. There's something nestled among its skirts. I smooth it out. It's another photo, taken inside the caves. It shows a still pool lit up by the flash and nothing else. At least, that's what I think at first.

Below the water's surface, there's a screaming face with its hair billowing around it and claw-like fingers stretching towards the photographer. I hold it up so Cameraman Carl can get a good shot.

"Oh. My. Giddy. Aunt," Python whispers. "Is that the Puckered Maiden?"

"Supposedly," Abbie sighs, lifting the photo from my hands. "This is a famous photograph taken in these caves. Famous among paranormal investigators, at least. It made the career of the man who took it."

"Is that what you want?" Marla says. "To be famous?"

Abbie shakes her head. "No. I want to know the truth."

"Well, I've always thought it was a fake," Liam says, then stops.

"You've seen it before?" I fight a smile. I can't believe he's still trying to keep up the ruse. Who does he think he's kidding, pretending this is the first time he's come to Umber?

"Think I saw it on some programme about hauntings, or something," he mumbles.

"What do you reckon?" I nod at Abbie. "Is it real?"

She stares at the photo, then hands it back to me. "I think so. It's a big lie, otherwise. I can't believe he'd choose a lie."

"Over what?" I say.

She glances at her temperature gauge. "The cold spot is the wall. It's maybe half a degree below its surroundings."

I reach towards the wall. I can feel the air change around the cold spot, like a cold breeze is passing across my skin. I hesitate, then touch the stone. It's damp. A trickle of water is seeping out through the rocks. Mystery solved.

"What if that's how she's moving about?" Python gasps. "Like, she can turn into water and hide inside the walls?"

"Oh my god, the cold patch looks kind of person-shaped," Marla says.

We squint at it. "It's more flying squirrel-shaped," Liam says.

"Do you feel that?" Marla whispers. "A cold breeze."

Liam shakes his head. "There's no breeze."

"There is," Python says. "I can definitely feel it."

I don't want to admit it, but so can I. We watch Abbie's temperature laser as the numbers creep down a fraction of a degree at a time.

A sharp, clacking noise makes the others jump.

"Where's that coming from?" says Python.

Clack, clack. Tap, tap, tap. It's like footsteps, but not human ones. Wooden limbs clicking together. *Clackity, clackity, clackity.* Increasing in tempo, like whatever it is has started to run.

"Wha ... what is that?" I say. "Oh my god, what's happening?"

"There's something coming," Python cries. "Something's coming, something's—"

"RARGGHH!" I cry, shaking the doll so hard that its limbs tangle together.

Python and Marla scream. Liam jumps back and clutches a hand against his chest. Abbie drops her device. It takes a good thirty seconds for Python and Marla to realize nothing is coming for them. I crack up with laughter and toss the Puckered Maiden at Python. He swats it aside and glares at me.

"It was you!" he snaps. "You're *not* going to be invited on *The Python Show* when this is all over."

"You bitch," Marla spits. She turns and storms back towards the fake town, Python following. Liam shakes his head at me, fighting a smile, and goes after them.

Abbie shoots me an exasperated look. "You don't take anything seriously, do you?"

My smile briefly falters as Cameraman Carl sticks his camera in my face. She has no idea how wrong she is. I take some things very seriously. I'm just good at pretending.

THIRTEEN

Everyone hates me now.

The others have built a campfire in the town square. Python and Abbie have collected up all the cardboard boxes left behind by the contractors; Liam has smashed up Victoria's empty coffin. Marla supervises; Cameraman Carl films.

I have a lighter, so I get to do the burning part.

The flames colour the cavern in shifting splashes of light. I can see more now. The ceiling reminds me of an upside-down mountain range, sharp peaks pointing down towards us. The walls are smooth lumps of rock, like melting columns of dirty ice. There are round pits in some places, where swirling whirlpools of long-gone water ate away at the limestone. Dark shadows could either be tunnels leading out of the cavern or dead ends, it's impossible to tell.

"Let's tell some scary stories. To get ourselves in the mood," I say.

"No," Marla says, shuffling as far away from me as she can get while still staying in Cameraman Carl's shot.

"There's something very wrong with you, Lex," Liam laughs.

"You mean very right. Come on. What's your scariest memory?"

"Nothing that makes for a good story."

Abbie is writing in her notebook, but she pauses and looks up. "It's the real world that scares me," she says. "Poverty, racism, police brutality. Not the supernatural."

"You're not even a little bit scared of ghosts?" Python says. "Not even a teensy-weeny bit?"

She shakes her head. "Show me someone who was murdered by a ghost. Until then, I'll spend my time worrying about real injustices."

"You're so serious all the time," Marla says, stroking her long hair like a pet.

"There's a lot of reasons to be. It must be nice to be able to pretend the world's a safe place. Not everyone has that privilege."

We all fall silent. It's awkward, but I'm OK with awkward. Besides, Abbie has a point. It's a weird world sometimes. If you think about it too hard, no one should ever get to be happy. There are people dying and getting sick, and wars and white supremacy and climate change and the richest one per cent owning over half the world's wealth.

You can end up feeling small and powerless. So you tell yourself there's nothing you can do – not about the big things or the little things. You look away. Enter a stupid reality TV show while the world burns around you.

The silence drags on. Python takes his hip flask out and swigs on it. He hands it to Marla, who takes a long drink while intently holding his gaze, then licks her lips. I catch Abbie's eye. She looks like she's regretting every choice that brought her here.

"Get a room already," Liam laughs, tossing a burnt lump of wood at the happy couple.

Marla wipes her lips, then leans back against Python, sitting between his legs. She wriggles to get comfy. "You're so warm! I'm turning into a block of ice in this cave. Ouch. Your chin is digging into me."

Marla notices Cameraman Carl focusing in on her. She stops complaining and instead pretends to brush a speck of dirt off Python's cheek. Python laughs nervously. I'm not sure if he's blinded by how pretty Marla is or if, like the rest of us, he's fully aware she's only pretending to like him. Perhaps it doesn't matter to him, so long as he can cling to the fantasy. It reminds me of my parents, playing make-believe that their whole marriage isn't a sham.

Liam bursts out laughing. "You two crack me up."

Marla frowns. "What's so funny?" she says.

"Oh, nothing. As you were. We could all do with some entertainment while we wait for something to happen. Are they going to keep us in the dark for ever?"

"My guess is Jackie wants us to spend some more time in this cave," Python replies. "The show usually tries to funnel contestants into areas where they hope we'll meet something ghostly. That's what the challenges are for."

"Oh yes, I forgot!" Marla says. "I mean, maybe there's something here that we're meant to do."

Python sits up straight, knocking Marla aside. "Wait! Perhaps that's it. I bet there's a puzzle or a game, hidden somewhere in the cave."

Marla dusts herself off. "A game?" she says woodenly. "That's so smart of you."

"For reals?" I jump to my feet. I love puzzles! One time, during the *before*, I did an escape room with my parents and I got so excited, I was sick in a bin. Good times.

"Shall we?" Python says, bowing deeply to me and putting on an old-fashioned accent. I accept his hand and let him twirl me away from the fire. It's time to go exploring.

Cameraman Carl films the five of us as we start at one end of town and I shine my torch into each building. The tea shop, the watermill, the mayor's house. All of them are painted facades nailed on to a shed. Inside are bare mud floors and splintering wood.

"Why don't we try the butcher's?" Marla says. I glance at her. Again, she sounds wooden. As though she's memorized a script.

We follow her to the end of the street. The butcher's shop is more substantial than the others. There's a swinging sign outside and a real door rather than an empty hole. I push it open and stick my head inside. It's like the Tardis – as big as a real shop and set up with plastic meats hanging from the ceiling and a glass display case full of more fake produce.

There's a table with five chairs around it placed in the middle of the room. It's topped with an ironed white tablecloth and a large candelabra. The chairs are all arranged on one side like on TV dining programmes. So a cameraman can get everyone into the shot.

Nothing's cracked or dusty. This set wasn't part of the Puckered Maiden Experience. It's a new addition.

"Oh, Jackie, you shouldn't have," I say.

"You think they're laying on a three-course meal for us?" Liam says hopefully.

Abbie circles the room, picking up props. There are bunches of dried herbs lying around the place, and candles that smell like sage. A little pot on the side contains salt, and there's a horseshoe nailed over the door.

"This is ridiculous," Abbie says. "I came here to look for real ghosts."

"Perhaps we should try to contact one. This looks like a séance." Marla's voice is a little too high-pitched. She sounds ... not scared, exactly. She's too excited. Stage fright, I realize. She takes a seat at the head of the table.

"You're very keen, all of a sudden," I say.

"Getting into the spirit of things, that's all." Her laugh is as brittle as glass. "Spirit, ha ha."

"Good one." Liam slumps into a chair. He nods at Cameraman Carl. "What's the deal? We do this séance for the cameras and Jackie will switch on some more lights? So we can go further into the cave system?"

Cameraman Carl grunts in reply. It's as close to a yes as we're going to get from him.

"I can't believe I'm being forced into this," Abbie says.

"It's going to be fun. Come on, Abbie, don't be so grumpy," Marla says.

Abbie curls her lip. "Séances are ridiculous. They make people act hysterical."

"We won't get hysterical, I promise," Python says. "Oh my god, oh my god, a séance!"

Cameraman Carl sighs and gets to work setting up his camera. We all take a chair. I lean back in mine and put my feet on the table.

"It won't work if you do that," Marla snaps.

"Tommy won't care about manners," Liam says.

"Um, so who shall we contact?" Marla babbles. "Um, Tommy? Yes, that's a good idea."

"You two are acting strangely," Python says. "Why Tommy?"

Abbie smacks my leg, making me move my feet so she can place one of her devices on the table. "Tommy was the butcher's apprentice and we're in the butcher's. I'm surprised you knew that, Marla."

"I didn't," Marla says, laughing nervously. "I know nothing. I mean, not *nothing*, but . . ."

"Argh, I'm SO excited," Python says. "Right. How do we do this?"

Marla picks up a little lacy veil, like a mini-tablecloth, and places it over her head. "Someone light the candles," she says. "And switch off that torch."

"What's going to happen?" Liam asks, obediently lighting candles.

"Who knows?" Python cries. His eyes are shining. "That's the FUN part! Not knowing."

"Quiet," Marla says. She places both hands on the table and nods at the rest of us to do the same. Then she closes her eyes and starts to hum softly under her breath. "Tommy, are you there?" she intones. "We mean you no harm. We only want to speak with you."

I smother a laugh. Marla is going in hard on the acting front. It's like she's practised every syllable a hundred times. This is an audition, I realize.

"Tommy? Tommy?" she calls.

Smoke swirls up from the candles, filling the air with a thick herbal scent. I'm not sure what's in those candles, but it's making me light-headed. I press my palms to my eyes and shake my head, trying to clear the fog.

"Bless us with your presence," Marla says, her voice slow and thick. "We welcome you into our circle. Please, share your secrets."

Something knocks loudly on wood. We all jump.

101

"Enter," Marla says. Her voice rises. "Enter and tell us what you saw. What really happened to Victoria?"

There's another bang. The table wobbles. I go to look underneath the tablecloth, but Marla quickly grabs my hand. "Concentrate! Focus on manifesting Tommy or he will not come."

"This is nonsense," Abbie says. She taps the dial on her device but the needle remains at zero.

"I can sense a presence. We're not alone," Marla whispers.

"Is it Tommy?" Python says. "Oh god, is he angry that they hanged him?"

Marla slides her hands off the table. "No, I ... I don't think it's Tommy." Her voice is shaking and I have to give it to her – her acting is improving. "I can feel someone else. They're here!"

She jumps up from her chair and backs away. The candles flicker. Something knocks on wood again.

"Who are you?" Marla cries. "Oh my god, what do you want with me?"

"And here we go," Abbie sighs, removing her hands from the table. She begins to pack away her equipment. "Nice try, Marla."

"No, this isn't right," Marla sobs. "What's happening? What—"

She raises her arms like she's trying to shield herself from an invisible attacker. Her body begins to jerk, limbs thrashing. Then she goes completely stiff and stands there, swaying. Her veil slides off her face and her mouth falls open.

"She's not such a crappy actress after all," I whisper to Liam. "I'd give her a six out of ten."

"Why did you leave me here?" Marla growls.

"Who are we talking to?" Python says, eyes wide with terror.

Marla's head whips around to face him. Her teeth are bared. "It's so, so dark here. Where am I?" she says, in a sing-song voice.

"You're kind of freaking me out, man," Liam says.

Marla turns to him. "*You*," she spits. "You left me. You abandoned me to the dark."

There's a screech as Liam pushes his chair back. "What is this?" he says, standing.

"Liam . . . Liam, where are you?"

He stumbles towards the door. "This is too much," he says as he trips outside.

"You left me behind!" Marla screeches after him. She rounds on the rest of us, looking as unlike Marla as it's possible for someone to look. She's suddenly all sharp edges and ugliness. Her hair is wild and stringy, like it's coated in stone dust. Her skin is chalky.

"Return Marla to us, you DEMON," Python cries. He takes out his hip flask with shaking hands and hurls alcohol into Marla's face like he's trying to repel a vampire with holy water. Some of it splashes on to the candles and they surge brightly.

"What the fuck?" Marla screeches. "Shit, that burns!"

And Marla is back. Also, the tablecloth is on fire. Abbie wearily smothers the flames with the salt.

"My eyes," Marla squeals, dancing around on the spot. "What did you do that for?"

"You almost had me there," I say, laughing nervously.

"It was certainly an interesting performance," Abbie says.

"You were POSSESSED!" Python cries.

Marla stops dancing and glares at us. "This was my moment and you ruined it." She stomps out of the room with a swish of her hair. Cameraman Carl follows with his camera trained on her face.

Abbie, Python and I remain standing around the charred tablecloth in silence. Marla's a slightly better actress than I'd expected, even if I didn't believe a second of it. But Liam's reaction? The fear on his face when Marla accused him of leaving her behind; his stricken expression? That part wasn't an act.

Which raises the question: who was it Liam left behind, alone in the dark?

FOURTEEN

We all gather around the camp fire again. The air is thick with smoke, irritation and so many lies.

Liam, hiding the fact he *knows* Umber. That he knows exactly who Laurie Cox is, despite his claims to the contrary.

And what about Marla? All over Python for the cameras. Playing the game. Persuading us to do a séance that clearly struck a nerve with Liam.

Then there's Abbie. There's an odd intensity to her ghost hunting. A desperation to prove the Puckered Maiden is real.

And finally, Python. A strutting, screeching peacock of a boy. But something doesn't quite ring true.

Work out their secrets; work out their weaknesses. And then the prize is mine, all mine.

Overhead the lights flicker off again. For a moment we only have the crackling campfire's glow. They buzz back on, first white, then blue, then pink, then red. Then all the colours light up together before settling on the sunset scheme once again.

"I thought something would happen after the séance," Liam says, throwing scraps of wood into the fire. "They'd open up the other caves or whatever."

"Something should have happened," Python says. "We've been in here for hours."

"There's something wrong," Marla says. "It isn't meant to happen like this."

"Don't worry, Cameraman Carl still got your big moment on film," I say. "It wasn't all for nothing."

"I don't know what you're talking about," she sniffs.

"It will be OK if we all stick together," Python says, squeezing her thigh.

She jerks away from him, then flushes. "Sorry," she says. "I'm just jumpy."

The lights flicker again. I glance at Cameraman Carl and, worryingly, he is frowning. Then the lights are back, this time in shades of blue like night is falling over the model town.

A whirring sound announces the projector has come back to life. The Tommy and Victoria soundtrack starts up. *"Thomas Brook, thou art brought here today—"*

The voice is cut off almost immediately but the projector continues to stutter on and off. It settles. The shadow of a woman appears, twenty feet tall. We all recoil. But then I see it. There's no woman. On top of the cafe, there's a doll. The light is shining right on her, casting a huge shadow.

I'm sure I would have noticed the doll if it had been there earlier.

"A clue," Python whispers.

"Maybe. Let's get her and look." I bend down so Python can climb on to my shoulders and I stand up on shuddering legs. He rocks perilously and squeals.

"Watch my hair," I snap.

He lunges wildly for the doll and unbalances us both. We go down hard. I am going to be covered in so many bruises by tomorrow.

I sit up and retrieve the fallen doll. It's the same one I keep seeing everywhere. Stupid Puckered Maiden. I examine it from every angle, but there's no clue here. I dangle the horrible thing by its leg and hurl it into the fire. That will stop it from messing with my calm.

Marla screams. "What did you do?"

The doll burns with a high-pitched hiss. First the straw-like hair, then the stuffed body, then her wooden limbs. All the paint and varnish on her face starts to bubble and melt.

Liam laughs nervously. "She's totally coming back all burnt and shit to haunt us."

"Don't," Marla whimpers.

"Lex is definitely going to die now," Python says.

"It's just a doll." I look at Abbie for backup. She looks up from her book to roll her eyes in exasperation. I don't know if it's a *stop winding everyone up* eye roll or a *now you've angered the evil cave spirit* eye roll.

"It's just a doll," I repeat more firmly.

"Or IS IT?" Python declares.

I wail and pretend I'm possessed. "I am the spirit of the Puckered Maiden, here to eat you all."

Marla squeals and clings to Liam for protection.

"You're proud of yourself, aren't you?" Python says.

"A hundred per cent." I grin at him. "You're just jealous that I'm the one who's going to look fun and exciting when the show goes out."

"A little," he admits. "I thought I would be braver than I am."

"Don't worry." Liam pats him on the back. "She's going to look chaotic, not cool. The viewers will hate her."

"No way, people love chaotic," I say.

"Not close up, they don't," Abbie says.

There's a thud from the next cavern. Then the sound of something breaking.

Abbie and I exchange looks. Both of us leap to our feet. The noise came from the cave where Abbie set up all her equipment. Maybe the camera will have recorded something. We run towards the tunnel, jostling to get ahead.

"Second place is for losers," I laugh, skidding on the wet stone.

"It's my equipment. My ghost!" she says, but she's smiling too. This is the most exciting thing to happen since we first came into the caves.

We're so busy trying to be first that we forget how slippery the portrait tunnel is. Abbie loses her footing with a scream and drags me down with her. We skid all the way to the bottom on our bums, in a big tangle of limbs and bumped teeth. We dust ourselves down and stagger to our feet. I direct my torch to where we left her equipment.

It's not there.

The thermal-imaging camera is smashed on the floor and the tripod is splayed open with one leg almost completely ripped off. The sound recorder has survived, but is metres away from where Abbie left it.

"The Puckered Maiden has previously been implicated in the destruction of property," she says. "It's why Mortimer Monk gave up on the Puckered Maiden Experience."

I think of Tommy and Victoria in the model town, their faces slashed. "You really think it's her?"

She chews her lip. "Unless it's proved otherwise."

She rolls the broken camera over in her hands, then yanks at a loose circuit board dangling from the twisted remains. She pulls it off, then cracks the plastic of the casing to extract the memory card.

"Is the memory damaged?"

"Not as far as I can see. I don't know if any footage will have saved."

She takes another camera out of her pocket and swaps

109

out the memory card. I lean over her shoulder as she scrolls through the files. It's recorded two bursts of activity. The first was us examining the cold spot on the wall. The second is from less than a minute ago. It lasts thirty seconds.

Abbie glances at me, then presses play.

The image shows an empty cave. We watch, but nothing happens. Water drips from the ceiling like tapping fingers.

Abbie sighs. "*Something* must have triggered the vibration sensor, but—"

She doesn't get to finish. A flash of white streaks across the screen and the picture turns upside down, spinning as the camera is violently smashed off the tripod and hurtles through the air. And then the recording ends.

The other three appear at the entrance to the cave, Python leading the way. He sighs in relief. "It's all good, gang, Abbie is OK. Oh, and Lex is here too."

I stick my tongue out at him. "Something was in here. It's destroyed Abbie's kit."

"What kind of something?" Marla says. "Like, a person or a ghost?"

"Maybe they're cross about being burnt alive by Lex," Liam jokes.

"Don't!" Marla spits.

Abbie retrieves the audio recorder and rewinds it. We listen in silence. It plays static for a few seconds, and then there's a slow scraping noise, like a knife being dragged against the rocky walls. Footsteps pad slowly, then stop. There's something else then – a whisper, too quiet to hear.

110

Abbie rewinds again and turns the volume up. The static hisses. The whisper is louder, but it's still difficult to decipher actual words. Abbie tries again. This time, the sounds rearrange themselves into words.

"You're all going to die."

It's followed by a scream – Abbie's scream as the pair of us skidded down the tunnel and into the cavern. We must have missed the whisperer by seconds.

Marla gasps. "This isn't part of the plan," she says. "Jackie said there'd be no other actors in here with us."

"They never use actors," Python agrees. "It would ruin the show's premise if they were caught faking an actual ghost sighting."

I glance over at Cameraman Carl. He nods once.

"I wasn't warned about this." Marla starts to back away. "I don't want to be here!"

"Wait, Marla," Python calls. But she skids away up the tunnel, hiccuping with sobs.

There's a scream, and a thud, and then nothing.

FIFTEEN

Extract from the transcript of the T-minus-one-day final interview with Marla Colombo [MC], contestant 3/5 *It's Behind You: Season 3, Episode 10 (Umber Gorge Caves)*. Interviewed by Jackie Stone [JS], producer of *It's Behind You*.

JS: What's your biggest fear, Marla?

MC: Hard toffee. Like, I always worry my teeth will become embedded in it and fall out.

JS: That's . . . specific. And why have you applied to be on the show?

MC: Well, I'm an actor.

JS: Oh, really? What sort of thing?

MC: I had this audition for a film called *Franky Stein*. It's about a teenage girl who investigates a spate of murders at her school and discovers the killer is her ex. It's like, she created the monster when she dumped him, you know?

JS: That's inventive. Do you think you might like to play the Puckered Maiden one of these days?

MC: Um, her skin is peeling off?

JS: It's delightfully macabre, isn't it?

MC: It's gross. I'm not really good with gross. Or scary.

JS: And yet here you are.

MC: I know, right? My boyfriend always says I wouldn't last five minutes in a horror. But I'll show him I'm not a coward.

JS: That reminds me ... [Sound of rustling papers] ... you mentioned him as a motivation on your application form?

MC: Did I? What did I say?

JS: "Who is basic trash now, DAMIEN? When Python sees me on the TV, I'll get to meet him afterwards and we'll fall in love and BANG IN A GRAVEYARD." It goes on ...

MC: Wow. Yeah. Um, wow. I guess I was kind of drunk when I applied? We'd had this argument. He

113

got mad about how much time I spend watching Python's channel. As research for my audition, obviously.

JS: Obviously. But you like him, right? Python.

MC: That's the stupid thing! I only said that because I knew it would make Damien mad.

JS: Oh. Right. Marla . . . this is not something I usually do, but I think there's a way we can both help each other. And make Damien seriously jealous.

MC: What do you mean?

JS: Let's have a chat off camera.

[Break in filming]

JS: Marla, why don't you tell the listeners about your feelings for Python?

MC: Oh my goodness, he's amazing. I love him. Actually love him.

JS: Perfect. And finally, do you think you can win, Marla?

MC: I thought you said –

JS: Whoa there, Marla. We're recording this, remember?

MC: Oh, of course. Yes, I can win! I'm going to show everyone there's more to me than the dumb pretty girl who is murdered at the end of Act One. I'll show Damien. I can be the final girl.

114

SIXTEEN

We find Marla lying outside the cheese shop, by the village square. She's on her back with her limbs splayed out and her eyes open and unblinking. I approach slowly. She doesn't move. Behind her, the campfire is burning low. The flames send freakish shadows flitting across her face. There's blood in her hair.

"Marla?" I whisper, crouching down beside her. I lower my head to listen for breathing.

"Oh my god, Marla," Python says. "Is she dead?"

Suddenly, there's an ear-splitting scream. Marla is not dead. She launches herself off the ground and clamps her arms around my neck. The girl's small but bizarrely strong. We roll over so she's pinning me to the floor, getting dirt and ash all over my already-filthy suit. She cranes her face towards mine. There's a vein on her forehead that looks ready to burst and she's baring her teeth like a zombie.

"This is all your fault!" she cries.

"Marla, calm down." Liam drags her off me and holds her around the waist while she kicks and screams, clawing at the air in an effort to disembowel me with her manicured fingernails. Cameraman Carl is the most animated he's ever been, following Marla's every flail with the camera.

"Oh my GOD, oh my GOD," Python says.

"Stop that!" Abbie orders. "You're acting like children."

"This is all her fault," Marla screeches. "She burnt that doll. She's made the Puckered Maiden angry."

She stamps hard on Liam's foot and he releases her with a yelp of pain. Blood dribbles down her temple.

"Marla, your head," Abbie says. "You're hurt."

"I fell over. I hate this place. And you know what? I'm done."

Marla turns and marches off, through the model town, then into the first cave with its fibreglass graveyard. We all trail after her as she feels her way past the angels and crosses. We follow her into the entrance tunnel. Cameraman Carl struggles behind us, panting under the weight of his camera. It's a sign of how pissed off Marla is that she doesn't check if he's still filming her. We reach the locked door.

Marla doesn't hesitate. She walks up to the sign that reads IT'S BEHIND ME, LET ME OUT and hammers on the door. Cameraman Carl jogs over to join us, swearing

116

under his breath. We all step aside for him in shocked silence. I always thought Marla would snap first; I knew I could break her. But even so, this is surprisingly dramatic.

I'm reminded of this time with my mum where I went an entire day answering "Why?" to everything she said. It was funny right up until the point she snapped. She screamed at me so loudly my dad came racing in from the garden thinking someone was hurt.

Marla *is* hurt, but no one's coming running.

"Let me out, I've had enough," Marla shouts. "Let me out. Please!"

There is silence. And I know then. No one's coming.

"Marla," I say. "There's no one there."

"What do you mean?" Python says. "This is how the show works."

They all look at me, confused. "You all sat through the health and safety talk, right?" I say. "The one with the risk assessment on licking mould?"

"So what?" Marla sniffs, pausing in her hammering.

"So, if the health and safety team are worried we might get an upset stomach from licking the walls, they must be crapping themselves over that head injury about now."

Mr Health and Mr Safety should be racing in with doctors and lawyers and release forms to sign. Marla should be in a neck brace with an air ambulance landing outside. Instead, silence. Cameraman Carl peers up at the wall-mounted camera over the door, lowering his own.

"You're right," Liam says. "If someone was watching us

117

from the outside, they'd already be in here to take Marla to the hospital."

There's a pause while the truth sinks in. The power cuts, the flickering lights, the fact that nothing happened after the séance. I'd thought it was all part of the show. But now I don't think it was.

"Oh my GOD," Python says. "We're on our own."

SEVENTEEN

The smoke from the fire is stinging my eyes.

We've torn down the wooden facade from the tea shop to provide more fuel, but the burning paint is letting off a terrible smell. So not only are we trapped in a dark, possibly haunted cave, but we're all going to asphyxiate. Feeling blessed right now.

"Some of the lights are still working. The ones in here, and the projector," Abbie says. "So there's still power."

"Then why isn't someone opening the door?" Marla says, rustling as she moves. We made her a bandage out of burnt tablecloth and I convinced her we should tie a strip of bubble wrap over the top for protection. It makes me giggle every time I catch sight of her, with her big padded head.

"I think something must have happened to the HQ," Liam says slowly. "That big truck with all the TV screens – that's where the production team should be, watching us. But for some reason, they're not."

"So anything pre-automated is working, but nothing that requires a human?" Abbie says.

"And even the automated stuff is shaky." Liam points to the ceiling and, right on cue, the lights flicker.

"What if it goes out for good?" Python says. "Lex's torch won't last for ever."

Python is huddling under the rest of the tablecloth. He's pulled it around his head, making him look like ET. He seems smaller and quieter. It's unnerving.

"We won't be in here for ever," Abbie says. "You're being overdramatic. Again."

Python's not listening. "What if we evolve into hairless mole people?"

Marla strokes her own hair protectively. "Doesn't the cameraman have an earpiece or something? How does Jackie communicate with him?"

Cameraman Carl sighs. He's put his camera down and is drinking from a flask. "I'd usually have a walkie-talkie but they don't work in caves. Too much solid rock."

"Brilliant, that's just brilliant," says Marla.

"Don't worry," Abbie says. "They won't leave someone like *you* in here."

"What do you mean?" Marla stops stroking her own hair.

Abbie looks her up and down. "Your pretty face would be on the cover of every newspaper in the country. It would be terrible PR for the production company. Whereas the rest of us—"

"Stop it," Liam snaps, in an uncharacteristic display of anger. "No one is getting left in here." We all fall silent, taken aback. He takes a slow breath and forces a grin. "Imagine what's happening out there. Jackie will be yelling at everyone. She'll get that door open."

"That she will," Cameraman Carl says. He takes another swallow from the flask.

Python tightens the sheet around his chin and Liam tosses pebbles at the fire, dislodging bursts of sparks. Marla rustles and Abbie glowers. We all sit there, waiting to be rescued like princesses in a tower. Game over.

Abbie abruptly tears a page out of her notebook. She screws it up and throws it into the flames. Then she places her face in her hands. "I can't believe I thought I could find her. This place is a joke. I wish I'd never even seen that photo."

I take out the photo I found hidden in the doll's dress. The one of the Puckered Maiden, swimming beneath the surface with her face twisted into a furious scream. "This one?"

Abbie takes the picture from me and looks at it, her expression unreadable. "It's been thirty years, and no one's been able to prove this photo was faked. I thought I'd come here and find out the truth."

"Why does it matter so much to you?"

She opens her mouth like she might answer, then her expression darkens. She tosses the photo into the fire and it burns with a fizz. "It's stupid," she says. "Who knows where this photo was even taken? These caves are so big."

"I know where it was taken," Liam says.

"Really?" Abbie turns to him. "How?"

"It doesn't matter. But I do."

"Can you show me the place?" Abbie jumps to her feet and starts shovelling her equipment back into her bag.

"Oh no. No way," Marla says, bubble wrap rustling in irritation. "You can't go off and do your own thing!"

"What's Jackie going to do?" I point at the overhead cameras. "We don't even know if anyone's watching. Come on."

Liam hesitates. "It's in the part of the cave system where the cave-in happened. It's not exactly safe."

"Tell me where and I'll go by myself," Abbie says. "Please."

"No. I'll show you." He stands up and glances over at me. "I take it you're coming too." Not a question. Sighing, he removes a head torch from his waistband and switches it on. Boy came prepared.

To my surprise, Python stands too. "I'm coming. I'm tired of being such a coward."

We all look at Cameraman Carl and Marla. Carl shakes his head and sips from his flask. "Show's over and I'm not paid enough to risk my life. But have fun."

"You can't leave me here with him," Marla whispers. "He has murder eyes."

Cameraman Carl lowers his drink and stares at her. One of his eyes is slightly bigger than the other and he can make it twitch on demand.

"Oh my god, wait for me." Marla hurries after us.

We leave Cameraman Carl drinking by the fire. Liam leads the way through the dark cavern where Abbie's equipment was smashed to pieces. Small pieces of plastic and circuit board lie on the ground where we left them.

We pass by the animatronic spiders and the wall of plastic hands. There are two routes out of this cave. One is marked with an unlit neon skeleton holding a large arrow. That's the way the Puckered Maiden Experience would have us go. The other is marked with a staff-only sign and the TV crew have blocked it off with reams of NO ENTRY tape, in yellow and black.

"We're not allowed down there," Marla says. "It was in the health and safety talk."

I pull the tape aside and duck underneath. On the opposite side, there's an empty tunnel. Despite all the warnings to stay in the approved caves, there's a camera hooked up in the corner, looking down on us as we sneak past the tape. It's like Jackie knew we'd come through here even though we're not meant to. It makes me feel uneasy, like Jackie's pulling our strings from a distance.

"Liam?" I start to say. "Does Jackie know that you grew up in—"

123

I don't get to finish. I turn a corner and nearly walk into a mouthful of razor-sharp teeth, inches from my face. It's a monster, with cracked white face paint, bright red lips and a red nose. A clown. We all scream, but Liam's the loudest. In the space of time it takes me to register it's a rubber prop, he's already fled, taking the head torch with him. We find him tangled up in the tape.

He extracts himself. "It's not real, is it?"

"Er, no," I say, trying not to laugh.

"Shit."

"Not a fan of clowns?" I say. "Don't worry. We'll take it back to the campfire and burn it."

"Don't you dare!" He's still breathing heavily but he manages a smile.

"You at least have to punch it in the nose. Face your fears." I gesture for him to go in front of me.

We edge back down the tunnel and approach the clown. Liam pokes it with one finger. It falls backwards on to the ground, revealing it was perched on top of a wooden box.

"I think it's a puzzle box," Python gasps. "I've seen these things on the show before."

It's really not sitting right with me that Jackie's put one of her props in part of the cave system we're meant to avoid, along with a camera. I think about the mysteries surrounding the other competitors – Abbie's obsession, Liam's lies, Marla's act and Python's secrets. And I wonder just how much Jackie knows about us all, and what she's using that information for.

"What does the box do?" Liam asks.

"There'll be something inside. Like food, or torches," Python answers.

"Food?" Marla bends down by the box. There's a door on one side. She rattles the handle. "How do we get it open?"

I circle the box. On the opposite side, there's a grid of twenty-four flat squares plus one empty space. The squares can be slid into new positions by moving one into the empty space, then another into the space the previous square has freed up.

"That's a sliding puzzle game," Abbie says. "Shuffle them all into the right places and it will make a picture."

"Man, I suck at that sort of thing," says Liam. "Never could do a Rubik's cube."

"I'm good at Rubik's cubes," Abbie says.

"Why does that not surprise me?" Marla mutters.

"There's a technique. You just have to learn the algorithms. Mind out the way." Abbie clambers over the box, then sits cross-legged on the floor. She starts to slide the squares, gradually shuffling their positions.

The pieces begin to slot into place. It's a photograph of a man. I can see the separate parts of his face. A pair of eyes watching me from opposite sides of the puzzle. Thin lips mostly obscured by a moustache. An ear. A nose. Abbie's expression hardens.

"Jackie is playing games with us," she says quietly.

"Yeah, I know. That's the whole point of the show," Marla grumbles.

"That's not what I mean," Abbie says.

"I know what you mean," I say.

"Who's the dude?" Python asks.

"I don't know." Abbie's lying.

Liam peers over the box. He squints at the picture and frowns. "But that's . . ."

"That's what?" I say.

He shakes his head. "I don't know. I thought I recognized him."

Abbie watches him with mistrust, then returns her attention to the puzzle. "Last piece. This one should open the box."

She clicks the final piece into place and it triggers the lock. Marla pulls the door open. Her lips curl in disgust. "There's no food here."

Python peeps over her shoulder. He squeals. "The diary cam!"

It's an old-school handheld video camera encased in a waterproof plastic case. It looks like it's been through many adventures of its own and I'm surprised it still works.

"I'm so excited. This is AMAZING." Python does a bizarre thrusting dance in celebration.

"Watch where you're flinging that thing around," I say. "You'll have someone's eye out."

He makes a heart shape with his hands and uses it to frame his groin. "Bite me, Lex."

"Eww," I say.

Python lifts the diary cam and points it at himself. An

expression of utter terror crosses his face. He presses record. "We're falling to pieces here; I don't know how much more we can take. Marla's badly hurt and we don't know what to do."

"Marla's fine," Marla mutters.

"What was that?" Python whips his head around, shaking the camera in the process. When he looks back at the lens, his eyes are wide. His voice becomes high-pitched. "There's something here with me. I can hear it breathing. I have to go . . . I can't . . ." He shakes the camera vigorously with both hands, then switches it off.

"Er, what are you doing?" Liam says.

"Booyah!" Python puts the camera on the floor and dances around it, pointing with alternating hands. "That's how you rock the diary cam!"

"You should be the actor, not me," Marla says.

Python misses her sarcasm. "Nah, that's your thing, babes. This is so cool. Let's go record some footage!"

"Don't you get it?" Marla says. "Something is very wrong here. The show's over."

Python winks at her. He's back to his old self and it's actually a relief. "Marla," he says, making a kissy face. "I AM the show."

EIGHTEEN

Extract from the transcript of the T-minus-one-day final interview with Keith Gough, aka "Python" [P], contestant 4/5 *It's Behind You: Season 3, Episode 10 (Umber Gorge Caves)*. Interviewed by Jackie Stone [JS], producer of *It's Behind You*.

JS: Python. Love your channel. It's going to be amazing having you on board for this extra-special, last-in-the-season episode. Can you tell the viewers why you wanted to come on the show?

P: You know exactly why, you bloodsucking, blackmailing parasite.

JS: Blackmail is a big word. I'm not forcing you to do anything.

P: But if I don't, you'll ruin my life. Have I got THAT right?

JS: [Laughing] You're being dramatic, which is what I love about you. That's what your fans love too. But let's adjust the attitude, shall we? Unless you'd rather I stick to the footage I already have of you?

P: You really are evil.

JS: You say evil, I say dedicated. I've built this show up single-handedly into something that made *your* career. You need me more than I need you.

P: Funny, because I heard the show was in trouble. Yeah, you're not the only one who can dig up dirt on a person.

JS: Listen here, you annoying little twunt. There's *nothing* I won't do to make this episode a success. Bear that in mind when you answer my next question. Because I can destroy you. Just. Like. That. [Clicks fingers]

P: Um, wow. You're going full psychopath, then? No build up, just straight in there.

JS: [Laughing] Let's start again from the top, shall we?

P: Fine. [Clears throat] Hey pals, Python here, ready to get the inside scoop on my absolute favourite show in the whole universe. *It's. Behind. You.* I'm so excited. Coming on this show is EVERYTHING.

JS: Perfect. And what's your greatest fear?

P: My greatest fear? Oh my GOSH, I am TERRIFIED of creepy-crawlies. Anything with more than four legs. Nope, nope, nopity nope.

JS: That's more like it.

P: It's bullshit, though. What I'm *really* scared of is insignificance. I want to matter.

JS: Don't we all. And what's your game plan, Python?

P: I'm going to go in there and be MYSELF. Hopefully the Puckered Maiden is a fan of my vlog and won't scare me too much. EEEEEK.

JS: Last question. Do you think you can win?

P: Win? I'm just trying to get through this thing alive, Jackie.

NINETEEN

We head past the puzzle box and along the tunnel, Liam leading the way. I can feel a faint vibration rumbling up through the soles of my feet. Like the sound of a waterfall. And then the rumbling stills and I realize it was the caves, moving and settling beneath us. It doesn't exactly fill me with confidence.

"This area is unstable," Liam says. "All the nineteenth-century excavations weakened the caves."

"How do you know so much about this place?" Marla asks.

Liam opens his mouth like he might lie yet again. Then his shoulders slump. "I grew up in this town."

"What?" Marla says. "Why didn't you say?"

He grinds his teeth together. "I lied to Jackie and the other producers about who I am so I could get on this show. I think Jackie knew, but she didn't say anything. At the time, I thought it was because it was too late to replace me, but now I'm beginning to think she was playing me all along."

"Not just me, then," Abbie says.

"What do you mean?" Marla says. "Who are you both?"

They walk on without answering.

The tunnel becomes narrower and littered with rocks and boulders. We're no longer on a human-excavated path, but something that formed naturally with no regard for my spine. As we edge through the cramped space, I think I hear a dragging, scraping sound behind us. I stop and listen, but hear nothing else.

Perhaps I'm losing my mind and hearing things that aren't there. It's preferable to the alternative, which is that we're being followed. We crawl under a huge slab of rock bigger than a car, pebbles and loose dirt beneath my knees and palms. I straighten up in a small, musty space filled with boulders and empty plastic bottles. There are filthy puddles around some of the rocks. It's very different to the beautiful caverns of the Puckered Maiden Experience.

Liam rests against the wall while the rest of the group catches up. "Everyone doing OK?"

Python responds by raising the diary cam to film Liam. "Tell us where we are, Liam," he says, doing an impressive Jackie impersonation. "And make it sound *exciting*."

Liam's mouth briefly twitches with a smile. "The tunnel we're about the enter is known as Big Boy's Terror after a local gentleman got wedged in here for three days in the nineteenth century. According to local records, it took two horses and eight men to free him."

"I can hardly contain my excitement," Marla says sourly.

"Don't worry, it's been widened since then."

Liam stoops down next to what looks like a solid wall of boulders and dirt. There's a small archway at the bottom half-filled with a puddle. It's big enough to crawl through, but barely so. Liam slides on to his belly and disappears into the hole. Python records Liam's feet shuffling as he pulls himself through, then gestures for me to follow.

I salute the camera before lowering myself into the stinky puddle. The hole opens up almost immediately, not into a tunnel as I'd expected but a series of spaces between rocks through which we have to climb and crawl. I start to worry Liam doesn't know where he's going. We could end up trapped, and no one would know where we were. I can hear the grunts and shuffles as the others follow behind me. It's no comfort to know I'm not venturing into the darkness by myself.

"We're having an adventure," Python narrates breathlessly. He's still managing to film himself with the diary cam. "Where are we going? Who knows. Will we survive? Also up in the air. But is it fun? No, it isn't."

"Do you need a hand?" Abbie says. She's talking to Marla, who's struggling.

"Don't touch me," Marla snarls. She's fine.

And then a low alcove opens up ahead. I crawl out and Liam reaches down to help me to my feet. My bravado is back before I've straightened up.

"You brought us that way so I'd spend ten minutes staring at your bum."

I think I manage to embarrass him, although it's hard to tell with his torch shining into my face.

The others emerge from the tunnel and we take in our new surroundings. There are no props or cameras here. Just a mud floor and a lake taking up half the domed cave. On one side of the cave, there's a mountain of rubble that's slipped in through what was once a tunnel. It reminds me of the set for a movie featuring another planet, except there are empty beer cans and plastic wrappers all over the place.

"Where are we?" Python says, still filming.

"This is Montgomery's Auditorium," Liam says quietly. "The Echo Chamber to locals."

"That's the name that . . . the man who took that photo used." Abbie clasps a hand to her mouth. "This is it! I can't believe I've finally found this place."

We step closer to the lake. I peer into the still water. "Isn't this where Victoria and Tommy met old Puckered Face?" I say.

"Some say this is where Sophia Kingston drowned, all her rage bringing her back as the Puckered Maiden," Abbie says. "This is so amazing!"

"You sound unfeasibly excited about this," I laugh. "I've never heard you so animated."

"If I'm going to prove she's real, then this lake could hold the key." She scurries off, already digging through her bag.

Python sweeps the camera around in a circle. "On a more troubling note, how many local teenagers have lost their virginity in these caves? I suspect it runs into the hundreds." He sniffs. "Ahh, you can smell the hormones."

"Why are you still filming?" Marla snaps.

Python lowers the camera. "I guess it's something to do. I'd cease to exist if there wasn't a camera."

I'm about to say this wouldn't be a bad thing, but something about his tone makes me hesitate. It doesn't sound like he's joking.

"Besides, there might still be a show, if there's enough good footage. Jackie is *particularly* dedicated to this episode."

That's a good point. I can't imagine her giving up. She'll probably fix whatever it is that means they're not opening the door and everything will revert back to her carefully planned schedule.

"Dare me to go in the water," I say. May as well give the viewers something worth watching.

"It's freezing," Abbie says. She's busy setting up her equipment by the water's edge.

"And that's where the Puckered Maiden lives," Marla adds. "Remember what happened to Victoria?"

I remove my shoes and roll up my filthy trousers. I eye

Python and grin at him. "Let's have a competition. See who can stay in the pool for the longest."

"Arggghh, nothing better BITE me," he says, handing the diary cam to Marla. "Make sure you get both our faces in the shot."

"OK, ready?" I say. "Loser streaks through the model village."

"YES!" he says. "I have the body of a GOD."

I aggressively twerk at him and he pretends like I'm firing bullets out of my groin that strike him in the chest.

Abbie looks up from her work. "You two are ridiculous."

"It's reality TV," Python says. "Ridiculous goes with the territory."

"How did you even get on the programme, Abbie?" Marla says. "You're not exactly . . . you know."

Abbie thinks about this. "I guess I fitted with Jackie's grand plan for the episode," she says bitterly.

"Are we doing this or not?" Python says, taking off his leggings to reveal tiny snake-print briefs. Eww.

"On three," I say. "One . . . two . . ."

Python's scream as he wades into the water is unlike anything I've ever heard. I'm sure it makes the cavern rumble, it's so loud. "Oh my god, oh my god! It's as cold as Lex's HEART in here."

"Four degrees," Abbie says. "I measured it."

Python stops screaming. "Lex's heart?"

"I have no heart," I say as the cold stabs at me with its

pointy fingers. "Ahhh. This water is nice now I'm getting used to it."

Python stares at me with his mouth open, then we both crack up laughing.

"Any sign of the Puckered Maiden yet?" I say, to keep my teeth from chattering.

"I'm trying to determine the angle that was used to take the photo," Abbie says. "It wasn't doctored, according to all the people who've tried to disprove its authenticity, but the photographer could have used props."

"My feet are turning to ICE," Python says. "It hurts."

"Get out, then," I say, gritting my teeth against the pain. "I could stay in here for hours."

Something rumbles. Ripples spread across the water towards us.

"Uh-oh, here comes the Puckered Maiden," I say.

Python eyes the ripples uneasily. "You know, maybe we really should get out now."

"*Here she comes with skin so white,*" I sing. "*Through the water, through the night.*"

"Lex, stop it," Python says. "You have a terrible voice."

"*A taste of love, then torn apart. Here she comes to eat your heart.*"

"Interesting you know that rhyme," Abbie says. "The man who took the Puckered Maiden photo also made a recording in these caves. That same tune."

A loose pebble drops from the roof and splashes near Python. He launches himself out of the water with a squeal.

Marla films him, getting a close-up of his expressions as instructed. I step out of the water at a leisurely pace, all the while thanking every god I can think of that Python gave in before I had to. My toes are going to fall off, but it was worth it to beat the little turnip on film.

"Oh no," I say dramatically. "Cameraman Carl's going to see your bare bottom."

"He'll love it," Python says. "You all will."

"Nope," Abbie says. She roots through her bag and pulls out a doll. The same doll that's been stalking me. The Puckered Maiden, with her wrinkly skin and sharp-toothed mouth. The same doll I burnt. The same doll that was on my bed in the B & B. The same doll as in the butcher's shop.

"Where did you get that?" I say.

"I brought it with me. To test a theory."

"No, I mean where did you *get* it?"

"The internet. The Puckered Maiden Experience had loads of them made to sell as souvenirs, I think. Someone find me a big rock."

Oh. That makes sense, I suppose.

Python picks up a rock, straining under its weight. Abbie ties a piece of fishing wire around the rock and secures the doll to the other end. She tosses it all into the deep water. The rock drags the doll down with it.

"You're trying to recreate the photo," I say.

"I think this could be how he took it." She frowns at the doll, just visible through the cloudy water. It's floating

138

beneath the surface, with its hair fanned out around it and its arms raised. "It could work, with the right lighting."

She sounds disappointed. It's clear that Abbie wants the photo to be real, although I still can't work out why it matters so much to her.

She steps back and takes a photo. It lights up the cave in a blinding flash. The water is so dark. Abbie takes a dozen more pictures, then examines them on the camera's screen. "It's not working. It looks totally fake."

"Sorry, mate," Python says, wrestling his leggings back on.

She looks up, her eyes shining. "This is great! It means his photo may still be real. *She's* real, and I'm going to prove it."

I turn away as she flashes another picture. That's when I realize that Liam isn't with us. He hasn't been since we first entered the cavern, but I was too distracted to pay it much attention. He's standing on the opposite side of the wide space, staring at the rockslide.

"Liam?" I say, walking over. "What's wrong?"

"It's nothing." He quickly wipes his eyes.

"It's clearly not nothing," I say.

Python hurries over. "Mate?"

Liam closes his eyes and shakes his head. His throat is twitching, like he's struggling to hold back the tears.

"Liam?" Even Abbie sounds concerned and steps away from her camera.

Marla places a hand on Liam's arm. "You want to tell us about it?"

"It won't go any further," I say. "Jackie will never know. Right, people?"

Python snorts, then turns off the diary cam. "Don't talk to me about Jackie. You have no idea what that woman is like."

"I think I do," Abbie sighs.

"Jackie is a cow," Marla says.

I fist-bump Marla. It's the first sensible thing she's said since I met her. The four of us are so different; the one thing we have in common is Jackie and all her games. It makes us ... not exactly friends, but close enough that no one wants to see Liam so sad.

"All right," he says quietly. "You all deserve to know why I'm here."

He walks over to a boulder and sits down. He rests his head in his hands. We all wait. He takes a deep breath. Then he lifts his head. "Two years ago, a girl was killed in these caves. Her name was Laurie Cox and she was my sister." He gestures to the pile of rocks. "This is where she died."

TWENTY

The diary cam lies on the floor. Abbie's video camera waits to record the silent water; the doll floats beneath the surface. We're all sitting cross-legged by the water, the Puckered Maiden briefly forgotten. Fairy tales don't hold so much horror when faced with real human tragedy.

"This was somewhere to come," Liam says at last. "Lots of us used to sneak into the Puckered Maiden Experience at night. Mess around with the exhibits, toast marshmallows, sit and chat. You know."

"Did you know the cave was unstable back then?" Abbie asks.

"Of course. These caves have been a death trap since the nineteenth century. There's a river running below ground and it's been eating away at the rock above it for millennia. Then the Kingston family put all these holes in the rock like cheese, and eventually it gave way."

"I'm surprised Jackie got permission to film here," Python says.

"I'm not," I say. The more I find out, the more I start to wonder just how far Jackie would go to save her struggling show. I remember Mr Health and Mr Safety saying something about Jackie not giving them the results of the structural survey. Her fudging the approval required to film in the caves doesn't feel too far-fetched.

"No, me neither." Liam smiles ruefully, but then the smile fades again. "That night, I was here with my sister and two friends. I had to head back to the entrance for a minute to phone my parents so I left them in here. But they must have gone through into the next cave, as they ended up trapped there when the ceiling came down."

"Where were you when the cave-in happened?" Abbie says.

"I was heading through the model village when I heard the sound." He closes his eyes. "I'll never forget it."

"Jesus," Python says. "It must have been thousands of tonnes of rock that came down."

"More, probably. It sounded like the whole gorge had collapsed. I tried to find the others, but I could hardly see for the dust. Eventually I realized they were trapped and I went for help."

"My chaperone said two of the teenagers escaped on their own," Marla says.

"Eventually." He swallows. "They separately found their way out days later."

"But not Laurie," I say softly.

"Not Laurie." He runs a hand through his hair. "The others told the rescue teams she'd been ... um ... she'd been buried."

"I'm sorry," I say.

He shakes his head and closes his eyes. "I should have tried harder to get to her. But I gave up."

"You couldn't have moved all of that by yourself," Abbie says, nodding at the rocks. "Not physically possible."

"The rescue team started to clear it," he continues. "But they gave up, too. They said the caves were too unstable and there was no evidence anyone was still alive on the other side."

He stands and paces over to the rockfall. He shines his head torch on the wall until he finds a small gap. It's barely big enough to slip a hand inside and goes on for metres. He sighs and closes his eyes.

"After the collapse, my ears were ringing and I couldn't see or breathe, but I was sure I heard her voice. Calling my name like she was looking for me," he says. "I couldn't see this gap through all the dust, but coming here and seeing that there really is a way I could have heard her? Maybe she did survive."

"You don't think she was buried by the rocks?" Abbie says. "You think she made it?"

"Honestly? I don't know. That's why I had to come here. I have to be sure. I've been trying to get in here for two years, but they closed off the caves after the accident."

"So you lied to get on the show?" Normally I'd high-five him, but it doesn't feel right given the circumstances.

"I used a fake name. Everyone in town knew me and my sister as Liam and Laurie Cox, but Cox was my stepdad's surname. My driving licence says Liam West, so that's what I used when the show asked for ID. No one questioned it."

"Even when you arrived in town and everyone recognized you?" I ask.

He shakes his head. "I thought the game was up. I was going to confess the truth to Jackie, but she cut me off. At the time I thought she was just desperate to get enough people for the show. Now I think she maybe knew more than she was letting on and *wanted* me to come looking for Laurie. That would explain the camera in the tunnel we weren't meant to enter."

I remember Jackie telling me the other contestants had better stories than mine. She totally knew exactly who Liam was. She played him in the hope his trauma would make exciting TV.

"What was your plan?" Python asks.

"I thought there might be evidence of what happened to her." He takes a shaky breath. "A body, maybe. I can't leave her here. Everyone else has given up on her, but I can't."

We fall into a brief silence.

Python's the first one to speak. "So you want to dig through all of that?"

"No. But if the others found a way out, then there's a way in. If I can retrace their steps to the other side of the cave-in, maybe I can find Laurie. There's an old route known as the Bone Road. It comes out close to where Laurie would have been trapped. If she survived."

"That's where you're heading? Is this Bone Road narrower than the path we came in through a minute ago?" Python asks.

Liam laughs in reply. "Just a little."

"Well, I'm coming," I say. "Not like I have anything better to do."

"What?" Liam's eyes widen. "But it's dangerous. Really dangerous."

"Still coming."

"Me too," Python says. "I have a sister. I can't imagine leaving her behind somewhere like this. I'll help you find Laurie if I can."

Marla sniffs. "I have a sister too. But I'm not coming."

"Someone needs to find out what really happened to her," Abbie says. "I'm in."

"Guys, you don't have to," Liam says.

"Sure we do." Python pats his shoulder. "We've bonded through shared terror and, right now, I'd die for any of you. Except for Lex."

"Feeling's mutual," I say.

"I'm still not doing it!" Marla says.

"You don't have to." Abbie starts packing up her stuff. "No one is going to force you."

Marla throws her arms in the air. "Arghh, all right, I'll come. Happy now?"

The entrance into Liam's Bone Road is in one of the museum caves we're yet to explore. So we head back the way we came in to look for it. We're most of the way through the passageway when there's a rumble. It's like a motorbike starting, only it intensifies. The vibrations surge through my hands where my palms are pressed on the rock. I can hear tiny pebbles skittering loose from cracks. Liam's torch lights concentric rings spreading across the puddles.

Liam freezes. Then he's moving again, vaulting over rocks and sliding through gaps. The rest of us try to keep up as the vibrations intensify. Every muscle in my body is bracing itself, like that might protect me if the ceiling comes down. My heart feels like it's going to turn itself inside out. The rocks scrape me as I pass, but I don't care. All that matters is we get out of this tunnel.

And still the rumble continues.

I scramble out from under the flat slab of rock and reach back with Liam to pull the others out one by one. Only, now that we're out of the tunnel, the rumble sounds different. I don't think it's a cave-in after all. It sounds more like a motor.

We collapse on the floor, trying to catch our breath. "What is that noise?" Abbie says.

We get to our feet and follow the rumbling sound.

Overhead, strip lights flicker on and off. Not the production crew's lights – it's the original Puckered Maiden Experience lighting that's sat here gathering dust for decades. I can't believe anything still works. The rumbling gets louder.

We track the source of the noise down to a small space hidden among jagged rocks off to the side of the tunnel. An old generator sits in a small puddle of oily water. It stinks of diesel. It splutters and the lights dim, then flicker back again.

"Someone just switched it on," says Abbie.

"Who?" Marla says.

We all exchange looks. I'm reminded of what Python said; the show never uses live actors. I glance up and down the tunnel. Whoever it was must have run back towards the public caves. Back where we're now heading.

"Maybe it was Cameraman Carl," I say.

The generator chokes out a loud thunking noise that makes me jump.

"Get back, she's gonna blow," Python yells, throwing himself on to the ground.

He curls up into a ball with his bum sticking up in the air. When nothing happens, he stands up shakily and dusts off the diary cam.

"And that, people, is how you pretend to be terrified."

I slow-clap him. "Amazing performance."

One of the strip lights fails with a pop. The others briefly brighten, then dim again.

"I think this generator is the power for the Puckered

Maiden Experience," Abbie says, stooping down to examine the wires snaking along the corridor.

"So?" Marla says.

"So this means we have light throughout the caves. We don't have to rely on the TV crew's lighting actually working."

"LIGHT!" Python cries, running off down the tunnel.

I smile at his excitement. I can't help but share a little of it, too. I flick up my collar and go after him.

TWENTY-ONE

I know what you're thinking. We're all acting like total idiots. We should be running terrified and hammering on the door until someone lets us out. Only, this is reality TV. Nothing real happens on reality TV.

By tomorrow, I'll be heading back to my old life, wishing I'd made more of my time here. There will be a boring explanation for all the weird stuff going on. Speakers hidden among the rocks, programmed to play the sounds of creepy laughter and footsteps. A mild ground tremor unbalancing Abbie's camera and causing it to smash into pieces. Our heads tricking us into seeing and feeling things that aren't real.

Sat at home, I'll be left regretting not having the adventure I came here for.

Besides, blocking out the truth is kind of my thing.

We sneak back into the Puckered Maiden Experience. To our right is the tunnel leading to the model village and Cameraman Carl. To our left is an unexplored passageway leading further through the cave system. We're heading left.

We edge past the wall of plastic hands and duck under the dangling skeletons. Now that the generator is on, the original scares have power. As Marla passes, a spider erupts from an alcove with a high-pitched cackle, making her shriek.

"I hate this place!" she complains.

I yank one of the plastic hands off the wall and stroke her hair from behind. "So pretty," I cackle.

She jumps and swats at the hand. "Choke on a testicle, Lex."

Abbie shushes us. "We don't want Carl deciding to act like a responsible adult and stopping us," she whispers.

"Yeah, Lex," Marla says. Another of the animatronic spiders springs out at her. She punches it off its pneumatic arm, leaving it dangling from wires with its legs twitching. She keeps walking like a badass bitch. It's kind of hot.

Liam whistles under his breath. "She's scary when she's angry."

"It's a big improvement," I say. "I'm finally starting to like her."

Abbie smiles. "I don't think the feeling is mutual."

The tunnel leading to the next section of the Puckered Maiden Experience is marked with a skeleton holding a big arrow. There's a speech bubble coming out of its mouth and it's meant to say *hello*, only the bulbs in the last letter are broken and it just says *hell*.

The TV crew have set up lights and cameras down here, but the lights aren't on. The Puckered Maiden Experience lights have power, although most of the bulbs are long dead. Those that are still working are hidden in grubby nooks and crannies and are coated in a thick layer of limescale or full of water. They cast more shadows than light, leaving plenty of places for creepy things to hide.

I'm lagging a little behind the others, posing the limbs on a skeleton, when I hear the hiss of a whisper. Pattering footsteps. I look back. The footsteps stop abruptly and all is quiet. Too quiet, like held breath. I walk on again, then jump around into a fighting stance. I think I see a shadow shifting, but it could be the ghosts of the flashing neon signs.

I squeeze through a crevasse between two gigantic rocks that are leaning against each other like drunks. My tummy flips when I emerge on the other side and the others are nowhere to be seen. There's a second where I'm left imagining what it would be like to be trapped in these caves all alone. But then I round the corner and find everyone waiting for me in the next cave.

It's an impressive space. We're on a natural balcony that encircles half of the cave, three metres up from uneven rocks that slope down to water. There's a mesh cage around us to ensure we stay on the walkway and don't tumble to our deaths. The cage forms a tunnel about thirty metres long that will take us through this cave and into the next.

As we circle the cave, I spot a beach-like area. The water is lit from within by blue lights, giving it a magical appearance. The walls are sheer cliff faces like someone's hacked at a block of chocolate. But it's the zombies that stand out.

I'm presuming they're more victims of the Puckered Maiden. One has climbed on to the mesh tunnel and is trying to grab us from above. Most are positioned around the cave, standing on rocks. These ones are all pointing at the water, at something hidden out of sight from our position.

"I want to get down to the water," Abbie says. "I'd like to set up a camera."

"How many cameras did you bring with you?" Liam laughs.

"Only eight," she replies.

"Only eight?" Python gasps. "Is that all?"

Abbie misses his sarcasm and shoots him a dark look. "Not all of us have rich families who can buy us expensive equipment. After my dad left, Mum could barely afford rent."

"No, I didn't mean . . ." Python starts to say. He stops himself. "That sounds tough. I'm sorry about your dad."

"I'm not sorry, I'm angry. I just wish I . . . it doesn't matter."

We continue along the tunnel. As we walk, I spot the Puckered Maiden half-submerged in the lake. Her hair's matted and her skin is white and peeling. One of her arms is moving like she's trying to pull herself out of the water. Or maybe she's trying to pull something in. Her latest victim is lying on the shore.

This dummy isn't in period dress like the others. It must be one of her more recent kills. He's lying on his back, surrounded by a pool of blood that looks black in the poor lighting. His arms are stretched above his head like he's been dragged towards the water's edge. It's all surprisingly creepy, I have to admit.

"So, so tacky," Python says. "I love it."

"Yeah, well, lots of the locals didn't," Liam says.

"I saw the protestors," says Python. "There was one old lady who seemed really pissed."

Liam nods. "Sally-Ann Kingston. Her ancestors owned these caves."

"My chaperone said Sally-Ann was part of the reason this place never opened," I say. "That, and the antics of the Puckered Maiden."

Liam chuckles. "Sally-Ann convinced a lot of the contractors this place is haunted. Mortimer Monk lost a fortune because the workers refused to finish."

"But you don't think it really is haunted?" Python says.

"Nah," Liam laughs. "There's no such thing as ghosts."

"There's no convincing proof," Abbie says. "It's not the same."

"Surely if the supernatural was real, someone would have found evidence by now," I say.

"You can't see the wind, but you can feel it," Abbie says. "And I can feel there's something here in these caves, waiting to be discovered. I just have to look in the right places."

"Ghosts are a lot like love," Python says earnestly.

"This is all bullshit," Marla grumbles.

As the others continue towards the next cave, I hang back. I can *feel* something, too. And then there's a scuttling sound I can't deny. I glance at the Puckered Maiden dummy in the water, its arm jerking back and forth. The coloured lights in the lake have cycled through several different shades. Now they're glowing red, turning the water into blood.

I hear the scuttling again. "I don't think we're alone," I call. The others stop.

"Nice try, Lex," says Python. "This is getting old."

"No, I'm serious."

The noise comes again and, this time, the rest of the group hears.

"There's something in here with us," Marla says, clinging on to Liam.

"It won't be able to get through the wire," Python says, his voice shaking. He sweeps the diary cam in a semicircle to take in the entire lake.

"Or we won't be able to get out," I say.

The footsteps echo through the cave again, this time chased by the sound of cackling laughter.

I back into Python. We all huddle together, except for

Abbie. She's holding on to the wire mesh and squinting down at the water.

"Look," she whispers. "Look at the dummy by the water."

We ignore her.

Laughter. Running footsteps that echo hollowly. "You're all going to die," a raspy voice taunts, like the static on Abbie's tape recorder. It seems to come from every direction. "I warned you, but you didn't listen."

"Who is that?" Python cries. He holds the diary cam aloft, hands shaking.

"It's coming from up there!" Liam shouts, pointing to a rocky outcrop that overhangs our cavern. There must be a hidden tunnel up there.

I think I see the edge of a filthy dress being dragged out of sight behind a rock. Like before. Like outside my B & B. My heart slams so hard in my chest I can't breathe. I laugh. This is terrifying and horrifying and amazing.

"Will you listen to me?" Abbie snaps. "The dummy by the water! Look."

The Puckered Maiden is still twitching away with her arm reaching for her victim. I look more closely at the body. A man with a wiry beard and blood-splattered skin.

"That's a freakishly realistic dummy." Python's fingers dig into my skin as he squeezes my arm.

A beat of silence. The water laps at the shore.

"It's not a dummy," Abbie says.

TWENTY-TWO

Wiry beard. Grubby combats. A reinforced support vest. Cameraman Carl. Dead.

A voice crackles in the darkness. I can't tell where it comes from, only that it's close. "You're all going to die," it echoes. "Just like he did; just like Laurie."

Fuck. There's something in here with us, and it's murdered Cameraman Carl.

It feels like all the air has vanished from the cave. Then everyone starts screaming. My internal organs attempt to escape my body like rats abandoning a burning ship. It takes a second for me to regain control of my limbs, and then I'm running back the way we came.

I'm fast and I leave the others standing. I don't look

back to check they're all right, but Python's gasping breaths follow me, and Liam's heavy footsteps, and Abbie's rattling bag, and Marla's sobs.

The next cave is metres away when I skid to a halt. There's a woman standing in a shadowy alcove, dead still like one of the dummies. She's wearing a filthy dress with a veil hiding her face. Her long hair is loose in tangled knots.

The Puckered Maiden.

We scatter like skittles. Everyone is screaming. I briefly imagine how we must look – like the top ten *It's Behind You* moments rolled into one. But I don't care. I need to get away from that thing.

"You're all going to die," the Puckered Maiden screeches in our wake. "Go on. Run, run away."

I don't look back to see if she's chasing us. The others follow me as I thunder along the tunnel and burst out into a new cave. It's like a museum, full of display cases and information panels. But I'm not paying attention to where I'm going and I trip. My feet fly out from beneath me and my hip smashes into a heavy wooden display case.

The case wobbles. It falls. The sound of breaking glass is deafening. Items from the display scatter at my feet as I trip through all the shards of glass. Sepia photos, a nineteenth-century pistol, a diamond necklace. I skid and slide, but somehow stay upright.

There's an exit nearby and I run towards it. A curved doorway cut into the rock. Leading anywhere but here.

"Wait," yells Liam. "Stop!"

We ignore him and bundle through the doorway. I stop. We're in a small domed room with no exits other than the doorway we came through. There are five large boxes on tall tables and nothing else.

A heavy metal gate slams down behind us, like the sort you'd expect to find in a prison. Thick bars and an electromagnetic lock that triggers with a loud buzzer sound. A red light flashes. I throw myself at the gate and try to pull it open, but it's no good. There's no way we're going to get it open without a key.

We're trapped.

TWENTY-THREE

"Stop it!" Abbie shouts. "For goodness' sake, calm down."

Liam's the only one paying her any attention. The rest of us? Well, Python is howling on his knees, Marla is hyperventilating and I'm screaming, because it feels like the right thing to do.

"We're all going to die," Python wails.

"AHHHH," Marla bellows.

"AHHHHHHH," I scream, louder than Marla, because I don't like to be outdone.

"What's wrong with you all?" Abbie says. She sounds frustrated to the point of tears.

"Oh my god, I can't think," Liam says, putting his hands over his ears. "They've all gone feral."

"ENOUGH!" Abbie bellows. "A man is dead. Pull yourselves together."

I stop screaming. Python does too, and contents himself with whimpering softly. Marla wipes her nose on her hand and hiccups.

"What was that?" Abbie says. "What did you think all that was going to achieve?"

"Letting off steam," I say. "It's been a traumatic ten minutes."

"More so for Cameraman Carl, don't you think?"

We all shuffle sheepishly, staring at the ground. I risk a glance at Liam. He looks *disappointed*. Oh, the shame.

"All right, now we have your attention, we need to work out what's going on," Abbie says.

Python raises a hand. "Um, what do you think happened to Cameraman Carl? Was he really dead?"

"I don't know," Liam says. "I wish we'd tried to help him instead of, you know ..."

My heart sags. We can't help Cameraman Carl because I led us all into a trap and now we're locked in this stupid cave.

"He was gone," Abbie says. "There was too much blood. Either he hit his head or someone hit him on the head, then dragged him down to the water's edge."

"It was her. The Puckered Maiden," Marla says.

"Maybe," Abbie concedes. "Either way, the important thing is to get out of this room."

Liam stoops to examine the lock. "The TV crew must

have rigged the door with a motion sensor to shut it behind us. Thanks, Jackie."

Python shakily points at the five boxes perched on five stands. "I know this game. The key will be in one of those."

I approach the first box and try to pick it up. It doesn't budge; maybe it's bolted down. The only way to find out what is inside is to stick your hand through a hole in the top and feel around.

"One time," Python whispers, "they put a live ferret in one of the boxes. Another time, there was a bowl of SICK. I mean, it wasn't real sick. It was curdled milk and lumps of carrot or something. One of the contestants was seriously terrified of puke, so she totally freaked out."

"That's a mean thing to do," Liam says. "This show is horrible."

"Everyone knows what they're signing up for." Python's smile fades. "Although I have to admit, tonight has veered a little off-piste."

"So we take one each?" Liam picks the one closest to him and pats the wood.

We all go over to stand by one of the boxes. I try to peer through the hole in the top, but it's obscured by a bundle of black fabric. I'm going to have to plunge my hand in and hope for the best.

Python jogs on the spot, psyching himself up. "Let's do this thing. Who's going first, then?"

Abbie shoves her hand into the box, all the way up to her armpit. She doesn't look happy as she roots around. But she holds it together and pulls something out through the top of the box. It's covered in fake spiderwebs. She brushes it off. A box of white wine, like the ones my mum drinks.

"No key," she says. "Next."

"All right, I'm going in." Python squeals as he slides his hand through the flaps of fabric.

"Oh my god, oh my god, it's wriggling. It's alive!"

He goes to pull out his arm, but Liam takes his other hand and squeezes it. "You've got this, man. You were born to do this."

Python nods dementedly. "I was. Argh, I hate creepy-crawlies! This is my worst nightmare."

But, to my surprise, he keeps searching. He's not as much of a wuss as I thought he was.

"I think I have something. If I can reach . . ." He yanks his hand out of the box, clutching a package. "I got it. I did it!"

I point at something crawling up his sleeve. "Um, you've pulled?"

Python glances down and spots a large cockroach waving its long antennae at him. It's a glossy, horrible thing with barbs on its legs. Python hurls his package in the air and flicks the roach across the cave. Liam catches the package; the roach scuttles to safety.

"It HAPPENED and it was HORRIFIC," Python declares, holding his chest and panting. "What did it get us?"

Liam picks up the package. It's wrapped in brown paper and tied up with string. Inside are several plastic-wrapped chocolate bars. "Oh, thank god," Liam says. "It's food."

162

"Food?" Marla snatches one of the bars. She stares at it, her nostrils flaring. She looks like she might implode. "This is chocolate-covered toffee. *Hard* toffee."

"Oh yum," I say. "Good find."

"I can't eat hard toffee." She hurls the bar at the wall camera with a shriek. "I am terrified of hard toffee, and you know that, Jackie, you witch."

"You're terrified of . . . toffee?" Python says.

"When I was seven, I got my first wobbly tooth. One day, I was eating a toffee and I felt this horrible tugging, popping feeling in my mouth. I took the toffee out and my tooth was stuck in it. Stuck in the toffee! My second-worst memory."

"What's your worst?" Liam snorts. "Did the liquorice allsorts man kill your family?"

"Very funny." She shoves her hands into the box in front of her. "There's nothing in here."

"There will be," Python says. "Reach in further, babes."

"There's noth—" Marla's eyes widen and she freezes. She slowly pulls her arm out of the box. She's holding a snake.

The rest of us leap back with a chorus of gasps. Marla looks at the snake. It looks at her. There's a breath of silence. Then she screams and hurls it at Python, which feels appropriate.

It's rubber. We all realize this except for Python, who wrestles with it frantically for a few seconds before he catches on. He chucks it on the floor.

"Oh god, this game is going to kill me," he pants, resting his head on the wall.

"Just you and me left," I say to Liam.

"All right," he says. "I'm going in."

"What's your greatest fear, Liam?" I ask, putting on a Jackie voice.

"Clowns," he says. "If Pennywise is in there, I'm going to cry."

He puts his hand in the hole, gritting his teeth and squeezing his eyes closed.

"Anything?" I say.

"Argh, it's wet," he says. "Wet and lumpy."

"Oh no, it's sick again," Python says.

"Don't say that," Liam says, retching. "Shit, it's cold."

"Oh my god, chilled sick," Python says. "One time, I was sick in the snow and the next day, it was still there, only frozen. And another time, I ate too much watermelon, and—"

"Will you stop it?" Abbie says, looking seriously queasy. "You are *not* helping."

"I'm sorry, I'm just nervous right now."

"I have something," Liam says. He pulls his arm out with a wet-sounding noise.

I pre-emptively gag, but there's no sign of sick, only a few baked beans and a lot of tomato sauce. Liam glares at Python. "Mate, you made that so much worse than it needed to be."

"Sorry," Python says sheepishly.

Liam unwraps the soggy package. It contains a plastic box in which there's a single head torch. "That will come in handy," I say, pinching it out of the box. Liam already has his own.

"The key must be in yours," Abbie says, nodding at my box.

I eye the hole at the top. If this is the box where the key is hidden, there will be something really bad inside. I'm regretting my choice. But everyone's going to think I'm a coward if I wait much longer. I roll up my sleeve and slip my hand through the fabric opening.

It takes a few seconds for the tips of my fingers to find anything. Whatever it is feels kind of cold and moist, like raw meat.

"Urgh," I say. "I think it might be pigs' hearts in here."

"What about a key?" Marla says.

I reach down to the bottom of the box. My fingers slip against the slick base and find a hard piece of plastic. I hook it up with a fingernail and pull my arm out. It's a key card, smeared with blood.

"Thank god," Marla says.

Abbie reaches over and takes it from me. She wipes it clean on her trousers, then walks to the door.

"Wait," Liam says. "Whatever killed Cameraman Carl is out there."

"And you lot are in here," she says, slipping the key card into the slot. "I'll take my chances."

TWENTY-FOUR

Everything is quiet. We creep through the museum, feet crunching on the smashed glass. There's a staff-only door marked with a no-entry sign. It leads through to the part of the zombie cave where Cameraman Carl is lying dead. We stop outside.

"He's gone," Marla says. "There's nothing we can do."

"We should still check," Liam says. "Cover him up, I guess."

"There might be clues. To how he died," Abbie says.

"Why does it matter?" Marla says.

Abbie ignores her and opens the door. I cling on to the outside of the wire cage and lower myself slowly on to the slippery rocks. Pebbles skitter beneath my feet as I descend.

We step down on to the beach area. The lake ripples as the Puckered Maiden dummy claws her way above the surface with the grinding of old gears.

I glance back up at the raised walkway and try to get my bearings. No, this is right. This is where Cameraman Carl was lying.

So why isn't he here any more?

Python turns on the spot. "Could we have mistaken one of the dummies for him?"

The walkway from which we first spotted the body is a long way away, and the lighting isn't great. Perhaps one of the dummies looked more real from up there. We'd been panicking, our minds all playing tricks on us.

"What about the Puckered Maiden?" I say. "You all saw her, right?"

The others exchange looks. "I started running because you were running," Python says. "I didn't see *anything*."

I was sure it was the Puckered Maiden standing there. But now that I think about it, I never saw her move. There's a dummy with tangled hair up near the entrance into the cave. The cave's creepy soundtrack combined with thinking Cameraman Carl was dead made me believe she was real at the time. But now?

"I think we might have got ourselves caught up in the moment," I admit.

"No," Abbie says. "I know what I saw and it was Cameraman Carl."

"From a distance, though?" Liam says.

"I know the difference between a dead person and a dummy!" Abbie snaps, angry but only for a moment.

"I've never seen a body before," Marla says quietly.

"I have." Abbie sits down on a rock. "My father, at his funeral."

"That's rough. I'm so sorry," Liam says.

"Don't be. I hadn't seen him for years. He left when I was a baby and I spoke to him just a handful of times." She pauses. "He didn't even look like me. Just some old white guy who picked his own ego over his family. Heart attack at fifty-four and that was it."

"That's so young," I say.

"He lived a hard life, I suppose. Drinking, travelling. It took its toll." She blinks. "I don't know why I'm telling you all this. You're not my friends."

She gets up and clambers over the rocks to reach the door. I check my surroundings one more time, but Cameraman Carl's not here. I catch up with Abbie in the museum.

"It *was* him," Abbie says. She pauses. "At least, I thought it was."

"Why would someone move the body?" Liam says.

"Perhaps we interrupted them," Abbie replies. "Then they had to wait until we were locked in that room to finish the job."

"The simplest explanation is he's fine," Marla says. "We imagined it all."

"I hope you're right." Liam gestures in the direction of

the model town cave. "Hopefully he'll be sitting by the campfire where we left him."

But when we get back to the campfire, there's no sign of Cameraman Carl. His camera and the hip flask are where he left them, but the man is gone. The fire has almost completely burnt out and the model town is lit up in shades of night-time. It feels cold and threatening.

It's a show, I tell myself. Nothing's real.

Jackie will surely have the front door open soon. Cameraman Carl will be found sleeping off his whiskey somewhere and we'll feel stupid.

As if mocking me, the faintest hint of laughter drifts through the cave. Footsteps scuttle somewhere among the fake houses and shops. I spin around. I think I spot something ducking out of sight, around the side of the tea shop. A burst of cackling follows.

"Oh my god, she's come back," Marla whispers.

"You're all going to die," a voice hisses.

We spin to face the shops behind us. Running footsteps echo through the darkness. It's impossible to tell where they are coming from. Someone laughs. "Die, die, die," the voice taunts.

Python screams. "Over there, over there." He points into the shadows.

My hands curl into fists. Enough tricks. Lex Hazelton isn't the cowering-in-fear type. I steel myself and march towards the fake houses.

"Lex, what are you doing?" Liam calls after me.

"If there's someone in here with us, I'm going to slap some manners into them."

The footsteps start to run, disappearing through the dark town. I run after them, shining my torch into each shop as I pass. My heart hammers so fast I can't hear myself think. Which is good, because my head would tell me to stop being so stupid. What kind of person chases after a ghost that may or may not have murdered our cameraman?

I hear something in the bakery ahead. A scrabbling and scratching. I slow my pace, and approach tentatively, my legs heavy and my breath catching in my throat. I reach the shop. Its painted wooden facade is decorated in shades of pink and pale blue.

I peek inside. The shop's empty, but there's a gap at the back where the wooden boards have been prised away from the shed's frame. Half of me is relieved I've not come face to face with the Puckered Maiden. Part of me is disappointed that I still don't know for sure if the laughter and footsteps are real or a recording.

I back out of the shop. Now the adrenaline has gone, I'm shaking. Then I realize it's not me; the *ground* is shaking. Dust and pebbles drop from above. The whole cave trembles like it's an earthquake.

"Cave-in!" Liam shouts. "Get under cover."

I hurl myself inside the butcher's shop. Of all the places I could have picked, I chose the one with metal hooks and giant plastic meats hanging from the ceiling. I huddle under the table as the caves shift with a sound like breaking waves. A deep rumble gets closer and closer.

The whole cavern makes a cracking noise, like a gunshot, and then silence. The rumbling stills. A few stray pebbles land. I wait, holding my breath, unsure if the danger has passed. Then I crawl to the door and poke my head out.

A section of the cave has fallen in. Tommy's coffin has been completely buried in rubble. Broken stalactites and the remains of huge limestone columns litter the fake cobbles and there's a huge crack running the length of the ceiling. Electrical wires dangle like tangled snakes, the original lights torn away by falling rocks. But otherwise, the cave is still standing.

I jog down through the town to join the others, who are all emerging from their hiding places.

"I thought this part of the cave system was safe?" Abbie says.

"It's meant to be," Liam says. "Perhaps the cave-in two years ago weakened this section."

"We need to get out of here," Marla says.

The rest of us hesitate.

"You're kidding, right? You're all so fame hungry or desperate to prove god knows what you'd risk being crushed to death?"

"No, you're right," Liam says. "Come on."

"We'll make our way back to the entrance and wait for someone to get the door open. They'll have felt the tremor in town," Abbie says.

171

We head up the street, towards the tombstone cave. We haven't got far when the rumbling starts up again. We freeze, but it's over as quickly as it started. A warning.

"We need to hurry," Liam says. Even so, he's the one who keeps glancing over his shoulder. Walking away means leaving his sister entombed here for ever.

We're almost at the low tunnel into the tombstone cave when I hear it. I hold up a hand for the rest of them to stop. There's a faint hissing noise, like someone whispering very far away. And then there's another noise. A clicking, tapping noise. Fingers rapping against stone, or wooden feet clacking together.

We exchange looks, then quickly duck inside the butcher's shop. There are plastic sausages and meats lying everywhere. I pick up one of the candelabras off the table to use as a weapon. Python goes for a salami. We wait. The noise grows louder. That tapping is familiar, although I can't place it. It gets closer. Someone is coming.

I peek out of the shop with my knuckles squeezed white around the candelabra. A pair of figures steps into the cave surrounded by light. I leap out from my hiding place with my weapon raised. Python jumps out behind me and throws the salami. It lands pathetically on the ground in front of one of the figures.

"There you are," a sharp voice says, kicking the salami aside with a fuchsia spike boot.

"Jackie?" Abbie says, peeking out from behind me.

"The executive board are being pussies," Jackie says. "So I'm here to save this show."

"Save the show?" Python says in a small voice. "You mean ... save us?"

"Like I always say, the people *are* the show," Jackie says.

"Ben?" Liam says, appearing on my other side. "What are you doing here?"

"They wanted people who knew the caves," Ben says. The light from Jackie's head torch picks out the definition in his arm muscles. He's wearing an action-star white vest despite the temperature. "And people who are good in tough situations."

"I'm surprised you'd come back here," Liam says. "It's like you have something to prove. Something to make up for."

"Maybe," Ben says. "Is that why you're here?"

Liam looks away.

Abbie frowns. "Is it just you two? I thought there would be a rescue team."

"They went back after that last tremor to wait for the professionals, but I couldn't leave you here." Ben pauses for dramatic effect. "Not again."

"Good for you," Liam mutters.

Jackie strides forwards to stand between Ben and Liam. I can't believe she's still wearing her heels and designer dress. That explains the clacking noise as she approached.

She smiles delightedly. "The chemistry between you two is sparkling."

"What do you mean?" says Ben.

"Oh, nothing. You signed that release form, right?"

"Yeah," Ben says. "You said I should in case I got caught in shot during the pre-show filming."

"Perfect."

"Um, Jackie?" Marla says. "We're leaving, right?"

Jackie nods. "Of course, but there's no rush. It was a little rumble. Nothing to get worked up about. Now, did you manage to—"

She stops. Stares up at the ceiling. There's a noise like the first drops of rain on the roof, and wind through the trees. A rumbling travels up my legs and vibrates in my chest. A thundering noise like the approach of a train gathers momentum, nothing to deafening in moments. It threatens to throw me off my feet. I try to speak and only then do I register how loud the noise is.

"Run!" Liam screams, but I don't hear the word. The world falls in around us.

TWENTY-FIVE

The noise goes straight through me and I feel it inside my teeth. A plume of dust erupts through the cavern and engulfs us all. It stings my eyes and catches in my nose and burns my lungs when I take a breath.

All I can do is curl up in a ball on the ground and hope it stops. But it doesn't. The thundering goes on and on. It's like the whole gorge is caving in and being swallowed up by hell itself. I'm sure it's only a matter of seconds before I am swallowed up too.

My heart beats so fast I think it might burst. I really, really don't want to die. All I can think about is how my parents will find out about my death from a kindly police officer knocking at their door. Teacups rattling in their saucers and my mum smoothing down her skirt again and again: a nervous habit she has. "Right," she'd say. "Thank you for telling me."

It would break her, and she's broken enough as it is.

It's not often I admit this to myself, but I can be massively selfish at times. I only stop to think about others when it's already too late.

At this thought, the rumbling and thundering stops. It feels like this brief moment of introspection paid a tithe. Like the cavern was testing me. I sit up and dare to open my eyes barely a slit. I can't see a thing.

I can hear someone coughing. I crawl around, groping around in the darkness. I find something. A leg, perhaps. I pat its length, looking for the rest of its owner. It's a skinny leg, clad in Lycra. Not moving.

"Python?" I say.

"Thank god," he replies, breathing out heavily. "I thought you were the Puckered Maiden. Why are you feeling me up, Lex? Now's not the time but later, maybe."

"Urgh, don't flatter yourself. Are you hurt?"

He coughs again. "I think I might be dead."

"You're not dead. Come on." We find each other's hands and feel our way sightlessly through the cave.

"Lex? Python?" It's Liam's voice. I walk straight into him: my face, his chest. Liam must mistake our collision for a hug, as he puts an arm around me and pulls me against him. "It's going to be all right," he says, squeezing me tightly.

"Can I have a cuddle too," Python says, angling himself between us and wriggling in close. "This is nice."

I laugh, despite the awfulness of our situation.

"Why isn't this radio working?" Jackie's voice asks. I can't tell where she is.

"There's no reception down here," Ben replies. "We're cut off."

Their voices fade to murmurs as they move away through the darkness.

"Abbie?" I call. "Marla?"

"I'm all right," Abbie says from somewhere nearby. She doesn't sound any different from usual, like this is a perfectly normal way to spend the night.

"Marla's here," Liam calls. "I've got her."

I follow his voice and nearly trip over Marla. She doesn't complain, which isn't a good sign. I drop on to my knees and check for signs she's breathing. She moans softly. She's not dead, but she's not exactly awake. Liam heaves her up, grunting with exertion.

Now the dust is starting to settle, I can make out his form. Something bright cuts through the darkness, although the light is muted. A moment later, Abbie appears beside us, using her camera flash to find us.

"Where are Ben and Jackie?" she asks.

"I don't know where they've gone. But I heard their voices and they're OK," I say.

"We need to get through to the next cave," Liam says. "Walk forwards until we hit the cavern wall, then follow it round to the right."

We edge forwards until the wall of the cave looms out of the dust. I trail my fingers along its rough surface and look for the tunnel full of all those old portraits. The wooden structure has collapsed, revealing the space behind. There's a hidden passageway leading off to another part of the caves, full of rocks and loose wires fizzing from the ceiling.

Movement. There's something down there, crawling over the rocks on all fours. I gasp and jump back, clinging on to Python. He holds me tightly, whimpering. The thing on all fours scrambles towards us, slipping and sliding on the loose stones like a newborn deer.

It has blood on its face.

Then Liam moves *towards* the thing, not away. "*Ronnie?*" he says. "Is that you?"

Ronnie? As in Veronica? What's she doing here? And how, and why?

The shock of seeing her gives way to concern. I help her off the pile of rocks and she sits down on the floor. She's covered in dust and there are tear tracks down her cheeks, merging with some of the blood seeping from a nasty cut on her cheek. One of her earrings is missing.

"The water's so cold," she sobs, her vision unfocused. "I can't go back there, not again."

"Veronica," I say, gripping her shoulders.

She jerks, like she's waking up. "Lex?" she whispers.

178

"What are you doing here?" Liam says.

"I . . . I was looking for you. After that first tremor, I saw most of the rescue team leaving and I panicked that no one would find you. So I snuck inside. I was looking for you up towards the Echo Chamber when the ceiling came down. Oh my god, not again."

"Looking for me, or trying to stop me?" Liam says coldly.

Veronica swallows. "I told you it wasn't safe! Why didn't you listen to me?"

I frown. There's something I'm missing, but I'm struggling to put the pieces together with all this dust prickling my eyes and throat. Abbie works it out before I can.

"Wait. You're *Veronica*. The girl who was trapped here by the cave-in that killed Laurie," she says, sounding excited at the realization. "And the boy with Jackie is Ben Brennan."

I stare at Veronica. Shy, law-abiding Veronica who wants to be a civil engineer and blushes red at the thought of even talking to a boy. She was one of the two teenagers who saw their friend killed by a cave-in and had to crawl through endless tunnels to escape. Wow, talk about not being who I thought she was.

I have a thousand questions, but before I can ask them, Liam speaks.

"We need to get out of here," he says. "Come on."

Through the hazy air, I can see the cave-in has

179

completely blocked off the tunnel leading back towards the entrance. Part of the model town has been swallowed up and the little houses poke out of the pile of rubble. I can just make out Ben and Jackie, looking for a way through. But it's no use. Like the cave-in that killed Laurie, there are thousands of tonnes of rock between us and the way out.

"Oi, Jackie," I shout.

"In a meeting right now," she says in that sing-song voice of hers. "Write me a memo."

"You know what, they can catch us up," I say.

Leaving Ben and Jackie to their futile task, the rest of us head in the opposite direction, climbing over wooden beams and the portraits now lying amongst the debris. The next cave looks like it's been picked up and shaken. Loose pebbles have skittered in and the animatronic spiders are skew-whiff on their perches. But the air's breathable.

Liam props Marla up against the rock on which Abbie had balanced her now-ruined thermal camera. Marla looks similarly bashed up, but she's conscious and as bad-tempered as usual.

"You all right, babes?" Python says, moving to tuck Marla's hair behind her ear.

"DON'T touch me," Marla says. "Oh my goodness, I'm so sorry. I think I'm really hangry right now."

Python sits next to Abbie instead, eyeing Marla with confusion. I notice that Veronica is standing against the wall, as far away from the group as she can get. She's stopped crying and her tear-streaked eyeliner is a *look*.

I have this picture of my mum from the early nineties, when she wasn't much older than me. She's dressed in a black vest top, with her hair dyed black, black lipstick and black sparkly make-up running down her face. She assures me she was happy and this was how she liked to dress. It's hard to believe that girl turned into someone so *grown-up*. I would have liked to know her when she was young and free.

I rub dust from my eyes. "You all right?" I ask Veronica.

She thinks for a moment and smiles weakly. "No, actually. Not at all."

"Me neither."

She looks around at the animatronic spiders and skeletons. "But at least I dressed appropriately," she says, gesturing to her earring and dress. The gauzy petticoat underneath her skirt has ripped and she's lost a few buttons from the bodice. She shivers and rubs her bare arms, so I give her my suit jacket.

"Um, everyone? Lex just did something nice," Python says, clicking his fingers to get the attention of the others. "I'm worried about her."

"She must have hit her head," Abbie says, managing a rare half-smile.

A weight lifts off my chest at their teasing. We're trapped, but we're still alive, and I still despise the lot of them. "I think you'll find I wanted to show everyone my guns," I say, kissing my flexed bicep.

"Poseur," Python says. He stretches his arms above his

head super obviously, then drops to the floor and tries to do a press-up.

Such an idiot. I laugh as he collapses on his face and lies there panting.

Footsteps sound and Ben clambers over the rubble. He has dirt smeared across his white vest, arms and on one cheek. He couldn't look more the part if he tried, and I'm thinking he tried quite hard.

"Everyone," he says. "I have some news—"

"Out of my way. I'm in charge here, remember," Jackie says, stepping in front of him. "So it turns out the route back to the entrance is completely impassable."

"What does that mean?" Python says. He must already know the answer. It's pretty damn obvious.

"It means we're trapped here," Ben says, glancing meaningfully at Veronica. He drops his voice to an ominous growl. "Like last time."

TWENTY-SIX

Extract from the transcript of local source telephone interview with Ben Brennan [BB], pre-show research for *It's Behind You: Season 3, Episode 10 (Umber Gorge Caves).* Interviewed by Jackie Stone [JS], producer of *It's Behind You.*

JS: Ben, thanks for speaking to me. My name's Jackie. I'm a producer on *It's Behind You.*

BB: I heard you were coming to town.

JS: I've been researching the caves and was hoping to ask you some questions. I came across your name in reference to an accident in the caves two years ago where a girl was –

BB: Whoa there. I don't think it would be appropriate for me to talk about this.

JS: Wait, Ben, don't hang up. My source also tells me your mother recently lost her job.

BB: You what?

JS: I thought you might appreciate a job offer. The TV crew offers a number of paid internships to local residents, and there's always the prospect of a full-time position for those who prove to be honest, principled individuals. That's you, isn't it?

BB: I try to do the right things, yes.

JS: And this job could help your mother, Ben. Isn't that what you want? I'd just need you to answer a few questions first.

BB: [Audible sighing] What are the questions?

JS: Perfect. So, you and two other teenagers were trapped in the caves, and one of them – Laurie Cox – was never found. What do you think happened to her?

BB: We were all separated when the ceiling came down. Laurie was crushed by the rocks. Veronica and I found our way out.

JS: Am I right in thinking you and Laurie were dating?

BB: How did you ...? Yes, we were.

JS: My condolences. And her brother was your best

friend?

BB: He *is* my best friend. Liam moved out of town but we're still in touch. He's a good guy.

JS: Oh. Right. That's a shame. I mean, um, it's a shame he moved away. So there's no bad feeling between the two of you? I heard you got into a fight soon after Laurie's disappearance and the police were called.

BB: He wanted to go into the caves to look for Laurie and I stopped him. It was too dangerous.

JS: I hadn't realized how heroic you are, Ben. Laurie would be proud, I think.

BB: What? Look, Laurie's death is still raw in this town. A lot of people would be hurt if you tried to turn it into entertainment.

JS: I would never do that, Ben. If anything, I want to understand how these caves have impacted the local community so we can ensure the stories we tell are respectful. I wouldn't want to inadvertently dig up something that would be better left buried.

BB: All right. Your contestants won't be going into the part of the cave system where Laurie died, will they? Because it's dangerous.

JS: Absolutely not. There will be strict protocol. Hey, what would you say to going in with them? As one of the contestants. You could make sure everyone is safe and confront some demons while you're there, so to speak.

BB: Are you kidding? No. No way.

JS: Let's just say you'll think about it. If you did agree, then ... Ben, are you still there? Ben?

[Call disconnected]

TWENTY-SEVEN

Jackie claps her hands together. "Let's all try to see this as an opportunity," she says. "You know what they say – the show must go on!"

Marla pushes herself up on to her elbows, wobbling unsteadily. Her bubble wrap has mostly unravelled and the cut on her head has been joined by a nasty graze on her cheek. "Wait, you're still worried about the episode?"

Jackie laughs lightly. "I know things haven't gone entirely to plan—"

Marla's expression hardens. "*Not entirely to plan?* I almost died. There's something in here, killing people."

"Don't be silly. No one is dead."

"We think Cameraman Carl might be, actually," Abbie says.

Jackie's perfect smile cracks. "Do you have anything on film?"

"What?" Python gasps. "No."

"Then I'm sure he's fine. He probably snuck out after that first tremor."

"No," Abbie says slowly. "I don't think he did."

Jackie put her hands together like she's praying. "So let's take that thought and stick a pin in it to deal with later."

"You know what? I don't care about Cameraman Carl," Marla yells. "I don't care about any of you, I just want to go home. I've had enough of rocks and dust and damp and putting my hand in boxes containing motherfucking *snakes*."

"Oh wow, you found the mystery boxes?" Jackie says, her eyes lighting up. "Please tell me you got some good footage."

"Shut up!" screams Marla. "I've had enough of this stupid show. This show can burn in hell. You can *all* burn in hell!"

"Go on, let it all out," Jackie says, fighting a delighted smile.

"Shut up, *Jackie*. Why don't you go stick a stalactite up your bum, and then the Puckered Maiden can eat you like a *fucking lollipop*. I'm done with this show."

She spins away and stomps out of the cave. Her bubble wrap snags on the rough wall, so she tears it off and stamps on it for good measure.

"Marla?" Jackie calls, going after her. "Marla, I don't think your story is complete. You signed a contract, Marla."

I wait until their voices have faded, then turn to Veronica. "I think Marla stole my in-cave baddie persona."

This raises a weak-tea smile. "You've not been embracing the clumsy sidekick role, then?"

Python puts an arm around my shoulders. "Lex is more of a . . . demon of chaos and danger."

It's the nicest thing anyone has ever said to me. "And you're the attention-seeking YouTuber who tries way too hard to make people like him."

"I really am!" he says, grinning at me.

"You guys are funny. Do me," Liam says.

"Oh, she totally would," Python says. I kick him in the shin.

"You're the likeable hot guy with a mysterious secret," I say. "Not the most exciting role, but the viewers need someone to perv over."

"I'll take that."

We all glance at Abbie. She barely looks up from her notebook. "I'm the boring one who everyone watching will hate based on the twisted standards of reality TV, not realizing that I am the only one here who is a normal human being."

"And what about Veronica and Ben?" Python asks.

Our brief moment of levity fizzles and dies. "I'm not part of her show," Ben says coldly. "I made that very clear to her when she tried to recruit me."

"She wanted you on the show?" Liam says.

"She called me up weeks ago, asking all these questions about Laurie."

"She called me too," Veronica whispers.

Liam shuffles uncomfortably. "That woman's been playing us all along. How much of this disaster did she plan?"

"Well, the fire and the power cut was an accident," Ben says. "She was furious when the HQ truck went up in flames. She seemed to think it was sabotage, but as soon as she found out that the cameras were still rolling, everything was about finding a way to ensure the show could go on."

"So the lights going out really wasn't deliberate?" I say. "And the locked door?"

"The lock was damaged in the fire. But I'm pretty sure she held back on getting it open. She kept disappearing to field calls from her boss. I overheard her arguing with him. He wanted all of you removed from the caves but she was determined that the filming continue."

"She's obsessed," Python says. "I heard this episode is make or break for her. If it doesn't do well, her career is over."

"And if we don't get out of these caves, our lives are over," I say. "How *are* we going to get out?"

Liam, Veronica and Ben exchange looks, like they're unsure whose turn it is to speak.

"We'll have to get out the same way Ronnie did," Ben

eventually says. "Take the Bone Road past the original cave-in and then we swim out."

"No, we can't!" Veronica cries. "We can't go back there."

"What choice do we have?" Ben says, his voice cracking. "Outside, they'll be arguing about whether it's safe to blast through the caved-in section and trying to convince themselves we're already dead. We're on our own."

"We can't stay here waiting for a rescue that won't come," Liam says. "The caves are too unstable."

Veronica's face darkens. "And this has nothing to do with you wanting to look for Laurie. You'd risk all our lives over this?"

"I'm trying to save our lives! Look, only one person needs to swim out of here. You don't have to do it again, I will. They'll have to send in divers to rescue us once they know we're there."

"I don't want you to get hurt, Liam," she says quietly. "We already lost Laurie and I don't want to lose one of you too."

"Yeah, you said all of this before I came in to the caves, Veronica. I know you're worried, but it wasn't your choice then and it's been taken out of our hands now. If we stay here, we're all going to die."

Veronica starts to cry again. Part of me wants to give her a hug, but I'm confused. Veronica, Liam and Ben have this huge shared history that they all tried to keep to themselves. Their pain feels private and I don't feel like I

191

can squeeze between them to console Veronica. But neither Liam nor Ben moves to console her, either.

There's a weird atmosphere between the three of them. Mistrust merged with familiarity. I still can't get my head round the fact that they were all here together on the night that Laurie was killed. I think about the way Veronica reacted when I joked about all the people who'd died in these caves. She lived through something terrible and she didn't say a word to me.

"What happened?" Abbie ventures quietly. "Last time. What happened to Laurie?"

"She was crushed by the rockfall," Veronica chokes out. Her face is puffy and red from crying. Liam and Ben both close their eyes.

Abbie nods. "Are you sure? Because I heard—"

"Don't," Ben interrupts. "You don't know what it was like. Trapped in the darkness for so long that you forget what the light is like."

"If it was so terrible," she says, "why did you come back here?"

Liam folds his arms. "It's a good question. You both tried to convince me that returning to the caves was a mistake, yet here you are."

"For god's sake, I'm here to stop anyone else from dying," Ben cries, slamming a fist against the wall. "I loved Laurie, and I can't bear the thought someone else could suffer her fate."

We're all silenced by Ben's outburst. Then Jackie clip-clops over with Marla skulking at her heels.

"And cut. Goosebumps," Jackie says. "Great intensity, Ben."

"What?" Ben says, looking bewildered.

Veronica's mouth falls open and her cheeks flush. "I'm not part of your show."

"Everyone's part of the show. You just have to decide how you want your story to be told – by you or by me." She clicks her fingers. "Now, let's move out. The dust is terrible for the shot and we have an episode to film."

TWENTY-EIGHT

The museum cave stretches out into a long, narrow cavern. We weave through the poorly lit exhibits as the cave lights flicker on and off. I can hear the old generator chugging away somewhere nearby. It's making a stuttering, juddering sound. I think it's running out of fuel.

The museum exhibits bring to mind a cluttered antiques store, full of old stuff. The silence makes me uneasy and I quicken my pace. But Jackie seems content to stroll between the display cases, reading information panels like this is a field trip.

"Abbie, did you know Sophia Kingston's father refused to speak to her for her entire childhood?" he says. "He was disappointed that she wasn't a boy."

Abbie hesitates. "I heard that, yes."

"Yes, I suppose you, of all people, would have." Jackie's using her stirring voice.

It's the voice she used on me during my sound bite interview when she kept asking about my mum. At the time, I thought she was just lucky in her choice of subject. Now I realize she knows everyone's secrets, from Liam's real reasons for entering the show to whatever Abbie is hiding from the rest of us. She dangles our secrets like bait, waiting to see if we'll bite.

"You've no doubt read all the books on her," Jackie continues. "My favourite is the one by Brian Tobes."

"Who's he?" I whisper to Liam.

He doesn't answer. Suddenly, he looks drawn.

"Let me guess. The man on the puzzle box?" I say. "I'm betting he took that famous photo of the Puckered Maiden, too."

"How'd you work that out?" he says.

"I'm beginning to understand how Jackie operates."

Liam pauses at one of the cases to look at a photo of Sophia Kingston. The woman who became the Puckered Maiden, if the legend is to be believed.

"Brian Tobes was obsessed with the Puckered Maiden's victims," Liam says. "He got hold of the report where I'd said I heard Laurie's voice. He was so excited that she might have survived the cave-in because that meant she could have been killed by the Puckered Maiden, instead. He kept calling me after she died and wouldn't let it go."

"Wow, that's harsh."

"It was horrible," Liam continues. "He asked me all these questions about her, what happened just before she died, who was she dating, was she in love. I'd just lost my sister. I didn't want to be part of his conspiracy theories."

Abbie strolls closer to investigate one of the other display cases. She's trying too hard to pretend she doesn't care about our conversation.

"Do you know what happened to him?" I ask, watching her out the corner of my eye.

Liam shakes his head. "No idea. He stopped calling me about a year ago. I figured he'd finally got the message."

Abbie abruptly strides away. Jackie watches her go with her shark's smile. She points Python's diary cam at me and Liam. "Maybe you should ask Abbie about Brian Tobes?"

"Maybe you should do one," I say, pushing past her.

We step into the next cave and fan out to take in the sight. Even Liam, Ben and Veronica, who must have been here dozens of times, are awed into silence. It's taller than a theatre, with multiple jutting rocks that form balconies looking down on an actual river. The river weaves through the cave, appearing from beneath a low overhanging stone and disappearing into an arched tunnel painted to look like a heart.

Sitting dead still on the silent water are four swan boats, like the sort you'd find in a theme park. They're all filthy and the paint is faded. One of the four has a large hole smashed into its plastic body, like someone's kicked it.

I look more closely. There's a rail system beneath the water that must propel the boats through the heart tunnel to what lies beyond. The cave's combination of beauty and tackiness takes my breath away. Not for the first time, I'm both horrified and impressed that Mortimer Monk took a natural wonder of the world and turned it into bargain-bin Disneyland.

"We have to wade through to the next cavern," Ben says. "Follow me."

"Why? We can take the boats!" I bound down the steps towards a control panel. The lights are on. The ride's still working after all these years. I hit the green button and the wheels beneath the water noisily turn. One of the boats judders along towards us. I bound on to the jetty. "All on board, come on people."

Ben jogs to keep up with the boat and clambers in. It tips heavily to the side under his weight.

"This could be your chance," I whisper to Veronica. "A romantic boat trip . . ."

"No, Lex. It's not what you—"

"Just get in," I say, giving her a little push.

Veronica trips slightly and has to take Ben's hand to stop herself from falling into the boat. As she sits, her skirts puff out around her. Jackie narrows her eyes.

"There are only three boats. Liam, you go in that one too," she says. "The three of you can catch up on old times."

Liam lets himself be guided towards the edge of the

jetty and he steps over into the boat. The boat stutters its way to the heart-shaped opening. The whole time Liam's glancing over his shoulder at Jackie. "You knew who I was right from the beginning," he says.

"You applied under your mother's maiden name," she laughs. "It wasn't much of a ruse."

"You set me up. You turned my sister's death into a soap opera."

"Yours is such a wonderful story. I simply ensured all the players made it on to the stage." Jackie looks pleased with herself as the boat disappears into the tunnel. "Python and Marla, you two lovebirds go next." She passes Python the diary cam with a sickly-sweet smile.

Marla doesn't exactly look happy, but does as she's told. She slouches down on to one of the benches in the next boat and Python squeezes in beside her. He holds the camera at arm's length to get both of their faces in the shot.

"Ahh, that's perfect," Jackie says as the boat leaves the jetty. The way she says *perfect* reminds me of a rattlesnake for some reason. Like the word is loaded with threat, waiting to strike. She purses her lips, like she's fighting a smile. "Marla, this is most certainly going to make Damien jealous."

"Damien?" Python says.

"Her boyfriend?" Jackie says. "Didn't she tell you?"

And there it is. The strike.

"Oh wow, she went there," I mutter under my breath.

"Yup," Abbie says, sighing. "I feel sorry for the guy."

"Why would I tell him *that*?" Marla whispers.

"So I'm kind of lost," Python says.

"Did I say something I wasn't meant to?" Jackie says. "Silly me."

The smile slides off her face a moment later. She stares at me and I think there is a challenge in her eyes. It reminds me of this girl at school, Amelia Rogers. She was big and mean and didn't hesitate to go for the eyes. One time, we all saw her trip this younger girl in the playground, sending her flying into a bush.

Amelia strutted off, looking pleased with herself, while Mitzi was left bloodied and sobbing. The look in Amelia's eye as she passed me was exactly the same look Jackie's giving me right now. *Go on, I dare you*, it's saying. If you think I walked away from Amelia's challenge, you don't know me at all. Just like I'm not going to let Jackie think she's top dog in this cave.

"Jackie, guess what?" I say.

"What?"

I walk backwards along the jetty, rooting around in my pocket. "I've got something for you, if I can find it."

Jackie crosses her arms and waits. I pull my closed fist out of my pocket and flip her my middle finger. Then I step backwards into the boat. Jackie glares furiously at me as we sail away, as slowly as tar. It's a whole minute of middle finger and my arm starts to shake. We finally edge around the corner into the tunnel.

I sit down opposite Python. He's still recording. Marla is

199

staring into her lap with those wide brown eyes of hers. She looks like she might puke. It's brilliantly uncomfortable.

"So, you have a boyfriend?" Python says cheerily. "Damien."

"I'm an actor," Marla says, as if that explains everything.

"A *paid* actor?"

Marla slaps her hands down on to her legs. "Fine. Yeah. Jackie paid me to pretend like I was possessed in that séance and to act like I fancied you."

"I can't believe you'd do that."

"You've known me for, like, a few hours. What, did you think we were going to get married and live happily ever after? Get over it!"

He pulls a confused face. "No, I mean *It's Behind You* has never used plants before. No scripts, it's a rule."

I laugh out loud. "That's the part you're pissy about?"

"This show is important to me, Lex. I get that it's a joke to you two, but I based my whole career on it and now I discover it's a lie?"

"You honestly thought it was real?"

"I thought it was *authentic*."

"Unbelievable," I say.

"Wait," Marla says. "You're not upset I don't actually like you?"

"Um, not really. You weren't very good at pretending, if I'm honest."

"Fine," she says coldly. "Thanks."

"Let me get this straight," I interrupt. "You're upset

because the boy you don't actually like also doesn't like you?"

She crosses her arms. "I hate both of you." Python's still filming her so she turns her back on us. Python laughs so hard he nearly drops the diary cam. We don't get to wind Marla up any further, though. The boat emerges into a small cavern and we're greeted by an epic sight. The space is lit with coloured lights, making it eerie and magical. The water is molten moonlight.

"Oh. My. Giddy. Aunt," Python says. "This is the best-worst thing I have ever seen."

To our right is a small beach area. Set up on a large fibreglass mound that's been painted like rock are papier mâché dolls. There are two main players on the stage – a man and a woman. They're standing on what's presumably meant to be Umber high street, a hundred and fifty years ago.

One time, I visited a model village with my parents, who walked around all the tiny houses at an excruciatingly slow pace, marvelling at how the tiny trains moved and the windmill's sails turned. This display is like that, only everything is terrible. The grass is ripped felt, the trees are plastic, the houses are mostly soggy cardboard.

"Marla, you should look at this," I say.

Marla ignores me. Her loss.

The boat triggers a lever beneath the water and there's the thunk of a mechanism hidden beneath the display's fibreglass base. Metal sticks lift and twitch and the dolls come to life. As creaky music plays, the dolls move towards each other. They twist and jerk like they're fighting demonic possession. The soundtrack kicks in, crackling with static.

"*Sophia Kingston*." The woman bows, introducing herself.

"*Tarquin Barleywood*." The man bows.

"I want one," I say.

Python snorts. "You know, I don't think it's possible to dream up anything as shite."

"*Why won't you love me?*" Sophia's voice says. "*I know you only want to marry me for my money.*"

"Ouch," I say. "Marla's not the only one with a mercenary approach to love."

"Shut up, Lex!" Marla snaps.

"It's kind of sad," Python sighs. "Why would she marry someone who she knew didn't love her?"

"I guess that's what some girls do," I muse. "All those expectations."

"Yeah, you're right. Maybe she was being pressured by her friends and neighbours to settle down. God knows I get it enough from my relatives and I'm not a nineteenth-century girl. 'Oh, Keith, when are you going to bring a nice boy home?'"

I turn to face him. "You're gay?"

"Nope," he says. "But you wear leggings and eyeliner around a ninety-year-old and they're going to make assumptions."

I gesture to my clothes and short hair. "With you there. My family don't accept that being bi is a thing, so they're waiting for me go full lesbian."

"They've clearly not seen you in Liam-letch mode."

I stick my tongue out at him. Poor timing. The boat carries us through the curtain and wet, stinky fabric slaps into my face. Great. Ancient mould, in my open mouth. It's like licking an old bath mat.

The diary cam shakes as Python films me spitting and gagging. I pull myself together and flick up the collar of my shirt, side-eyeing the camera. I think I got away with it.

We emerge into another cavern. It's a similar setup to the last. A river running through a domed room, half of which is dedicated to another craptastic puppet scene. This time, there is a third figure. She and Tarquin stand together next to a field of cows, while Sophia stands to one side.

"*I have changed my mind,*" the man declares. "*I am going to marry Mary.*"

"Who the fuck is Mary?" Python says.

"The doll with the yellow hair," I say. "Keep up."

"Our girl Sophia can do better," he says. "She'll find someone else."

"*You will pay for humiliating me!*" Sophia screeches. "*I will never recover from this slight and you will suffer for all time.*"

"Or maybe not," I say.

The puppets stop moving mid-twitch. Mary clatters on to her side. The strip of tape that had been holding her on her pole has peeled away.

"Who made this car crash of an exhibit?" I say. "Because I want to buy them a milkshake."

"I want to marry them," Python says. "This place should be number one on TripAdvisor for the entire country. It's amazing."

The boat hits a bump. With an awful grinding sound, it half-detaches from the rail. The wheels keep on pushing us forwards, only now we're sort of going sideways, with the hull of the boat dragging noisily along the wall.

"Oh my GOSH!" Python yells, fanning himself with both hands.

"What have you done, you pair of shit buckets?" Marla screams.

"Did you call us *buckets*?" I grab the edge of the puppet display and shove us straight again. The boat clunks back on to the rail.

Python clutches his chest, hyperventilating. "Scrub my previous comment, this place is a massive health and safety risk. I can't believe Jackie thought it was acceptable to send us in here. Jackie, you SUCK BUCKETS."

I catch myself laughing — with *Python*, of all people. Wow, I've changed, and I'm not sure I like it. I splash Python with cold water, making him squeal and me feel momentarily better.

We approach another curtain and, this time, I'm ready. No stinky curtain face for me. But, as we're fighting our way through, someone behind us screams. I'd blame it on Marla if it wasn't for the fact that Marla is with us.

Python and I grab at the walls, trying to slow our boat. It slips off the rails and the wheels grind against the base. Another boat emerges into the cave and the puppet scene activates. It's Abbie and Jackie's boat. And it's empty.

TWENTY-NINE

Extract from the transcript of the T-minus-one-day final interview with Abbie Bailey [AB], contestant 5/5 *It's Behind You: Season 3, Episode 10 (Umber Gorge Caves).* Interviewed by Jackie Stone [JS], producer of *It's Behind You.*

JS: Hello, Abbie. It's lovely having a ghost hunter on the show. Can I start by asking who is your favourite ghostbuster?

AB: Um, Winston Zeddemore. But I'm nothing like the ghostbusters –

JS: Winston? No one likes Winston.

AB: I do.

JS: Abbie, we want the viewer to identify with you. And Winston is ... kind of boring.

AB: Boring?

JS: It's not a criticism, but you come across as rather uptight. Let's try to show your fun side, hmmm? Tell me, what's your greatest fear?

AB: I'm scared of lots of things. Climate change, global pandemics, police —

JS: Those are worthy replies, yes. But I'm talking about you. The visceral, selfish terror that sends your heart racing and your stomach churning.

AB: [Sighing] I guess ... never knowing.

JS: Never knowing if ghosts are real? Why does it matter to you?

AB: I just ... I don't want it to have all been for nothing. Can we talk about something else?

JS: Of course. What does the name Brian Tobes mean to you?

AB: What do you mean?

JS: He was a ghost hunter, wasn't he? Like you. I believe he took a photo in the Umber Gorge caves that divided the paranormal community.

AB: Right. Yes. He was a paranormal investigator, with a particular interest in the Puckered Maiden. His photo is considered by many to be real evidence of the existence of the paranormal.

JS: He also spearheaded a conspiracy campaign claiming the truth behind a recent death in the cave was being covered up and was proof the Puckered Maiden exists. What do you think about that?

AB: I don't know. That's one of the reasons I am keen to take part in this show.

JS: Professional curiosity?

AB: Exactly.

JS: And that's all it is?

AB: Of course. Why are you asking me these questions?

JS: Trying to get an idea of who you are. Sometimes the real story is hiding just below the surface. In the things someone *doesn't* say. Those stories are the ones viewers want to see played out and it's my job to encourage them to be revealed.

AB: I see. In that case, why don't you tell the viewers why you're here?

JS: Excuse me?

AB: *Boring, uptight* people have one big strength, Jackie. We don't spend our time wrapped up in ourselves, meaning we see things other people miss. Like, how there's a reason you want to get into those caves and

it's not just because of the show. You and Umber
Gorge have history.

JS: Let's not . . . how do I switch this off?

[Break in filming]

JS: Welcome back, Abbie. Can I ask you one more
question?

AB: Get on with it.

JS: Do you think you can win?

AB: You and I both know I'm not here to win.

THIRTY

Our derailed swan rocks precariously. Water sloshes inside, lifting a thick film of grime into dirty soup. The swan's wide eye with its off-centre pupil looks vaguely surprised, like it doesn't appreciate being dragged out of retirement only to crash within minutes.

"Um, guys?" Python says.

Too late. The empty boat collects us and shoves us through the next curtain with an awful grinding noise. We tilt and a splurge of cold water hits my feet. I grip the wall to steady us until we come to a halt. Our boat ends up jammed between Jackie and Abbie's and the display.

"What are they playing at?" Marla says.

There's a quiet click and a musical soundtrack starts up,

all gloomy and full of menace. The lights dim and fade into purples and blues.

"What's happening?" Marla says.

"It's just the puppet display starting up," I say.

On the fibreglass mound against which we're wedged, two puppets raise themselves off the floor. One's a man in a fancy suit, the other's a woman dressed like a bride. She's holding a bloody knife and her hair is a matted, straw-like nest.

"It's the Puckered Maiden," Python says in awe. "Before she puckered."

"*Stop, no, please*," the man says, his voice crackling like the speakers are full of water.

The puppet drops to his knees while the bride – Sophia Kingston, aka the Puckered Maiden – stands over him. She jerkily waves a knife around.

"*Someone, help me*," the man pleads.

"*No one's coming to help you*," Sophia cries. "*You broke my heart and now I will cut out yours.*"

"She didn't take being dumped very well, did she?" I say. "Dressing up in a wedding gown and attacking your ex-fiancé with a knife is kind of extra. The sort of thing I can imagine Marla doing."

"Shut up, Lex," Marla says. "How are we going to get out of here now?"

"There must be a way out. Otherwise where did Jackie and Abbie go?" I shakily stand up in the boat, making it rock. As I thought. There's a tunnel running along the back of the puppet caves, linking them together.

211

"Can we climb over the display?" Python says.

"I don't want to get wet," Marla snaps.

"You'll be fine." Python steps bravely into the water, trips, then quickly scrambles up the display, putting a knee through a brittle hill to reveal the white fibres inside.

Marla sniffs in indignation. "I'm not moving."

"Don't, then." I climb over to join Python with more grace than he managed. We crawl past the struggling puppets, now lit in bloody shades of red as Sophia hacks at poor Tarquin.

"It could be dangerous and neither of you are taking this situation seriously," Marla wails.

"Fine. Wait here in a spooky tunnel. Alone," I say. "Makes perfect sense."

Marla's eyes widen as the realization sets in. But credit to the girl, her stubbornness prevails and she doesn't budge. She tilts her nose into the air and folds her arms. "Send someone back to help me get this boat working again. Ben will know what to do."

I salute her, then put on my head torch. I shine it around the cave, illuminating the parts that aren't reached by the museum's dusty lights. We find a narrow tunnel. It's small and damp and smells like old trapped water. There are puddles at my feet and the walls are slimy to the touch.

"Abbie?" I whisper. "Are you in here?"

There's no reply, but there's a faint clacking noise up ahead. Like a wooden doll being shaken. Python switches on the diary cam. "Abbie has disappeared and we think the Puckered Maiden might have got her," he says.

"Do we?" I say.

"There's something up ahead. Something evil. I can SENSE it," he says.

"No you can't."

"Quit that," he hisses, "or they'll have to edit you out completely." He does some heavy breathing, his gasps catching in his throat.

"You're such a terrible actor!" I tell him. "And if you think they're still going to turn this into an episode, you're as deluded as Jackie."

He lowers the camera and turns off the recording. "Second to screwing, real danger is what the audience wants to see the most. Of course Jackie will get to make her episode, and you know what? It will be EPIC."

I have to admit he has a point.

"Let me have my fun and I promise I won't cockblock you with Liam. How's that for a deal?" He switches the camera back on, looking smug.

"I don't want ..." I stop. I can't deny his accusation on film, otherwise Jackie will twist it around to make it look like I'm pathetically crushing on Liam and Python's offering me relationship advice. He knows this, too, the game-playing bastard. "Fine, carry on."

"Abbie?" he calls out with a wavering voice. "Stay strong, we're coming for you."

But if he wants drama then that's what he's going to

get. "She was the best of us," I sob. "Please let her be OK, please, please."

"Rein it in a notch," he mutters, splashing on ahead.

The tunnel gets narrower and narrower. We squeeze through a vertical slit. The cave on the other side is like something from another planet. If it wasn't for gravity, I'd have no idea what was up and what was down. The floor rises and falls like sand dunes, except they're water-worn rock.

There are gaping holes in the walls, leading into adjoining caves with steep, sloping floors. Giant rocky outcrops jut out above our heads. In the torchlight, I can make out a huge pool of water. It looks impossibly deep and menacing. It's a deep blue that blooms black as it disappears beneath a low ceiling.

"This is creepier than I'd imagined," Python whispers. "Where are they?"

"I don't know," I reply. "This place is massive."

A clacking noise makes me jump around. It came from one of the tunnels. We creep towards the sound, my torch bobbing shakily. We find a tunnel hiding between looming rocks. As we follow it, my palms start to sweat and my chest tightens. Maybe something bad *has* happened to Abbie and Jackie. It's hard to imagine anything good existing in this place.

We round a corner as a figure vanishes at the opposite end of the passageway. I don't see their face, only the creepy way they're feeling their way along the walls with both hands. Palms spread, footsteps slow and juddering.

"I heard that the Puckered Maiden's blind," Python says. "Her eyes are all cloudy from the salt in the water."

I pick up a rock from the ground and edge down the passageway. Python grips my shoulder, pressed up behind me. He holds the diary cam out in front of us both. We peek around the corner. There really is a person down there, it wasn't just a trick of the light. Only . . .

I let out a slow breath and shrug Python off. It's Abbie, not the Puckered Maiden. Not some killer prowling the tunnels for her next victim. She's standing dead still, peering over a large rock behind which a light bobs. She hears us approach and holds a finger to her lips for us to be quiet. She gestures over the rock.

I'm taller than both Abbie and Python so I can see more easily. It's Ben and Veronica, standing in a small side cave, having a whispered conversation. We silently edge closer.

"Why did you really come here?" Ben says. "What are you trying to prove? That you were a good friend to Laurie after all?"

"I *was* a good friend to her. And you left her here, too." Veronica sounds like she might cry. "We both did, and maybe if we hadn't, Liam wouldn't have come here and we'd all be safe at home right now."

"He came here because he knows we're hiding something."

"Don't," Veronica says. "What happened two years ago is over. We have to move on."

She reaches out to take his hand but he snatches it away.

"That's good advice. Leave me alone, Veronica. Or I'll tell Liam exactly what kind of friend you were to Laurie."

"Secrets!" Python whispers, poking the camera around the corner to film them.

Only, Python's version of a whisper is as quiet as a yappy dog when it sees the postman. Everyone in the cave must hear. Veronica and Ben hurry out of their hiding place, both red cheeked. Ben shoves the diary cam away.

"Get that out of my face," he says.

"Were you spying on us?" Veronica asks, her wide eyes meeting mine. She looks hurt.

"Um, yes?" I say. "But in my defence, Abbie started it."

Abbie glares at me in exasperation. "I was looking for Jackie," she says. "She ditched me without a torch."

"We found your boat," I say. "What happened?"

"We heard a noise, like footsteps inside the walls. And creepy laughter again. Jackie *lost* it."

"*Jackie* was scared?" Python says.

"No, angry. She started ranting and raving about how she wasn't going to let anyone ruin her show or sabotage her career. Before I could do anything, she'd grabbed hold of the display and nearly derailed our boat."

"Where did she go?" I say.

"She took off down the tunnel at the back of the puppet scenes, taking our only torch with her. I tried to follow her but she vanished into this massive cave and left me in the pitch dark. I had to find my way with my camera flash."

216

"All right. Let's get back to Liam and we'll work out what to do next," Ben says.

"Why are you down here by yourselves?" I say.

"Ben wanted to talk." Veronica hiccups with the beginnings of a sob, then rushes past us with a hand clasped to her mouth. I guess Operation Beronica is a bust, then.

"Should someone go after her?" Abbie says.

Ben hesitates and when he speaks again, his voice isn't as sharp. "It's hard for her, that's all."

"Because of what happened before?" Abbie says. "What is it she's scared of?"

"Her best friend died. Isn't that enough?" He leads the way back to the end of the boat ride. Liam's waiting there, staring at a tunnel marked with an unlit neon arrow. The tunnel is completely blocked off with rubble.

"You all right?" I ask.

"This tunnel collapsed in the original cave-in," Liam says. "I remember running round here thinking I might be able to get to Laurie from this direction, only to find it impassable too."

"We did the same on the opposite side," Ben says. Then he quickly clears his throat. "You know, maybe I should find Veronica." He walks away, wiping his eyes.

"It would be nice if everyone would stop storming off." I throw both arms in the air.

"He knows his way around. He'll catch up," Liam says.

"In that case, we should look for Jackie," Abbie says. "As much as I'd love to leave her behind."

The four of us – me, Python, Abbie and Liam – search the big, scary cave behind the boat ride. It's huge and we spend the best part of an hour clambering between the various caves and tunnels. The cavern's arranged like a tentacled monster, with tunnels heading off in every direction. Some are dead ends, others are interconnected like a rocky maze. We find nothing. The whole time, I have this vague feeling that I'm forgetting something, but I can't think what it is. I put it down to tiredness.

I'm searching a small alcove when my torch starts to fail. Sighing, I rejoin the others. They're standing at the edge of the lake, staring into the water.

"I think we need to call this a day," I say. "Someone should go and find Ben and Veronica. If they haven't murdered each other."

Liam looks up sharply. "Why would they murder each other?"

"They were arguing," Abbie answers. "Veronica doesn't want us to go any further."

"No. She doesn't." Liam's hands tighten into fists. "All right. Let's look for them."

Python picks up a rock and tosses it into the water with great ceremony. "Goodbye, Jackie," he says. "I wanted to say a few words."

"No you don't," I say. "Besides, Jackie's a cockroach. She'll come back."

"Yeah, true," Python agrees. "Let's enjoy the peace while we can."

We clamber back up the sloping cave floor and make our way through the maze of tunnels leading to the end of the boat ride. Liam's plastic swan bobs sadly by a wooden jetty.

"Shit, Marla!" Python says.

I laugh. *That's* what I forgot about. "I can't believe we left her waiting in the boat."

"No," Python says, grabbing my arm so hard I'll have bruises. He turns me around so I can see into the tunnel.

There, floating face down in the water, is another of the zombie dummies. Only this one isn't a dummy. It's real.

"Marla," Python repeats. "It's Marla."

THIRTY-ONE

Even in death, Marla manages to look pissed off. I know I sound cold and heartless. I *feel* cold and heartless. I'm just so . . . numb.

We drag Marla out of the water and stand in a circle around her, staring. She's staring, too. Like she can see a world that's invisible to people who are still alive. I can't believe she's dead.

"This is our fault for leaving her behind," Python says. The diary cam is hanging from his hand, no longer recording.

"She wouldn't come with us," I say. "I thought we'd be right back."

"Only we forgot."

"She must have been wading through the tunnel," Liam says. "The rocks are so slippery. It would be easy to hit your head and drown."

"Oh my god, it really is all our fault." Python squeezes his eyes closed.

Footsteps approach across the cave. It's Ben and Veronica. "Marla?" Veronica whispers.

Her eyes are puffy and her cheeks blotchy. It's obvious she's been crying, but she's tried to redo her make-up to hide it. She's put on so much black eyeliner she looks like she's playing fancy dress as a skull.

"What happened to her?" Ben says, his face grim.

"I think . . ." Abbie starts. She takes a deep breath. "I think we need to consider the possibility this wasn't an accident."

We all stare at her. Veronica's chest heaves like she's fighting tears again.

"Someone murdered her?" Python says. "But who'd want to kill Marla?"

I laugh bitterly. Everyone *wanted* to kill Marla. She was a nightmare. But that doesn't mean I'm happy she's dead.

"You think it was the Puckered Maiden, don't you?" I say, narrowing my eyes at Abbie.

"We need to be open to every possibility."

"The Puckered Maiden isn't real," Liam says.

"Isn't she?" Abbie watches Ben and Veronica, like she's waiting for one of them to agree with her, but neither does.

"We need to move on," Liam says. "Our torches won't last for ever."

"Liam, please," Veronica says. "It's not too late to turn back."

"And do what?" he snaps.

"Wait for someone to rescue us! We don't have to go further into the caves. We can't go further into the caves."

"No one's coming," Liam says quietly. "We're on our own."

"And Jackie?" Python says.

"For all we know, she's dead too," Ben says. "Like we'll be if we don't try to find a way out."

As if to make a point, the caves rumble and a fine sprinkling of dust rains down on us. Each of us nods, except for Veronica, who shakes her head and wipes away a tear.

"What about Marla?" Python says. "We can't leave her here."

"And we can't carry her through the Bone Road," Ben sighs. "It's not possible."

"Someone help me lift her," I say, taking her ankles.

Liam takes her arms and we carry her to the swan boat. She feels much heavier than I expected and we keep scuffing her off the ground. We splash out into the water and manhandle her over the side of the boat. She slumps into the footwell with her face pressed up against the seat. Liam tries to rearrange her, but the boat keeps rocking.

I climb back out of the water. My feet are freezing. "We should set it on fire," I say. "Like a Viking funeral."

"Everything's too wet," Abbie says.

"Um, does someone want to say anything?" Liam asks.

No one says anything.

We stand there, staring at the water. It's so dark and deep and *final*. The cave rumbles and a series of ripples spreads across the surface. The water laps against the boat.

It's funny, I used to believe death was this big deal, and that the whole world would stop turning when it happened to someone I knew. Recently, I've started to think death is endless hospital corridors, and finding change for the car park, and boredom. So much boredom you start to wish something – even the worst thing – would happen so you can walk away and stop staring into that abyss.

Death is not knowing what to do and, at the same time, knowing there is nothing you can do. There should be thunder or fireworks or the world should stop spinning for one tiny minute. Only it doesn't, and your feet still hurt and you need a piss, and you're trying so hard to act like you care but something's stuck inside you and it doesn't come.

In the end, you have to walk away.

THIRTY-TWO

The Bone Road is a series of caverns interconnected by tunnels barely wide enough for a person to squeeze through. Ben tells us it was discovered in the early twentieth century by an explorer who started crawling and found he couldn't turn back, so was forced to keep going in the hope the tunnel went somewhere.

I stare at the tiny space through which he wants us to scramble. It's not so much a tunnel as a series of gaps left behind by an ancient rockfall, leading to a passageway eaten away by the flow of long-gone water. Experienced cavers would baulk at crawling inside. I look at our ragtag bunch. A YouTuber dressed like a member of Whitesnake. A girl in a gothic party dress. A budget action figure. A cynical ghost hunter. A nerdy hot guy. Me.

"So we're screwed," Python says, filming the entrance to the Bone Road with the diary cam. "This, people, is where we all DIE."

"Do you have to be so dramatic?" Abbie says.

"Um, yes?" he says.

"Stupid question," she mutters. "Are we going in, then?"

Ben leads the way, leaving me and then Python to bring up the rear. I wink at the diary cam, then drop to the ground and drag myself into the hole. There are a few seconds of heart-exploding terror as I feel all that rock pressing in on me from every direction. The walls drag against my shoulders and my chest and my thighs, and I can barely move.

"Slither, Lex," Python shouts from behind me. "Slither!"

"I'm trying but it's tight." I inch along painfully slowly.

"Maybe if you try slithering instead of wriggling," Python says.

I breathe out slowly. This is going to be a long crawl with him behind me.

I try to not think about where I am, or how much rock there is surrounding me, or how massively out of our depth we all are. Instead, I focus on putting one arm in front of the next and dragging myself onwards. My own breath is warm and cloying as I rebreathe the air I just exhaled.

I stop to regather myself. Breathe in slowly for four, out for eight. One of my mum's tricks for staying calm.

"Lex? Lex?" Python says. "If you slither, then—"

"Say slither one more time," I say, surprising myself with the venom in my voice.

Python shuts up.

The tunnel goes on for ever, or that's how it feels. My knuckles have been rubbed raw on sharp rocks and they sting as I splash through cold pockets of water. Every muscle aches.

"I can't go on," Python declares dramatically. "Leave me behind and go on without me."

I try to look back at him, but it's too tight and I can't turn.

"I'm going to lie down here and become a stone."

Crap. The others are still crawling on ahead, oblivious.

"We're going to be stuck here for ever. There's so much rock and we're going to suffocate and die. This is it, we're all going to die."

All right. I need to get him moving again. "In situations like this," I say, my own voice coming out raspy, "I like to ask myself, W.W.J.D.?"

Python stops gasping. "What would Jesus do?"

"What would *Jackie* do."

Python manages a weak laugh.

I put on her sing-song voice. "The show must go on! And if you must die, make it spectacular for the cameras."

"Have you considered your near-death persona?" Python continues, doing a better impression of her than me.

"What *story* do you want to tell, Python?" I say.

He chuckles to himself. "Not one where I die in this stupid tunnel. Oh, right. I see what you did there."

"I'm not just a handsome face," I say. "Come on then. Get slithering."

We continue on. The tunnel rumbles like a hungry monster, making my insides squirm. But the rumbles taper out and the monster sleeps, for the time being. I wish I knew how long we have left. Minutes, hours, days, months, years. The not knowing is the worst, like with everything. Any time now, the world could come crashing down on top of us. Or maybe it won't, and I'll have wasted my time on worry and what-ifs.

The tunnel grows narrower. It feels like the walls are closing in on me. I dig my elbows into the floor to pull myself along. Dust catches in my throat and makes me want to cough, but coughing would mean clouding up the stale air even further. I try to ignore the tickle in my chest and keep moving.

After what feels like an eternity, I scramble out into a huge cavern full of dagger-like stalactites and a rugged floor. There are small pools hidden among the sharp rocks, and steplike formations that hide all manner of dark nooks. It feels ... dead. Like we're among a mere handful of living things that have ventured down here in tens of thousands of years.

Ben helps me up. "Where did you get to?"

"Someone thought it would be fun to stop and take in the sights," I say, glaring at Python.

We find places to sit in the torchlit dark to eat our hard

toffee and drink some water. I find myself next to Ben. "We must be almost there, right?" I say.

He looks at me sharply. "What? We've only been crawling for fifteen minutes."

"Is that all?" I pull a face. "It feels longer."

"It feels like for ever. Like I never left."

There's an awkward silence that, for some reason, I feel a need to fill. I guess I don't want to be alone with my own thoughts: thoughts about how we might never escape this place, thoughts about Marla. I say the first thing that comes into my mind. "What's going on with you and Veronica?"

Ben's face darkens. "What do you mean?"

"She mentioned something about you two back in the town and . . ." I tail off. I'm dangerously close to embracing Jackie's suggestion I play the supportive friend. Since when do I involve myself in that kind of drama?

"Stay out of this," Ben says. "It's none of your business."

I leave him to his mood and crawl over to sit with Veronica. Her expression is tight and drawn.

"You sure you like that guy?" I say. "He's a bit intense at times."

"I hate this," she whispers. "We used to be so close, and now he can barely look at me."

"You remind him of what happened here," I say.

She nods. "When we're together, he remembers her. And I hate that I can't change how he sees me."

"Is he one of the reasons you want to get out of Umber? When you civil engineer your way to a new life?"

228

"I used to think he'd come with me. He won't, though. I need to leave it behind — Umber, the tragedy. Liam and Ben. Start afresh without the past holding me back."

"Attagirl," I say, patting her on the back. "Come travelling with me and find yourself a nice boy with no baggage, or maybe ten."

She stares at me with her lips parted in surprise. "Go travelling with you? Do you mean that?"

"Sure." I laugh at her expression. "I'm not asking you on a date. I just thought if we both happened to be on the same train out of this country then we could sit together. It'll be a laugh."

She nods slowly. A faint, pleased flush creeps up her cheeks. "All right," she says, grinning.

"But first we have to get out of this place alive."

Her smile drops like a lead weight. She clasps my hand. "We can still turn back, Lex. Maybe the others will listen to you."

There's a shuffling sound and Abbie scoots over to join us. She's holding her notebook in her lap and frizzy curls of her hair have escaped the ponytail.

"This must be hard for you, Veronica," she says, rather stiffly. I narrow my eyes at her. Abbie offering comfort doesn't sit right with me. She's up to something.

"You could say that," Veronica says.

"This route takes us past the cave-in tunnels, back to where you were trapped? Where Laurie died?"

Veronica glances over at Liam. "Near there, yes."

229

"Do you know *exactly* where she's buried, though?"

Veronica's eyes well up and I glare at Abbie. "Not cool," I say.

Abbie shuffles back and scribbles something in her notebook. If I wasn't so knackered, I'd be curious about what she's playing at. She's been acting differently ever since Ben and Veronica arrived. But I can barely keep my eyes open. I try to get some rest against the uncomfortable rocks. I've almost dozed off when scurrying footsteps wake me. I sit up. Everyone else has fallen silent.

The footsteps come again. They're followed by a burst of laughter. "You're all dead," a voice rasps. "Dead like her, dead like him, dead like her."

The voice bounces off the walls of the cave, echoing so it sounds like it's coming from every direction. The echoes fade to nothing. We all sit in silence, broken only by the drip of water.

"Do you think that's one of the audio tracks they set up for the show?" I say at last.

"Down here?" Python asks.

"We should move on," Liam says.

We clamber up on to a ledge and Ben points us towards the next portion of the route. Once again, the tunnel is so narrow it's barely passable. I eye the rest of the cavern. There must be dozens of other tunnels hiding in all the twisty corners and hidden alcoves.

"The tunnel is narrow but easy enough to follow," Ben

says. "I'm going to go last this time to make sure no one gets left behind."

Liam moves to go first, then hesitates. He looks so scared. "After Laurie died, I had nightmares that started like this," he admits.

In a moment of bravado, I push past him. "I've got this," I say.

"I've been to these caves before. I should lead," Liam says in a small voice.

"And if you freeze, everyone behind you will be stuck. I'm doing this for me, not you."

He nods, sagging with relief.

I pull myself inside. Straight away, it's clear this section is going to be harder than anything that came before. Python tries to keep up a steady stream of stupid questions and films snippets of our journey. But soon everyone falls quiet. This tunnel is far too narrow for us to go back if we hit a dead end. We're all trusting Ben with our lives.

We go on, and on, and on. Through gaps so narrow we have to force one arm through first and then wiggle the second free once our shoulders are clear. Between slabs of rock that have cracked apart. Our fingers splash in dirty water seeping in through the walls. Our knees are rubbed raw by jagged rocks. We crawl up through narrow shafts eaten away by long-gone rivers. We slide head first through tunnels with walls like driftwood.

When it narrows further, I'm forced to twist around on to my back so I can use the ceiling to pull and push myself along. I brace my legs against the walls for more grip. It's so tight I can barely move.

Cold water trickles down my back, inside my shirt. "Urgh," I say. "This literally couldn't get any worse."

In retrospect, this was a stupid thing to say. Because *of course* it's possible for things to get worse. A few metres further on, the tunnel starts to slope downwards and I feel water against the back of my head and my neck. Only this time, it doesn't let up. Instead, it gets deeper. And deeper, until my hands splash when I try to move.

The tunnel is flooded.

THIRTY-THREE

We all lie there in the tunnel, as still as death. Cold water seeps through my thin shirt and makes the fabric stick to my skin. I close my eyes and will myself to wake up. When I open them again, it's still torchlit rock I see, and my breath clouding in the cold air.

"We have to keep going," Ben eventually says. "We can't go back."

"What if the tunnel's full of water?" Python says.

No one answers. This is why the route's called the Bone Road. If the tunnel's completely flooded, we'll all become skeletons littering the tunnels like those old-time explorers who came before us.

"Does anyone want to record a message or something?" Python says.

"No one would ever find the camera," Liam says.

Silence again.

"I still wish I could say goodbye to my parents," Python says.

Me too. I try to not think about what this will do them, but my brain goes there anyway. Will they hold a funeral even though my body will remain entombed down here for eternity? What goes in the coffin if there's no body? A few possessions and a bunch of flowers? Maybe they'll stuff one of my suits, like a scarecrow.

"If I don't make it, then . . ." I tail off, unsure what to say.

"Yeah, us too," Python says.

I nod once, then brace my feet on the walls to push myself into the dip. The roof is a few centimetres from the tip of my nose. It's a strange feeling descending head first. Like going down a slide on my back, only this time with water sloshing against my hair and the back of my head.

I pull myself further in. My head torch shines on a small area of rock directly above my nose. The water comes up to my ears. I move slowly, not wanting to make a wave that would cover my face. One tiny movement at a time, I inch my way around the dip.

I stop. The water's getting deeper. There's less than four inches of air and I have to tilt my head back to make sure my nose and mouth remain clear. Water laps at my chin. I can hear my heart whooshing in my ears, far too fast and far too loud. I can't move. I'm frozen where I lie, and I can't go back but I can't go forwards either.

I'm reminded of this time when I was little and I went to the beach with my parents. I was playing in the rock pools when a big wave crashed against the rock and knocked me over. I cut myself on the barnacles and I can remember sitting there, butt-deep in water, crying over the blood bubbling from my knee. My mum ran over to help me but she couldn't reach my rock.

"Jump across," she said. "I'll catch you."

Only I couldn't make myself get up. I was too scared of the waves and my knee hurt too much.

"Come on, baby," Mum said quietly. "It's all right. You're OK."

I staggered up. The gap looked so wide and the sea so violent. But my mum was holding her arms out to me. I jumped. Like she'd promised, she caught me and I don't remember what happened next so presumably everything was happy and fun again.

Sometimes you just have to be brave. I imagine she's here with me, telling me it's OK. Telling me I can do this. I take a deep breath and kick off the walls. The water splashes into my nose and my eyes and my mouth. There's nothing but water. I kick and kick, my mouth and eyes squeezed tightly closed, but the water has swallowed me up.

I'm going to drown. I'm really going to drown.

Then the roof of the tunnel abruptly lifts and I'm lying in shallow water, gasping for air. I scrabble on to my hands and knees and throw up my hard toffee, sobbing snotty bubbles.

"Lex?" comes a muffled voice.

I wipe my eyes and take a deep breath. I'm alive. I'm wet and cold, but I'm alive.

"Hold your breath and come on through," I yell back. "There's less than half a metre to go."

As I wait for them to gather up the courage to follow my lead, my torch starts to flicker. I take it off. It's filled up with water during that short period when I was submerged. I shake it and some of the water comes out. The bulb fades and fails. I'm plunged into darkness. "Great," I mutter. "I see Jackie spared no expense when she bought this thing."

At first, I'm not scared. The others will be here soon, and three of them have torches. But the minutes drag by and no one comes through. With my eyes out of action, my other senses are heightened. I am sure I can hear quiet laughter, as if the walls themselves are mocking me. I know nothing can have crept up on me, but I'm convinced something is in the cave with me. Its fetid breath is inches from my face.

I can't move. I can't breathe. The thing creeps closer. Its fingernails quietly tap on the ground as it crawls. I imagine its mouth, wide and grinning, with a black tongue that slowly licks its peeling lips. Something touches my neck, as gently as a stray hair tickling my skin. The tip of a fingernail trailing against my throat.

And then there's a splashing, struggling sound and

someone erupts from the tunnel, coughing and spluttering. A hand grasps my ankle and I stiffen, but it's only Python. The sense that something is touching my neck vanishes.

"Lex?" he sobs. "Where are you?"

"I'm right here," I say, reaching down to find his hand and pulling him up. "My torch died."

"Oh my god, that was horrific," he says. "I am traumatized for life."

He's quiet for a second as he fumbles around in the dark. Then a small red light comes on, followed by the bright light of a screen.

"Seriously?" I say.

"We nearly DIED," Python says into the camera. "How does it feel to still be alive, Lex?"

"Don't you get tired of all that?" I say.

"All what?"

"Come on, we both know it's all an act. Don't you ever want to be yourself?"

He lowers the camera to glare at me and I think maybe he's going to say something real. But I guess he's as committed to the lie as I am. "This is who I am. Why would I want to be anyone else?"

I wave him away. "Yeah, whatever."

Liam comes through next. Thankfully, his torch survives its brief dip in the water. I go to sit next to him as he recovers. He's shaky and drawn, and his eyes are ringed in red. He looks broken.

"You know, I'll still think you're hot if you cry," I say.

He smiles weakly. "You think I'm hot."

"Well, you're not wholly awful," I say, backtracking.

"You're not wholly awful, either," he says. "When you're not being an arsehole."

We smile at each other. It's kind of nice.

Veronica erupts out of the tunnel, tangled up in her gauzy petticoats. She scrambles out of the water and lies face down on the rocks, sobbing noisily. She looks like a doll left out in the rain, only with watery blood making a map on her legs. Liam looks away.

"Are you all right?" I say.

She nods and sits up shakily. Soon afterwards, Abbie emerges through the tunnel and immediately roots through her bag, takes out her black notebook and flicks through the pages, visibly relaxing as she discovers it is still dry.

"What is that?" I say, gesturing to the book.

She quickly tucks it away. "Just notes. My research."

"Research into the Puckered Maiden?"

"Mostly. But there's not much modern-day information out there. Witnesses don't tend to talk about their experiences." She looks over at Veronica as she says this.

Veronica fixes Abbie with a smudgy stare.

"There's something in these caves, I know it," Abbie whispers. "And I think you know. Why are you so frightened to go back? What did you see?"

Veronica shakes her head. "The caves are dangerous. I'm scared someone's going to get hurt. I *know* someone's going to get hurt."

"No. I think you're scared of *her*."

"Of who?" Veronica whispers.

"Did the Puckered Maiden kill Laurie?" Abbie's eyes burn with a feverous determination I've not seen until now.

"Are you serious?" Liam snaps. "Laurie died because the caves fell in. The Puckered Maiden is just a story. Trust me, I got enough of this crap from Brian Tobes, with his ridiculous obsession. Don't you start too."

"It's just that—"

"No. Stop. Just stop."

Abbie opens her mouth like she might say something else, then thinks better of it. A moment later, the uneasy quiet is interrupted by Ben emerging through the waterlogged tunnel. He immediately jumps to his feet and clonks his head on the ceiling. He pretends he's fine.

"Not far now, people," he says, in a voice that's all bravado. "Let's move out."

We gather ourselves together to follow him. Veronica catches my hand. "Lex, no one else will listen to me. If we go to the other side of the caves, people are going to die," she says.

"People already have died." I pull my hand away.

"Veronica, pack it in," Liam says.

"For god's sake! Can't you see I'm trying to warn you? Why won't any of you listen to me?"

"Because we've come too far to turn back," Ben says.

"Then I'm sorry," Veronica says, tears running down her face. "I'm sorry about what's going to happen next."

THIRTY-FOUR

We've been crawling through tunnels for the best part of three hours now, and once you've seen one tunnel, you've seen them all. Sure, *It's Behind You* is a roller coaster of excitement and emotion, but only when you're watching from the comfort of your sofa. Clever editing tightens and twists the reality into something entertaining. The truth is far more boring.

Finally, we emerge out of the endless tunnels on to a small ledge that's not much bigger than my bathroom at home. We're all filthy and shivering in our wet clothes, with smears of blood across our dusty foreheads and hands. I straighten up painfully, holding on to the wall so my shaking legs don't buckle beneath me.

We're in a narrow space that's not so much a cavern as a crack between two immense walls of rock: ten metres across, endlessly long and so deep that I can't see the bottom. I can hear a river, though, gurgling past more than three storeys beneath us.

"I've always wanted to visit the Grand Canyon," Liam says. "It's colder than I imagined."

I manage a weak smile. All I can think is that there's nowhere to go. The path just ends.

"There's a bridge to the other side," Ben says, reading my mind. "But to get to it, we have to cross to that ledge over there."

He points down, to another rocky outcrop similar to the one we're on, half-swallowed by darkness. To get to it, we'll have to horizontally scale five metres of the wall, then drop on to the ledge. I eye the wall. It's a rocky version of a playground climbing apparatus. There are narrow cracks that double as footholds. Small rocks jut out to form natural handholds.

"I'll find the best route across," Ben says. "Liam, train your light on the wall so we can all see where we're putting our feet."

Liam salutes him, looking visibly relieved he doesn't have to go first.

Ben rubs his hands together, then tentatively reaches out to swing himself off the ledge. His feet scrabble into a long crack and he edges his way along, finding places to grip hold of. One of the jutting rocks crumbles at his touch and

241

he's left swinging one-armed. But he quickly finds places to brace his feet and reaches for a new handhold.

"All right," he says. "Who's coming next?"

No one budges. I roll my eyes. "Fine. Watch and learn." My shaky voices betrays my nerves. "I do this all the time."

I reach out a hand to grip one of the rocks. I squeeze my foot into a crack and my weight swings out over nothing. My arms shake as I cling on with everything I have. I mean, I have *a lot*. But now I'm wondering if it's enough.

"There's the next foothold," Liam says, using his torch to direct me. "You got this."

Next in turn, Python jiggles up and down on the spot. "She's going to fall, she's going to fall."

"Shut up, dickweed," I snap, irritation briefly making me forget how scared I am.

"She's slipping! Oh my god, I can't watch."

"Nah, she's fine," Liam says. "She looks like she's having a great time. See how happy she is?"

I'd give him the middle finger if it didn't mean letting go of the rock. And there's no way I am risking it. I edge my foot into the next space and pull myself along. Muscles I didn't know I had tense at the sheer effort.

"You don't understand," Python says. "Both of us have outlived our horror movie parts. Characters like us aren't meant to make it past the first twenty minutes. We're too annoying."

"Er, speak for yourself," I say.

Python continues to ramble. "Marla started out as the

242

most likely candidate for last girl, but she turned herself into the hate sink by being awful to everyone. That's why she died soon after poor Cameraman Carl, who, let's face it, was cannon fodder from the start. None of us knew anything about him! He didn't even get a backstory." He takes a deep breath. "And now it's Lex and me who are going to die."

"Except this isn't a horror film," Liam says.

"No, it's worse," I say. "It's reality TV."

"Exactly," Liam laughs. "The only form of media where annoying characters get to win."

Python stops jiggling and nods slowly. "I guess that could be true. As long as I redeem myself later by revealing a heartfelt secret from my past, I could make it to the end."

"That's the spirit." Liam pats him on the back. "You're next. To cross. Not to die."

"Lex, come on," Ben says. "You're almost there."

I nod and concentrate on following Ben across the wall. Inch by inch, the next ledge gets closer and closer. But my head keeps spinning back to what Python said, and Veronica's comments about how you can't change how someone sees you. For the first time, I'm wondering if I'm playing the part I want to play. It feels too late to back down now.

"That's it," Ben says, taking my hand to help me onto the ledge. "You're over."

My feet step on to solid ground and it feels even better than when I dragged my sorry arse out of that flooded tunnel. I dance around until I remember how high up we are, and press myself against the wall instead. The others make it across, too. We all cluster together on the small ledge.

Ben nods ahead. "There's the bridge."

It's not a bridge. It's two fraying ropes strung up with one about a metre above the other. Top rope for your hands, bottom rope for your feet.

"This was left behind by the original explorers," Ben says. "It's over a hundred years old, so be careful."

"Good advice," Liam says. He tentatively pulls on the upper rope, testing its strength. He pauses to remove his head torch and passes it to me. "In case I fall."

"You're not going to fall," I say, rolling my eyes at him.

"Shine it on the ropes so I can see where I'm putting my feet."

He edges out along the lower rope. It's like another obstacle from a children's playground. Easy enough to cross when you're only five inches off the ground and not dangling way above a rushing river. He rocks perilously from side to side, at one point hanging horizontally with his feet braced on one rope and his knuckles white on the other. But he makes it over.

Ben goes next. He's heavy and the rope stretches noisily under his weight, but he makes it. Veronica, Python and Abbie do too. And then it's just me. I put the torch on and edge out across the bridge. I keep the light directed at the lower rope so I won't misplace my feet. I move slowly. It takes a surprising amount of strength in my arms to keep myself upright.

I pause halfway across. "Keep going, not much further," Liam says, reaching towards me.

I turn my attention back on to the lower rope. Less than two metres to go. I'm almost there. Then, out of the corner of my eye, I spot Veronica's torch – one of the only two head torches we have left – flickering on and off. Another casualty of the flooded tunnel. It lights the group up for a second, then drops them into darkness. My own torch is now the only light.

There's a scream. Something yanks hard on the rope and my legs slip off. I dangle with my arms as my body thrashes about like an animal in a snare. I can't get my feet back on to the rope. My torch throws panicked slashes of light through the darkness.

Everyone is shouting, "Hold on, hold on, hold on!" Only it's not just me they're worried about. Python is hanging from the lower rope by one hand. His fingers are slipping.

Veronica's torch comes on again and there's Liam, lying on his stomach, desperately trying to reach Python. But he's too far away. Python's fingers let go.

THIRTY-FIVE

Python twists and flails like a cat as he falls, in his leopard-print leggings, bleached hair fanning out around him, diary cam still clasped in one hand. The little red dot flashes as Python's final moments are caught on film. My torch lights him briefly as he drops, then he's a shape in the hazy darkness, and he's gone. There's a quiet splash, then nothing.

I look up at the rope from which I'm dangling. My feet are still kicking, trying to reach the lower rope. My palms are burning and my arms are shaking. My fingers slip and there's nothing I can do to hold on. The rope slides from my grip and then it's gone.

There's rushing air and screaming. There's the walls

246

of the ravine, my brain picking out surprising details like the red tones of the rocks and streaks of white and green limescale where water once trickled. And then there's water, so cold it feels like it's crushing my skull and boiling my blood. I can't think. I can't do anything.

My lungs scream at me to take a breath and it's only dumb luck I manage to wait until I break the surface to start gasping like a suffocating fish. My limbs are trying to move, but they're uncoordinated and I slip under the surface again. My clothes are so heavy, they're pulling me under. I struggle but I'm too cold to swim and my heart's beating so fast it might split in half and I need to breathe but then I know I'll drown and I'm sinking and sinking.

I kick off the wall, but only succeed in rolling over in the water. All I can see is rocks overhead. I've drifted into a submerged cave. There's no air. My fingers drag against the rough rocks, clawing for a way out.

There's nothing but water.

I push off the riverbed and – thank every god I don't believe in – I'm breaking the surface again. I can't make out where I am. It's like I'm in a glitching video game, glimpsing half-rendered images of rocks before I dip back underwater.

Next time I surface, I grab hold of one of the rocks and drag myself out of the water on my belly. I lie there, trying to catch my breath while my whole body shakes painfully and my teeth clench.

Python! He's here too, lying nearby with his legs

submerged and his face turned away from me in an inch of water. I scramble over to him and roll him on to his back. The head torch gives him a bluish-white tinge and I think he's drowned, but then he blinks against the light and raises an arm to shield his face.

"Lex?" he says, his voice hoarse. "You came for a swim too?"

"Thanks to you." My teeth are chattering so much it's hard to speak. "D-d-d-dick."

He manages a weak smile at this. He crawls out of the water and we huddle in dripping balls on a ledge. The ceiling is so low I have to tilt my head to one side to fit. I feel like one of the dolls in my B & B. I'm so cold I think I might die. I mean, I really might die, now I think about it. Hypothermia, starvation, Puckered Maiden. But mostly hypothermia.

"We should take off our clothes," I say. "We'll be less cold than if we're soaking wet."

"Are you trying to get me naked?" Python says, but it's half-hearted, like some of the Python-ness has been washed out of him.

We remove our dripping outer layers, stiff fingers fumbling with the buttons. My shirt and trousers are plastered to my skin and I have to peel them off. I'm not any warmer in my underwear.

Python holds out his shaking arms to me. I almost tell him to get lost. But I'm *that* cold. I edge closer to him and we huddle together like penguins. His skin is icy cold and damp, and it's like cuddling a salmon fillet straight from the fridge.

"My whole life flashed before my eyes," he says, his voice slurring. "And it was shit."

I didn't even get a near-death showreel. Is that a sign I have nothing to show for my entire existence? I came on the show because I was worried I would die having never had any real adventures, having lived my life on the default settings. Like my parents, with their two-bed semi, rebellious teenager and boring, grown-up jobs.

The irony is, the cave might kill me and I'm not sure the adventure is worth the price.

"I've got millions of fans but not one of them truly knows me. I'm nineteen and I've never been in love," Python continues. "What's the point of anything if I've never found that one person who loves me for me?"

"Bleugh. Who wants to fall in love?" I say. "That shit's boring."

He ignores me. "I guess I want to find someone who *gets* me. The real me."

"Ha ha, I knew it! You're such a faker."

"Duh." He smiles weakly. "But I've been doing it so long I don't know where Python ends and Keith begins. I don't even know if there's any of me left for someone to fall in love with."

I think about reassuring him that not only will we find a way out of this mess but he'll meet that special someone. Only, it's not me and I can't do it. "Love is overrated," I say.

"We're better off on our own. Relationships tie you down and trap you into lives you don't want to live."

He removes his cheek from my collarbone and cranes his head around to look up at me. "You're so cynical. What's up with that?"

I don't answer. I think about my parents, and their screwed-up marriage, and how my mum might not get another chance to fall in love with someone who makes her happy. She's wasted all those years on this small, furniture-polish-scented life and it might be all she gets. I will never, ever be like her.

"A faker knows a faker," Python says gently. "I know there's more to why you're here. It's pretty damn obvious."

I open my mouth to tell him to do one, but I'm suddenly fighting tears. It's the cold, I tell myself. I shuffle away from him and clamp my mouth shut, closing my eyes until the feeling passes. Lex doesn't do crying.

"Sorry, forget I said anything. Let's talk about something else. Who's your favourite Tik Toker?" he says, patting his hands on his bare legs.

"My mum's sick," I say. "Cancer."

His hands still on his thighs. "Shit, Lex. I'm sorry. That sucks."

"It's OK," I lie. "She's finished chemo and chances are she's going to be fine. There are all these stats on the internet. Five-year survival rates and stuff. And they all say she's got a ninety per cent chance of a good outcome, but it's that ten per cent I keep thinking about."

"I should say something about focusing on the time you have together and not the worst-case scenario, but sometimes you need to do some serious dwelling."

"I'm not good at dwelling," I say, managing a smile. "I entered a stupid TV show instead."

"It's certainly been a distraction from the realities of life," he says.

"It's not just that. It's . . . I don't want to end up like her. Facing death and wishing she had something to show for her life. All she has is a crappy marriage, a job she hates, and me. Lucky, lucky her."

"Did she say she was unhappy?"

"No, but . . . how could she be happy?"

He watches me with narrowed eyes. "Lex, darling. I bet if your mother had the chance to do it all over again, she'd do it exactly the same. One tiny change would mean she wouldn't have had you. You're a miracle."

I laugh loudly, but it comes out angrier than I expected. "Miracle or not, I'm hardly much of an achievement."

"I'm going to tell you a story. My parents are doctors and they wanted me to become a doctor too. I worked so hard at school but my GCSE results weren't good enough to do the subjects I needed. Telling them was the hardest thing. I blubbed like a baby because all I'd wanted was to make them happy and, instead, I thought I'd disappointed them. But you know what my mum said?"

I try to sneer at him but my face is too cold. "Are you trying to make me cry? Because I'm not going to."

Python rolls his eyes, then puts on a terrible attempt at a woman's voice. "I want the best for you because I love you, but I could never be disappointed in you. Keith, YOU are what makes me happy."

His hand has snuck over the gap between us to clasp my own. Huddling together for warmth was one thing, but this is too much. He notices my glare and removes the hand.

"Anyway, I got into vlogging and my mum watches every single episode and tells all her friends about me. I'm, like, her biggest joy in life, no matter what stupid shit I do."

Wow. I hadn't expected this story. I'd presumed someone as desperate for fame as Python came from a miserable home. In reality, his family sounds boringly happy.

I nod slowly, trying to pretend I understand the point he's trying to make. Something to do with love overriding all the disappointment that comes with not living your life to the full. But all he's done is prove my argument. Love is an anchor. I'm the one holding my mum back.

"There's a type of spider where the mummy spider feeds her young by puking up her own liquefied internal organs," I tell him. "Then when she's nearly dead, the baby spiders pierce her with their mouthparts and suck her dry."

His mouth falls open. "You what?"

"Those spider mummies love their children so much they're willing to sacrifice themselves for a light snack. And that makes them idiots if you ask me."

He throws his arms in the air. "You really do have no heart. There's no hope for you."

"I'm not sure there's much hope for either of us." I gesture at our surroundings. Dark water. Dripping ceiling. Sense of impending doom.

Python thinks about it, then he shakes his head. He reaches for his wet clothes and wrings them out. "I have far too many people who'd miss me if I died. We're getting out of here."

Python is right. We have to keep moving. I put my damp clothes back on. Python puts on his top and jacket but can't squeeze himself back into his leggings. The last thing I'm going to see will be his snake-print Y-fronts made borderline transparent by the water.

We clamber up a slope of fallen rocks that make a steep staircase out of the cavern. At the top, there's a narrow gap in the wall through which we can squeeze. We scrabble our way into the gap. It's narrow but doable, and the movement warms me slightly. But not much.

"Ouch," Python complains. "Half-naked caving is not fun, Lex. I am not pleased with this route."

"Maybe you should have thought about that before falling off a ledge."

He stops moving. "I didn't fall. I was pushed."

"Seriously?"

"When Veronica's torch went out, someone pushed me."

"Why would someone push you? Actually, scrap that question."

"Ha ha, thanks. But it doesn't make much sense. You're the only one mean enough to do something like that."

"If I wanted to push you off something, I'd look you in the eyes when I did it so you'd know it was me."

"That's ... reassuring. Thanks. You don't believe me, do you?"

I hesitate. I believe he thinks he was pushed. But it's more likely someone bumped into him. "Who were you standing next to when you fell?"

"When I was *pushed*, I was on the edge of the group, near the tunnel. Liam was the closest, I think. He was leaning out past me to watch you."

"He was?" I ask too quickly. "Did he seem worried about me?"

"Why do you care? You're not into love."

"I don't want him for his heart."

"Lex!"

I fight a smile and walk on. Love might not be on the cards for me, but I said nothing about becoming a nun. "Come on though," I say. "You can't really think Liam pushed you? He's a marshmallow with abs."

"There's another side to everyone here," he says. "I overheard Liam arguing with Ben and Veronica. Those three have some serious history."

This is true. But murder? Nah.

I realize we've stepped out into a small cavern. It's kind of pretty, but I'm over the whole cave thing now. Unless there's a big flashing neon sign reading EXIT, I'm not interested.

That's when I realize. It's a dead end.

I step back and turn in a circle. The torch light reveals nothing but stone and – strangely – a single doll propped up against the wall. I crouch down in front of her. It's the Puckered Maiden again. I can't see how she got into the cave.

I look again as panic rises inside me. But it's no use. There's nowhere else to go.

THIRTY-SIX

I try to stay calm. But I keep thinking we're destined to be trapped here for all eternity, like that Puckered Maiden doll, staring into the dark.

"This sucks," Python says, slumping down against the wall.

"Yup." I sit opposite him.

"The others better be mourning us," he says. "I want tears and wailing."

I jiggle the doll up and down on my knee, and put on a squeaky voice. "Maybe you should have tried to be less irritating, then."

Python mimics my voice. "Actually, Lex is the most annoying. No take-backs."

I throw the doll at him. "Like I care."

"Sure you do."

I don't bother replying. He's right, if I'm being honest. But it's a bit late to regret everything I am. Besides, I'm suddenly ridiculously tired. I close my eyes and my head starts to loll.

"Blackmail," Python says. "That's why I'm here."

This is enough to bring me startling back to consciousness. "Jackie? Spill everything," I gasp. "Did you kill someone?"

"Nothing that exciting," he says quietly. "Years back, when I hadn't been posting videos for long, I reviewed an early episode of *It's Behind You*. One of the contestants had a slight stammer that got worse when she was scared and I did this really mean impression of her that went way too far. When I posted it, I immediately got a comment saying I should take the video down and *rethink my brand of humour*."

"That's the internet for you."

"No, they were right. I was being cruel and I'm glad I removed the video before more than a few people saw it. Before the girl I'd mocked saw it. She'd have been so hurt."

"Ah. Right. I think I can see where this is going."

"I still can't work out how Jackie got hold of it."

"Nothing surprises me about Jackie," I say.

"I had to come on the show, otherwise she said she'll release the video. I know I deserve to be held accountable, but I've changed so much in the past three years. These days, I campaign for kids with stammers and work with anti-bullying charities."

I think of all the stupid things I said and did when I was younger. I'm glad there's no video evidence of some of it.

"Not that it matters now," Python says. "I'm going to die and she'll show everyone, and the last thing people will think of me is that I'm a terrible, terrible person. No one will ever know the real me."

At least he knows who the real him is. I still feel like a work in progress and now it's too late to be anything more than I am.

I let my head fall back against the wall with a hollow-sounding thud. I swear I can hear distant voices. I must be imagining them; sound waves can't travel through solid rock. They fade in and out of existence, lulling me towards sleep.

"Do you hear that?" Python says, crawling across the cave.

"Is it the Puckered Maiden?" I laugh softly.

"No, you dumbass." He knocks his fist on the wall behind my head. "That's not rock."

"What?" I shake my head to clear it. I shine my torch on the wall. I can see a small door, like something out of *Alice in Wonderland*. It's made of painted wood. That's why it thunked when I knocked my head on it.

I hammer my fist on the fake wall, then feel around the edges for a way to pull it loose. Python finds a gap and sticks his fingers inside. Something clicks and the door swings open to reveal a narrow tunnel barely big enough to crawl through.

Python and I jostle to be the first into the tunnel. I win and crawl rapidly through the space, already forgetting about death and all that sentimental rubbish. The tunnel has to lead to safety. It has to. Python keeps pushing me on the bum, trying to make me move faster. I attempt to kick him in retaliation but mostly I'm laughing. We're not going to die, we're not . . .

I collide with the end of the tunnel. The torch smacks into the back of another secret door. It's easier to see it's not rock from this direction. I undo the catch and push it open. The bottom drags on the floor and I have to give it a firm shove. I tentatively crawl out and straighten up. Python pulls himself upright using my leg.

"Where are we?" Python whispers.

"I don't know." I sweep my torch around the small cave.

The cave has a homely feel to it; there's a faded chaise longue in the corner and a wooden desk up against the wall. Lying on the floor is a three-legged chair, with its fourth leg beside it. Beneath our feet, there's a patterned rug with washed-out colours and fraying edges.

"It's like someone has been living down here," Python says.

"Perhaps it's the Puckered Maiden's lair," I joke.

He narrows his eyes in thought. "Do you think she's real?"

"Nah. But Abbie certainly does."

"You know, I'm a bit of an expert on obsession and there's something weird about how Abbie's so into the Puckered Maiden."

I remember Jackie in the museum cave, her eyes on Abbie, making her unsubtle digs. "Jackie kept mentioning that guy, Brian Tobes. He took that creepy photo of the Puckered Maiden and was convinced she's real. He even harassed Liam about what happened in the caves when Laurie died."

"Huh?" He stares at me with his mouth open.

"You don't pay attention to anything, do you?"

He winces. "Not really, no."

I think for a moment. "Abbie's here for a reason. And I think she's on to something. She's always scribbling in that notebook of hers. Have you noticed how weird she's been around Ben and Veronica?"

He shakes his head and I sigh.

"Honestly. The Puckered Maiden herself could creep up behind you and . . ." I break off. Footsteps. There's someone in this cave with us and, this time, we can't blame it on a spooky soundtrack.

I hold a finger up to my lips, then creep over to a doorway leading into a tunnel. All I see is a brief flash of dirty fabric as the figure darts past.

"Oh no you don't!" I say.

I race down the tunnel while Python shouts at me to wait. I skid around the corner, but there's no one there. Only a long, dark tunnel stretching into the distance.

Python breathlessly catches up with me. He's recording with the diary cam once again.

"You're still playing Jackie's game, after everything?" I say.

"No, but if you're going to get your heart eaten by the Puckered Maiden, I may as well get some footage."

"If it's the Puckered Maiden, then why does she keep running away from us?" I say.

We continue to follow the tunnel. It weaves, rises and falls, sometimes narrowing to the point we have to crawl, then widening out into a space the size of my living room. Eventually, we come up against another dead end. This time, though, we don't succumb to panic. Instead, we hunt around for another secret tunnel. As my fingers find a smooth panel, I hear a voice. I press my ear up against the door.

"I don't care if they *all* die," the voice says. "Just so long as I get what I came here for."

I'd recognize that voice anywhere. Jackie.

THIRTY-SEVEN

"Thank goodness," Jackie says as we climb out of the secret door. "I was so worried."

I glance around. We've made it back to the Puckered Maiden Experience, if the tackiness of the cave is anything to go by. It's set up like a horror-film scientific laboratory, with dusty bottles full of eyeballs and severed fingers placed in backlit alcoves. There are dangling skeletons and car batteries hooked up to zombies as they lie on metal trolleys.

In the centre of the room, there's a glass tank full of old water. SUBJECT 13: THE PUCKERED MAIDEN, reads a sign. The tank's empty.

I can't see anyone except for Jackie. Who was she talking to? And in what world does Jackie worry about people? I look her over. Her green dress is dusty and her knees are bloodied. She's lost one of her towering pink heels.

She limps over to Python and snatches the diary cam from his hands. "I thought this was lost for ever. Please tell me the memory hasn't been damaged."

Oh, right. That makes more sense. If anything, it's reassuring to know she's still the same old mercenary Jackie.

"We're fine too," Python says. "In case you were interested."

"Marla's not." I fold my arms and glare at her until she stops fussing with the camera and looks up at me.

"I'm aware. Did anything happen between you two? We can still spin a tragic love story out of the footage."

"What? No. And didn't you hear what Lex said? Marla's *dead*."

"Oh, I know. It's terrible, tragic." Her eyes are gleaming. "Perhaps you could describe what it was like finding her body?"

Python stands there, unmoving and unspeaking. Me too. I have a pretty low bar when it comes to Jackie and yet she still manages to limbo underneath it at every opportunity.

"It's just you two? I suppose that will have to do." She walks off around the side of the tank.

"Was she always *this* fixated?" Python whispers. "Or has she really lost it?"

"This way," Jackie barks. "We need to set up the love in."

"The what?" I say.

"Love in," Python says. "It's when two contestants get to spend some alone time together, usually with a glass of wine and some chocolates. It's one of the show's set pieces."

Jackie beckons us round the corner and, reluctantly, we follow. One of the science lab benches has been set up for a romantic date. There's a bottle of the unlabelled local alcohol I remember from the town festival, a skull-shaped candle and a plate of beef jerky arranged into a heart shape. It would all work better if the bench wasn't splattered with fake blood.

"Come on then." Jackie clicks her fingers at us. "I'll film the segment on the diary cam seeing as Carl has let me down yet again."

"How dare he get himself murdered," I say. I don't know for sure, but it feels increasingly likely that he really is dead.

She ignores me and lights the candle. "When we edit the episode, we'll make it look like the other contestants have voted for you to share this special time together."

"Um, how can I say this?" I pretend to consider it. "No fucking way."

Jackie slowly faces us. The flickering light from the candle makes her into the scariest thing in these caves. "What was that?" she says, grinning her shark's smile.

"Marla is *dead*. Cameraman Carl is missing. Python and I almost died falling into a freezing cold river and the others are who knows where in these caves. There is not going to be a date."

She cocks her head at Python. "Oh, I think there is, don't you agree, Python? We need to make sure we have enough footage, don't we? Otherwise Jackie might have to share what she knows."

Python swallows heavily. "You know, maybe we should have a drink."

"Nope, not doing it." I cross my arms and stare Jackie down.

"Look, you little toenail," Jackie spits. "This show is going to be the best fucking show I've ever made, and I don't care about stupid cave-ins, or unreliable cameramen, or bitchy actresses who were too stupid to not die."

Python gasps. "You're so mean."

Her grin widens to painful dimensions. "Please sit down, you intolerable pair of shitheads."

"Make me," I say, winking at her. "I'm going to try and find the others."

"You two, get back here," Jackie snaps, but we ignore her. "Please. Pretty please? Get the fuck back in here!"

I duck through an archway and find a small cave full of soggy cardboard boxes. They contain unused props, light fittings and costumes. They must have been left here by Mortimer Monk when he abandoned his plans for the caves. Perfect. I root through a couple of them until I find what I'm looking for.

"I barely dared to dream," I say.

I pull out a nineteenth-century men's suit, complete with waistcoat.

"Nice," Python says. "I reckon that was meant for the actor who would've played Tommy."

"Maybe you can be Victoria and then we can fall in lurve," I say.

He makes a gagging noise. From the next cave, Jackie calls out to us. "That could work. Get changed and we'll talk over some conversation starters."

I shake my head in exasperation. I quickly pull off my wet, ruined clothes and put on the shirt and trousers. The suit's mostly dry, even if it smells like an old person's attic. I'm so happy, I dance around the cave like a ballerina.

Python laughs at me as he pulls on a new outfit of his own. An indecently tight Lycra skeleton bodysuit. He does a few Ben-style flexes and stretches. I bow and offer him a hand, then twirl him around between the boxes.

"Has romance blossomed in the dark?" Jackie says, sticking her head around the corner.

"Oh my god, do you ever stop?" I say, releasing Python abruptly.

"This show won't get made if I stop. And where would we be then?"

"Still stuck in an unstable cave with no way to escape."

She waves dismissively and limps back into the laboratory. "Please. Ben knows the way out."

I follow her. "You say that like you know where Ben is."

"The Bone Road comes out in the next cave. I'm sure he'll be here soon."

It takes me a second to catch on. We're in the final caves

266

of the Puckered Maiden Experience. We've made it to the other side of the cave-in, despite our watery detour.

And so has Jackie.

"How did you get here?" I ask.

"Hard work and dedication. The TV industry is tough, but I persevered—"

"To this cave! The Bone Road's meant to be the only route."

"Clearly not," she sniffs.

I open my mouth to grill her further. Then I process what she said a minute ago. The Bone Road comes out in the next cave. The others are heading our way! I rush out of the laboratory into a wide corridor lit by colour-changing lights. One end is cut off by a pile of large rocks that must have come down during the cave-in.

The corridor is taller than it is wide. It's like the open atrium of a modern building, and we're standing on the ground floor. Overhead, there are dozens of small caves and twisty passageways hewn into the rock. I think I hear something, but maybe it's wishful thinking. No, I definitely hear voices, drifting towards us from somewhere in the distance.

I find a part of the wall where the rocks jut out enough to climb. I dig my fingers into gaps in the rock and scrabble my feet on the rough surface until they find purchase. "Lex, get down here," Python says. "You're going to break your arse."

"Just as long as we get it on camera," Jackie says.

I reach a small ledge. Above me, the wall slopes inwards,

making it impossible to climb. But there's a rocky outcrop about six feet away, protruding from the wall. My earlier climbing success story has given me confidence in my own abilities. Some would say overconfidence. I take a running leap.

I slam into the outcrop with my belly. It knocks all the air out of me and I'm left scratching at the rocks as I slip. I manage to dig my fingers into a crack and dangle there, with my legs hanging out over nothing and my chest barely keeping me on the rocks.

"I'm not catching you," Python yells. "I'M NOT CATCHING YOU!"

I manage to worm my way on to the platform. I examine my forearms. I've lost quite a bit of skin and they're bleeding hideously, blood dripping on to the floor. But my sacrifice wasn't in vain. I've found something. There's another cavern back here. It's a big open space with a floor that slopes down through slanted rocks and dark cracks. It looks like it goes on for ever, all the way to the centre of the earth.

I squint into the darkness. Is that a distant light, flashing on and off? It's so faint I can't tell if it's my eyes conjuring sparks out of nothing. Or maybe it's sweet, desperate hope, and the memory of Liam's face.

No, it's totally a light, bobbing around like a floating lantern.

"Wooo," I scream, my voice echoing. "I am the ghost of Lex Hazelton come to eat your hearts."

The flashing light stops moving. It shines in my direction, but it's far too weak to reach me.

I make a roaring noise, enjoying the way it echoes in the cavernous space. "RARRRRGGHH!"

"Lex, quit that," Python calls from the ground. "You're being weird."

"Rarrrgh, rarrgh," my echo replies.

"I think it's the others," I say. "I can see a light."

"Why are you roaring at them, for goodness' sake! Switch on your head torch. Try to signal them using Morse code."

As if I know Morse code. But I do reach up and switch on my head torch. It sends a bright beam deep into the cavern. I'm basically a lighthouse, only better looking. The flickering light bobs closer and I squint to make out four figures clambering up towards me.

"Lex? Is that you?" a voice calls.

Liam, Veronica, Abbie and Ben step out of the darkness. They're dusty and muddy, and have the weary looks of people who've been through a lot. Which they have. Believing I was dead must have been hard on everyone. Liam grins crookedly at me. He can't pretend this isn't the greatest moment of his life to date.

"Gang? Is that you?" Python shouts up.

The other four rush over to the mouth of the cavern and wave happily at Python. They climb down surprisingly easily considering I nearly died getting up here.

I stand on the outcrop, watching as Jackie films the five

of them exchanging smiles and greetings. For a second, I'm hit by a strange feeling. A sense that I don't belong. I'm used to being the loud popular one, but it suddenly feels shallow. None of them truly know me.

Liam looks up, shielding his eyes against the brightness of my torch. "You coming down?" he says.

My weird moment of introspection vanishes. "Catch me," I say, tensing like I'm going to jump.

"No, don't!" Liam cries, rushing forwards with his arms outstretched. Sucker.

I laugh at him and clamber down, letting him help me at the bottom. He takes a moment to release my arm. "I'm glad you're OK," he says softly. "Really glad."

"Ahh, did you miss me?" I say, when what I really mean is "I'm glad you're OK, too." I almost say it, but I can't get the words out. Despite everything I've been through, I still default back to that game-playing arsehole who can't bring herself to let anyone get close.

That way, it can't hurt when I inevitably lose them.

THIRTY-EIGHT

"Let's vote for our favourite couple!" Jackie says, clapping her hands together.

"You what?" Abbie says. "No thanks."

Ben and Veronica are both staring at the pile of rocks cutting off the corridor. Ben's expression is grim; Veronica's bottom lip is shaking. Of course. This is where they were trapped.

Ben turns away from the cave-in to fix Jackie with a dark look. "We're getting out of here. No one's risking their life to make your show."

Jackie smiles sweetly at us all. "The lake isn't far from here. What harm will it do to record a few interviews to camera first? Maybe a quick Ouija board."

I place a hand on Jackie's shoulder. "I think it's time to let this thing go," I say. "There will be other shows. New contestants for you to terrorise."

Her face contorts into the ugliest thing I've seen. "Except there won't be. This is it. The last episode. My last chance to show her."

"Show who?"

"I know something about each and every one of you. Don't you forget that."

"And I know plenty about *you*, Jackie," Abbie retorts. "Don't you forget that."

"Show's over," Liam says, squeezing past her.

We head to the laboratory cave while Jackie calls after us, sounding increasingly desperate. We all ignore her. I slump down at the date table and help myself to some beef jerky. "What's the plan?" I say.

"Let's rest for fifteen," Ben says. "Then we'll move on."

I hold out the plate to Liam. "You look like you could do with something to eat."

He shakes his head. "No, I ... I need a few minutes alone." He heads back out of the cave.

Python sits opposite me. "Arm wrestle?" he says, flexing.

He wins three in a row, not because he's stronger than me, but because my mind is elsewhere. I sigh, rubbing my bicep. I glance around the room. Ben and Veronica are hunched in their respective corners, looking haunted and drained of colour. Abbie is sitting on a bench with her black notebook on her lap. Liam hasn't returned.

I slap my hands on the table. "I'm going to check on Liam."

"Right after you bow down and admit I'm the arm-wrestling champion of these caves," Python says.

I pretend to bow. "I'll make you a crown later."

"Real gold, please. Love you." He blows me a kiss. I pretend to swat it out of the air and stamp it to death.

"If I'm not back in ten minutes, I've been murdered by the Puckered Maiden," I say.

I find Liam sitting in the tunnel, with his head resting back against the wall and his eyes closed. "Am I interrupting?" I say.

"No. I was thinking about my sister and I could do with a distraction."

"I am distracting." I sit down next to him.

"It's been two years, so rationally I know she's dead. But . . . I guess there was part of me that hoped I'd find her here. Alive. Waiting for me to rescue her."

"Hope isn't always rational. But it keeps us going."

He stares at me with one raised eyebrow. It's like he's waiting for something. "Sorry, I figured there was more. Something mocking and flippant."

"I'm running low on wit."

"It's fine, I don't like you for your personality."

I laugh and nudge him with my shoulder. He smiles, but it doesn't last.

His gaze goes past me to the rockfall at the end of the corridor. It's a mixture of huge slabs of rocks and boulders, cracked along fault lines and crumbling where they've smashed to the ground. The gaps are filled with smaller stones and hardened mud. The pile looks like it's flowing towards us through the mouth of the tunnel.

"That tunnel used to split into two. To the left, it led to the boat cave. To the right, the Echo Chamber." He points to a crack in the wall. "There's the gap through which I imagined I heard Laurie's voice."

"Imagined?" I say.

"The thought that she's dead is just too much. Believing that she survived the cave-in let me deny the truth for the past two years. But no matter what, she's gone." He rubs his face wearily. "I guess this is the point where I'm meant to have some big moment of revelation where I imagine her ghost saying she'll always be with me."

"Is that something Laurie would tell you?"

He laughs. "Nah. She'd laugh and tell me to sort myself out."

"I like the sound of her."

"Yeah, you two would have got on. Or you'd have been mortal enemies. One or the other."

"Both are acceptable."

"She was so much fun. And impossible and infuriating. All I wanted when I grew up was to be like her. Now I'm older than she was when she died and it feels way too young."

"I don't have a brother or sister, but she sounds like a good one."

"She'd like that I'm here, I think. She was always telling me to stop thinking about things and just do them. *Life's too short*, she'd say."

"What do you think she'd say to you now, if she was here?"

He grins at me. "Life's too short. Stop thinking about things and just do them."

"And what do you want to do?" I say. I'm thinking about boring stuff like going to university and work placements and learning to drive.

It turns out Liam isn't thinking about any of these things.

He leans over and kisses me. I'm surprised for a second, and then I'm kissing him back. His soft lips, and our fingers finding each other's and knitting together. He loops a hand around my waist, pulling me closer. Our bodies are pressed tightly together. Our fingers trace each other's cheeks and arms and the bare skin where his T-shirt has ridden up.

He pulls away and clears his throat. "Sorry."

"Are you apologizing for kissing me?" I laugh.

"Maybe? I mean, it's not the greatest timing, is it?"

"Works for me." I move to kiss him again, but something strikes my arm. "Ouch!"

A pebble ricochets off Liam's forehead. We scramble to our feet with our arms shielding our heads and dive for cover. Seconds later, a boulder smashes on the floor, landing where we were sitting just moments ago.

I rub my arm and scan the atrium, trying to work out where the rocks – small and large – came from. "You think that was an accident?" I say.

Liam doesn't get a chance to answer. Appearing from the mouth of one of the caves is a figure. It's too dark to see her clearly, but I make out a filthy wedding dress. Her hair is a bird's nest of tangles. This time she's undeniably, impossibly real. The Puckered Maiden.

"You're all going to die," she cackles, with a voice like burning wood.

We don't hang around. We run to the laboratory and skid to a breathless halt by the empty tank. Abbie and Python are where I left them, but Ben and Veronica have gone.

"What is it?" Python gasps, shooting to his feet.

"We saw her," I say. "Properly, this time."

"She tried to crush us with a massive boulder," Liam adds.

"Oh. My. Gosh," whimpers Python. "The Puckered Maiden."

Abbie looks oddly thoughtful and quiet. She checks her watch. "I wonder where the others are."

As if summoned by dark magic, Jackie appears. Her hair is dishevelled and her head torch wonky. She's still limping, still smiling. She's reapplied her lipstick and it's smeared on her teeth like she's been eating raw meat.

"Tarot cards!" she says, producing a box from behind her back. "Let's do this thing."

"Have you seen Ben and Veronica?" Liam asks. "We need to get out of here. Someone just tried to kill us."

"Kill you?" she mutters, frowning. "Why would she want to kill you?" She sways unsteadily.

"You all right?" Python says.

"I'm wonderful. Never better. Never—" She doesn't get to finish as she's sick all over herself. It's all liquid and stinks like the local rubbing alcohol everyone was drinking at the festival. It leaves a dark wet patch on her purple dress. "Oopsie."

"Juice cleanse, my arse." I go to the side room and grab one of the boxes of old costumes. I return and dump it out on to the floor.

"I'm not wearing polyester," Jackie says.

"Stay in the sick dress if you want. I don't care. But, so you know, you smell terrible."

Jackie drops on to her knees and starts rooting through all the costumes. I've managed to pick a box without anything nice in it. She's left with a choice between a chimney sweep's outfit and a stiff dress that would suit a Victorian governess. She picks the latter and steps behind the tank of dirty water to change.

I go to pick up the clothing now strewn across the floor. But then I notice the look on Liam's face. He's staring at something among the costumes and it's like all the blood has drained from his face.

"Liam?" I say.

Slowly, he reaches down to retrieve a woolly bobble

hat. It looks homemade, with pointy ears sewn on the top and buttons for eyes. One of the buttons is hanging loose on purple thread.

Liam glances up at me. "This was Laurie's hat. She was wearing it the night the cave collapsed."

Just then, Ben and Veronica step into the cave. Veronica spots the hat and puts a hand over her mouth. Ben stands there, frozen to the spot.

All of us stare as Liam helplessly clutches the hat. Its mouth is a grinning seam from which a red tongue lolls. No one needs to say what this means; we all know.

If Laurie's hat is in this box, then she can't be buried under a hundred tonnes of rock.

THIRTY-NINE

A small red light shines through the darkness like a star. It hits the tank of dirty water and splits into a dozen shimmering beams. Jackie's spotted the drama and is filming Liam with the diary cam. Her black governess's outfit swamps her figure and rustles like dry leaves as she limps closer.

"Laurie didn't die in the cave-in," Liam says, still staring at the hat. "You lied to me."

Ben shakes his head. "We were separated. I looked for her, but there was so much dust. So I presumed she'd been buried."

"She could have dropped the hat before the cave-in," Veronica whispers. "It doesn't mean she—"

"Don't." Liam's voice is so full of simmering anger that Veronica falls silent.

The tension is like the intake of breath before bad news. A knot in my stomach is tightening and tightening. I know any moment something will snap. And then will come the feeling of free-fall, like when my mum told me about her diagnosis.

It's Abbie who moves first. She steps forwards and takes both of Liam's hands in hers. He doesn't resist. She's smiling, which is unusual for Abbie.

"Do you know what this means?" she says. "It means he was right."

"Who?" Liam says.

"Tobes. Brian Tobes! If she survived the cave-in, then what happened to her? Think about it. She was young and in love; a girl who strayed too deep into the caves. Her disappearance is classic Puckered Maiden—"

"Don't you dare," Liam yells, ripping his hands away from Abbie's. "That man called me up daily after my sister died. Asking me endless questions I couldn't and didn't want to answer. Now you, too?"

"Who is Brian Tobes to you?" I ask Abbie, as the pieces start to fall into place. Abbie's fascination with the photo of the Puckered Maiden and the man who'd taken it. The puzzle box. The story of the father who abandoned her as a baby . . .

"Brian Tobes is Abbie's father," Jackie says triumphantly. "He's why she's here."

Abbie closes her eyes. Liam takes another step away from her.

"It's not what you think," she says. "He was no father to me. He was so obsessed with the Puckered Maiden, he left me and my mum. And that's why I need it to be real. If I can prove Laurie was killed by the Puckered Maiden, then him leaving won't have been for nothing."

There's a desperation in Abbie's voice that makes me feel nauseous.

"Don't you want to know the truth?" she pleads, but Liam won't even look at her.

"Abbie, drop it," I say.

"I can't! I've spent every minute since he died piecing together his work – his theories." She holds out her black notebook. "After he took that photo, half of the supernatural community called him a fraud. He spent the next thirty years trying to convince people that the photo was real. Even having me wasn't enough for him to forget his obsession. The last time I spoke to him, he said if he could get into these caves, he'd find proof Laurie was taken by the Puckered Maiden."

Liam looks between Abbie's face and her notebook. Then, quick as a flash, he snatches the book from her and hurls it across the cave. Abbie cries out and grabs at the book as it passes, but it arcs through the air and falls into the tank of water. The book slowly sinks, bleeding ink into the dirty water.

"My sister isn't a game. She's not some stupid conspiracy theory," he yells, so loudly Abbie recoils.

"But don't you want to know the truth?" Abbie says, tears running down her dusty face.

"Yeah," he says, his voice gruff. "Yeah, I do."

He storms out of the laboratory cave with his hands in tight fists. Jackie limps after him, still filming his every move. Her grin is terrifying.

"Liam, stop," Veronica pleads, weaving around Jackie. "Laurie's dead! You have to let her go—"

"Enough, Veronica." He pushes her away and she stumbles, falling against the wall.

"Liam, slow down," Ben says. "You need to stop."

Liam doesn't stop. He runs to the cave-in, dropping to his knees where the flow of mud and stone meets the cavern floor. He tosses rocks aside one at a time.

"Stop," Ben repeats, his voice barely a whisper.

"I'm finding my sister! I can't bear the not knowing. I can't do it any more."

"She's gone. Laurie's gone." Veronica's arms are wrapped tightly around her stomach like she's hugging herself.

"I'm not like you. I can't stop caring because she's dead."

"We never stopped caring," Veronica says.

We all stand there while Liam digs through the rubble with his bare hands. His fingers are bleeding. And we're just standing there.

"Liam, stop. Enough." Ben tries to pull Liam away from the rocks, but Liam swings at him. His fist connects with Ben's mouth. Ben shoves him back, but he pushes him too hard. Liam's ankle goes out from under him and he falls to the ground. Even as he's gasping in pain, he's still dragging himself back towards the cave-in, to claw at the hardened mud.

"She's not here," Ben yells, blood outlining his teeth. "Listen to me. She's not here!"

Everything stops.

"Ben, don't," Veronica says. "Please."

Liam manages to stand back up, supporting himself on the wall. He turns. "What did you say?"

"She's not here," Ben whispers. "She wasn't killed in the cave-in."

I go to Liam and take his dusty, bloody hand in mine. Veronica shakes her head and stares at her feet. There are tears dripping from her face, splashing on the dry ground.

"I have to know," Liam says. "Ben, please. You have to tell me."

Veronica holds a hand over her mouth to stifle her sobs. "Please don't, Ben. He'll hate us."

"What happened?" Liam says.

Ben glances over at Veronica. "There was an argument. Laurie didn't want me spending any more time with Veronica. She thought there was something going on between us."

"Was there?" Liam says.

He doesn't answer the question. "The three of us ended up screaming at each other, saying all these things we didn't mean."

Liam nods slowly. "And then what happened?"

"There was a noise unlike anything I'd ever heard before. The cave filled up with thick dust and the floor was shaking so much we couldn't stand. It went on for what felt like an eternity, and then it stopped."

Ben looks at Veronica again. She's stopped crying but her chest keeps heaving when she takes a breath.

"I wanted us all to stick together and look for a way out," he goes on, "but Laurie was still furious. She was screaming all this stuff. In the end, I . . . I . . . ."

"What did you do?" Liam says.

Ben locks eyes with Liam. The two boys are silent for a moment. We all hold our breath while we wait for Ben to answer. "I walked away," he says. "I left them both. I headed for the Bone Road and eventually I found my own way out. I thought she'd follow me. I thought there'd be time to make up, but I never saw her again."

"You left her here. You left her behind." Liam glances at Veronica. "And you did too."

Veronica wipes her eyes. "She kept yelling at me. Saying she knew I was after Ben. I couldn't make her listen to me, so I left. I tried to find the Bone Road but I got lost. Eventually I found my own way out swimming through the underwater tunnels into Shepherd's Lake."

"That means Laurie wandered around the caves until she, what? She died, somewhere in this place, all by herself?"

"I guess so," Ben says in a small voice. "I know I shouldn't have left her—"

"You were her boyfriend! You were meant to help her."

"I know. Liam, I'm sorry. I'm so sorry."

Liam shakes his head. He takes his hand from mine and he limps away. We all let him go.

FORTY

The cave grumbles beneath our feet. A single pebble skitters down the pile of rocks and rolls at my feet. The tremors are getting closer together. A reminder that we're on borrowed time.

"We should catch up with Liam," I say. "No one should be wandering around these caves by themselves."

Jackie claps her hands together. "Hide-and-seek, haunted cave edition?"

"Why don't you hide, and we'll all forget to find you?" I say.

She laughs dramatically. "I was right. You *are* the comic relief. So fucking funny."

"Better than the clumsy sidekick," I mutter, setting off after Liam.

We find no sign of him, just unlit tunnels stretching into the distance and dozens of passageways snaking off to the sides, leading into any number of cosy crawl spaces where he could be hiding.

"I'll check the laboratory and all the passages beyond," Ben says.

Abbie and Veronica go with him, perhaps not wanting to venture away from the lights of the Puckered Maiden Experience. Python, Jackie and I reach a metal gate marked as no entry. It's standing ajar so we step through. The ceiling's low and Jackie and I have to tilt our heads to fit.

These tunnels aren't like the ones of the museum. They remind me of natural passageways of the Bone Road. There's no beauty down here, only rocks and puddles and mud. I direct my torch into all the hidden alcoves, but there's no Liam.

"Come out, come out wherever you are," Jackie sings, holding the camera at arm's length as she films us. She still smells of alcohol and puke.

I hear the distant ghost of a voice. I pause and listen. Whispering, maybe. It sounds like it's coming from the walls. But the harder I listen, the less I hear. I begin to think I was imagining it.

Then Jackie abruptly shoves the camera at Python and rustles off at speed. "Keep recording. I'll be right back."

"What on Earth is going on?" Python says.

"I have no idea."

We round the next corner, but Jackie is gone. It's like she's vanished into thin air.

"One of the secret tunnels, maybe?" Python says.

I sweep my torch in a circle. There are small alcoves everywhere, any one of which could be hiding one of the wooden doors. I direct the light overhead and find a chimney-like structure pitted with dozens of holes, like a dovecote. A cold breeze swirls down towards us, making me shudder. "Let's find Liam and get out of here."

"What about Jackie?"

"She knows her way around. She'll find her own way back."

We reach a fork in the path. I shine the torch down each route. They both lead deeper into the cave system. I pick the path to the right. Water drips from the ceiling, forming stalactites so fine that they shatter when I brush against them.

"This tunnel makes my top five creepy moments of the night," Python says. He films the stalactites as we pass.

"Creepier than that cave full of zombies?"

"God, that feels like a lifetime ago. The séance is top for me, though. I was so scared."

I chuckle, remembering when Python threw vodka in Marla's eyes and set the tablecloth on fire. Thinking about Marla feels like a punch to the gut. Surrounded by horror house exhibits and clever lighting, it felt like her death was just another trick. But here in the dark, it's all too real. She's gone, and when this show is over, she'll still be gone.

I duck beneath an overhanging rock and weave through several fleshy-looking stalagmites. "I feel bad," I admit. "If I'd been nicer to Marla, then she wouldn't have stayed in the boat by herself."

Python doesn't reply. I guess he blames me as much as I blame myself.

"Do you really think it was an accident?" I say. "This place is messing with my head and I don't know what's real, what's all in my mind, and what's one of Jackie's games."

Silence. I turn around and Python's gone.

I sweep the torch through all the rocks. The cave looks bigger from this direction, full of places where he could be hiding.

I fold my arms. "I'm not playing," I say. "We're meant to be looking for Liam."

Something drips from above and a cold splash on my neck quickens my pulse. I retrace my footsteps, peering behind all the rocks. I even force my face into an expression of boredom so when he catches me with the diary cam, I won't look surprised. Only there's no sign of him.

"Python?" I call.

Water gurgles somewhere among the rocks. I duck back into the tunnel where I last saw him. Only it feels unfamiliar. The path is sloping downwards, taking me even deeper into the cave system. I stop. Try to get my bearings.

My heart is beating so fast and my head is spinning. I

can barely breathe. It feels like the day my mum told me she was sick. I can remember wanting to run away as fast as I could but, at the same time, I was panicking too much to move. So I just stood there, rooted to the spot.

That's what I'm doing right now. I want my mum here with me now, calm and rational, with an answer for everything. Her cool palm on my face, her thumb stroking my cheek.

"Lex, it's going to be fine," she'd said, a quiet laugh in her voice. "I know it feels scary right now, and too big to deal with. But we can get through this one day at a time. One step at a time if we have to."

I'd stared at her, still unable to say a single damn thing. I should have been reassuring her, not vice versa. I guess selfishness has been a theme of my entire life. I close my eyes.

"One step at a time," she whispers, kissing my forehead. "You can do this."

I nod. OK. I've got this. I don't have to fix everything in one go. I only have to retrace my footsteps until I reach something familiar. And then I'll move on to the next problem. I wipe my eyes.

"The darkness can't go on for ever," she says. "Even if that's how it feels right now."

"These caves would beg to differ," I say, finding that saying the joke out loud makes me feel a little bit braver, even if it shatters my mother's spectre like those ancient stalactites.

I jog back the way I came and stop at the mouth of the cave. All the rocks look the same. There are several dark alcoves that could lead to a tunnel. Did I duck when I walked in to the cave? Or did I weave around rocks? I can't remember.

I pick a direction and start walking. Just then a voice speaks. Not my mother's voice. It's the same voice that's been stalking us through the caves. "Not that way. You'll be lost for ever."

I spin around, but I can't see anyone. "Who's there?" I shout.

"Take the next tunnel, and maybe you'll get there in time. Maybe not."

"Why should I believe you? Maybe you want me to get lost."

"Maybe I do." The voice cracks up into choking laughter. There's something about it. A roughness, like whoever it is either hasn't talked for a long time or has talked too much. Their laughter sounds unpleasantly wet.

"Where are you?"

There's no answer. I wait, turning on the spot so my torch throws stretching shadows off the rocks. Whoever it was is gone. I hesitate, then I pick the tunnel the voice directed me towards. I can always double back if it's unfamiliar. But from the first step, I know this is the right way. And when I reach the broken stalactites, I breathe a sigh of relief.

That's when I hear the scream.

"Python?" I call. "Python!"

I start running along the dark tunnel. I shine the torch across the walls, looking in all the little alcoves, but I don't see him.

What did the voice say? *Maybe you'll get there in time. Maybe not.*

I burst through the metal gate. I've nearly reached the laboratory cave when someone steps out of the shadows.

"Lex!" Liam says. "Are you OK? I heard screaming."

"It was Python," I say breathlessly.

We run up the passageway until we reach the laboratory cave where we left the others. And Python's standing at the entrance, with the diary cam hanging from his hand, recording the floor. He's fine. The total bastard is fine.

"What's with the screaming?" I say. "Someone with a heart would have been worried."

He doesn't answer. Instead, he points into the cave. Ben and Veronica are standing in the opposite doorway, but he's not pointing at them, he's pointing at the tank of dirty water.

At Abbie.

"Oh my god," Liam says.

Abbie's lying at the bottom of the tank. Her hair is the only part of her that is floating. Wet tendrils stand tall, like underwater plants. The rest of her is still and heavy.

"Is she ... she's ..." Python says.

"She's dead," Liam finishes.

Part of me wants to dive into the water and haul her

out. Press on her chest like they do in the movies until she pukes up all the water she's inhaled. But I know it's too late.

Her eyes are wide open and the water around her is a hazy pink colour. It reminds me of how the ink seeped from her notebook when Liam threw it into the tank. Only this time, it's a cut on the back of her head that's bleeding into the water. The book is still in there, lying open to a page washed clean of words. It looks like Abbie is reaching out for it with her limp fingers.

I could almost believe this was an accident. That Abbie was trying to retrieve the book and fell. Except, scattered on the steps leading up the side of the tank, there's a smashed laboratory flask. A heavy thing, with a thick bottom. There's blood on the broken glass, shining like rubies.

Someone crept up behind her as she peered into the water. Someone hit her on the head and left her to drown.

There's no denying the truth now. There's a killer in these caves with us. That's when I notice that our party is missing one person.

"People?" I say slowly. "Where's Jackie?"

FORTY-ONE

Extract from the transcript of pitch to executive board for *It's Behind You, Season 3, Episode 10*; Umber Gorge Caves as a potential location, as proposed by Jackie Stone [JS], producer of *It's Behind You* and adjudicated by David Moore [DM], managing director Spooktastic Productions.

DM: Is there a reason you've brought, um . . . what is that?

JS: Pickled pigs' hearts on toast, Dave. I wanted to get your attention. This episode will be the last in the season, after all. It's a big deal.

DM: [Sighing] I'm going to level with you, Jackie. The numbers aren't looking good. Season three hasn't lived up to expectations based on the popularity of the first two seasons. The problem's originality. Viewers know what to expect now, and they're getting bored. The team think we should cut our losses.

JS: Which is why I have something amazing in store for this episode. Something to reignite the public's excitement and maybe even secure a fourth season.

DM: Let's not get ahead of ourselves. But go on then, shoot.

JS: I want you to picture a cave. Stalactites, gleaming pools of water, dark corners where all manner of scary things could be hiding.

DM: A cave would be an interesting change of scenery. Is Health and Safety on board? Because I can foresee some issues with uneven floors, falling rocks, those pools of water.

JS: Oh yes, everything is covered. These caves were converted into a tourist attraction years ago. They're set up for the public to visit.

DM: I'm listening.

JS: These caves are home to a particularly gruesome local legend. The Puckered Maiden is a ghost who tears out the hearts of the young and in love.

DM: The pigs' hearts make slightly more sense now. And what scares are you thinking of?

JS: Just the usual challenges. Throw in some clever lighting and some sound effects, and we're good to go. The expenses will be kept to a minimum and I can guarantee the contestants will be terrified.

DM: It does sound intriguing, I will give you that.

JS: And I have Python. The YouTuber who reviews all our episodes. He's big. Huge, even. Over a million followers.

DM: Wow. OK. That does make a difference, but I still don't know.

JS: I can personally guarantee this will be the best episode ever. I'd stake my job on it.

DM: You will need to, Jackie. Unless the filming goes without a hitch, I can't see us keeping you on, I'm afraid. Are you sure this is the hill you want to die on?

JS: It's a gorge, not a hill. And yes. This episode is ... important to me. There's nothing I won't do to make it the scariest one to date. Heart, anyone?

FORTY-TWO

I can't look away from the tank – from Abbie – even though I wish I could.

"Abbie said she knew something about Jackie," Veronica whispers. "What if Jackie was trying to stop her from talking?"

"I can't believe Jackie would kill someone," Liam says.

"You can't?" I say, raising an eyebrow. "I'm not sure there's anything she wouldn't do for this show."

Ben nods slowly. "When both Marla and Abbie died, she wasn't with any of us, was she? She has no alibi for either of the murders."

"Wasn't she still outside when Cameraman Carl vanished?" Python says.

"She knows these caves," Veronica says. "Somehow, she's moving around without anyone knowing how she's doing it. If she knew of another entrance, she could have snuck inside during all the chaos of the fire."

"It's possible," Ben admits. "She kept going off to field calls from the production company bosses."

"But why?" Python says.

"Maybe it wasn't intentional," Veronica says. "Maybe Carl just saw something he wasn't meant to see."

"And the Puckered Maiden?" Liam says. "Is that her, too?"

"It wouldn't take much for her to throw on a costume to torment us, then disappear back into those tunnels even you locals didn't know about," I say.

I think about something that's been bothering me. How the mystery woman tried to drop a rock on my head, only to rescue me when I got lost an hour later. It didn't make sense at first. But what if she was thinking about what grisly fate would look better on camera? Maybe she has something special saved for me . . .

"Oh my god, Jackie's trying to kill us," Python whispers. "What are we going to do?"

"We stick to the plan," Ben says. "We carry on through the caves and we get out of here. The police can deal with Jackie."

"Do you think they'll investigate?" Veronica says. "They refused to come in here, last time. It was too dangerous."

"They didn't come in last time because you both lied to them," Liam says.

298

"Liam, come on." Ben tries to take Liam's arm, but Liam slaps him away.

"Get off me!" He glances contemptuously at both Ben and Veronica. "Laurie's dead because you both lied. I'll never forgive you for that."

"We get it," Ben says to Liam. "You hate us. And that's fine. But we need to get out of these caves before they fall in on us or some deranged TV producer kills us for ratings. So how about you act like a man and help me make sure no one else dies?"

Liam steps towards him so the two boys are nose to nose. "You're right. I'll work with you to escape, but after that? I'm going to make sure everyone knows what happened to Laurie. If it's the last thing I do."

He breaks away and heads for the tunnel, still limping badly on his injured ankle. The rest of us move to follow, but then we hear something. The tell-tale clicking of Jackie's one heel.

"Quiet," Ben hisses. "Everyone behind the tank. Quick."

We duck down low, hoping the filthy water will hide us. Through the dirty glass, I see Jackie step into the cave and stop. We all duck down lower. Python bites my shirt to stop himself from crying out. Although he is still managing to record Jackie with the diary cam. Devoted to the cause right to the end.

"I'm making a TV show," she yells, raising both arms in the air like a conjuring magician. "The greatest TV show in history, and none of you maggots are going to ruin it. You hear me?"

Python digs his fingers into my thigh and stares at me with wide, terrified eyes. Jackie swishes closer, and closer, and closer. We all wait, motionless, as she approaches our hiding place. When she speaks, her voice is babyish and creepy. "How can Jackie make her show if you're all hiding from her?"

Closer, still. I think she's spotted us as a slow grin spreads across her face. But suddenly she cocks her head like she's heard something. Her grin twists into fury.

She sets off at a run. "I'm going to kill you if you fuck up my show."

We wait until her footsteps fade. "I've had enough," Veronica says quietly. "I want to go back to my life and forget about these stupid caves."

"Sounds like a plan," I say, squeezing her hand.

We walk for close to an hour in exhausted silence. We don't hear or see Jackie, and I start to think we've lost her. But we're moving slower and slower. Liam's face twists in pain with every step. Veronica keeps stumbling. Python's diary cam mostly records our shuffling feet.

Ben eventually stops walking with a sigh. Her sweeps a hand over his short hair. "All right, team, we're going to have to take a break."

"No, we keep going," Liam says.

"I'll keep watch while the rest of you sleep. I'm fine but you all need to rest."

"I don't need to rest." But Liam slumps down on to the floor anyway. "Just a few minutes," he mumbles.

I sit down against a rock and Python lies down with his head on my legs. "You're going to stay awake, right?" I say, eyeing Ben suspiciously. "I don't want Jackie creeping up on me in my sleep."

"I've got this."

My eyes blink slowly. I know I'm going to regret this tiny snippet of sleep when I wake – it will only serve to remind me how tired I am – but it's too late to stop myself.

The walls are whispering in my dreams. They're angry and bitter and they think I can't hear them, but I can. *I know what you did*, they're saying. *I know who you are.* Scuffling footsteps, muffled cries. *Don't threaten me. Keep your mouth closed, or . . . or . . .*

I shift in my sleep and drift too close to wakefulness. The voices stop. More footsteps. I drift down once again and, this time, there's silence.

I wake up desperate for a wee. I stagger to my feet, stiff and achy from lying in the same position on a hard surface for too long. I stretch out my arms. It's then I notice Ben and Veronica are gone. So much for Ben keeping watch.

But there are more important things to deal with. Such as not wetting myself in front of hot Liam. He's spooning with Python on the floor. I leave the head torch hanging from a rock for them. I'll use what little juice there is left in my key-ring torch because I'm nice like that. I hurry around the back of a water-eaten rock for some privacy.

I'm finishing up and about to return to Liam and Python when there's a noise. I pause while buttoning up my trousers. "Veronica? Ben?"

There's no answer.

I shine my torch through a low alcove into a neighbouring cavern. The beam is too dim to pick much up, but I think I see movement. "Who's there?" I say. "That better not be you, Jackie. Because I am done with your nonsense."

Nothing. I start to think maybe I imagined it, and move to go back. Then there's this strange noise. Like someone tossing a heavy bag on to the ground. A quiet splash.

"I know someone's there," I say. "I should warn you, I'm armed."

I look around for something I could use as a weapon. I settle on a fist-sized rock. I glance back over my shoulder, but Liam and Python are out of sight. I venture through the alcove into the cavern. There's nobody here, just gently rippling water and arches of stone making doorways through into yet more caves.

"You're losing your mind, Lex," I say.

I sweep my torch around again, catching all the sharp edges of the limestone. It feels dreamlike. Haunted, even. I'm heading back to the others when I nearly step on something. A tiny skeleton with wire joints and wooden limbs. Veronica's earring. My stomach drops.

No, not Veronica.

I bend down to pick it up. I sense a presence behind me

and freeze. I want to tell myself it's all in my head, like in that cavern along the Bone Road. But this time, I can hear them breathing and I know it's real. They smell like clothes that have been damp too long. My mind fills in the blanks. Skin hanging in tattered strips. Sharp, triangular teeth. Claws protruding from blackened fingers.

I move to stand up, only something clouts me on the back of the head and I'm out of the game.

I'm in and out of consciousness. Everything's in flashes. I can hear voices. Muffled shouts. Laughter. I stumble between rocks and splash into the shallow water. I lose my footing and fall to my knees. I touch the back of my head. Blood. Like Marla. Like Abbie.

Someone tried to kill me?

I sway unsteadily. The mirrored water makes it impossible to tell which way is up. I'm not sure if I'm real or if I'm the reflection.

Voices again. I stagger to my feet. Veronica's here, out in the water. She's tussling with the Puckered Maiden, or is it Jackie in costume? My head lurches with every thought. I can't think straight.

My vision clears briefly. The Puckered Maiden's dragging Veronica along by the hair.

"Stop," I manage to say. I try to move towards them, but I'm too dizzy and my limbs won't listen to instructions from my brain. I trip off in the wrong direction, losing my balance and splashing down, down, down.

There's nothing I can do but watch helplessly as the

Puckered Maiden yanks a sack over Veronica's head. Holding her around the waist, she drags her away through the shallow water, into the cave beyond.

FORTY-THREE

I wake up with my head in Python's lap and Liam clasping my hand. I must have passed out, but for how long? With Liam's help, I shakily sit up. My vision splinters into sparks at the pain in my head.

"They tried to kill me," I say, surprising myself with how slurred my voice is.

"Was it Jackie?" Python says.

"I don't know." I wince as another stabbing pain sears through my head. Liam's head torch is far too bright. "I didn't see them."

"We heard a scream," Liam says.

I sit up straighter. The movement makes the world tilt

and threaten to tip me off. "Veronica," I manage to say. "Veronica was here. The Puckered Maiden took her."

"Took her where?" Python says.

I point into the still water. The roof of the cave makes a doorway over the shallow pool. I think it was through this archway that the Puckered Maiden dragged Veronica away, although I'm sketchy on the details.

"Where's Ben?" Liam asks.

"I have no idea," I reply. "I woke up and he and Veronica were gone. I went for a wee and I thought I heard voices, but then someone whacked me on the head. I think she would have killed me if Veronica hadn't turned up."

"God damn it." Liam runs a hand through his hair. "All right, I'm going after her. But you need to stay here."

"No way," I laugh. "We're not letting you go by yourself, are we, Python?"

"Um, I guess not?" Python says, pulling an unsure face.

"You can't even stand up," Liam says.

I unsteadily heave myself upright, clinging on to him for support. "I'm up," I say, wobbling dangerously. "Anyway, you're the one with a broken ankle."

"It's not broken. That's what I'm telling myself, anyway."

I laugh, then immediately regret it when I nearly pass out from the pain in my head. "We're a great team, aren't we? My skull's in pieces, your foot's going to fall off, and Python's a wimp."

"I really am," Python says.

Liam smiles. "Together, we're a complete human."

I point to my key-ring torch so Python can pick it up for me. I shakily lead the way into the water. It's icy cold and seeps into my already wet shoes, making my socks unpleasantly sloshy all over again. But it isn't deep. We duck beneath the arched ceiling and follow a wide tunnel. The water covers the entire floor and the disorientating reflections remind me of a carnival mirror maze.

Liam and I grab at the walls to stay upright. Python unhelpfully paws at our clothes for emotional support.

"What if she's already dragged her underwater and drowned her?" Python whispers. "Or eaten her heart?"

Liam shoots him a dark look. "None of those stories are real."

"It doesn't matter if you believe or not," Python says. "Jackie strikes me as the sort of person who *commits*."

He has a point. I quicken my pace as much as possible.

The tunnel opens out. We switch off our torches and peek around the corner. I can see Veronica illuminated by the light of an old oil lantern. She's sitting next to the water with her knees tucked up against her chest. Her dress is dripping a puddle on to the ground. Compared to the columns of stone and cavernous ceiling, she looks tiny. She's not tied up, so I don't know why she's not moving.

But then the Puckered Maiden aka Jackie steps into view. Her filthy wedding dress is sodden and leaves a wet trail behind her. She's holding a meat cleaver.

I duck back so she won't see me. "What are we going to do?" I whisper.

"I'm not sure I'm going to be much use in a fight," Liam says.

"Me neither," I add. We both glance at Python. No one needs to say anything.

"All right, fine," Python says. "How about we create a distraction?"

"That could work. Well done for volunteering."

He takes some deep breaths, then scurries over to hide behind a rock. Every time Puckered Jackie's back is turned, he runs to the next rock.

"What does she want with Veronica?" I say to Liam. "It looks like they're talking. I'm going to get closer."

"Wait, Lex, that's not the plan."

But I'm not listening. I creep around the edge of the cave, sticking to the shadows. The lantern is throwing just a small puddle of light that doesn't reach the walls. If I keep quiet, no one will know I'm here. The water laps gently against my ankles.

I get as close as I can and duck down behind a rock. I stumble and have to catch myself with one hand in the water. Puckered Jackie whips her head around. I stay dead still, holding my breath. She turns away.

"I warned you last time," she says. "You shouldn't have come back here."

"I never wanted to!" whispers Veronica. "You don't understand."

"I understand perfectly."

She transfers the cleaver from one hand to the other and

it's all I can do to stop myself from gasping. Because her fingernails are gnarly and her skin wrinkled. I was wrong. There's no way it's Jackie.

"I had no choice." Veronica eyes the cleaver. "Please. What do you want?"

"What do I want? Ha! What I *want* is for you people to get out of my caves and never come back."

"That's what I want, too. By dawn, I'll be gone and you'll never see me again."

"And the others?"

Veronica doesn't answer. I'm struck by the feeling they've spoken before. And then I realize: maybe they have. The last time Veronica was trapped here. Oh god, maybe Abbie was right. Maybe the Puckered Maiden really does exist.

"These are my caves," she says. "I'm done with you bringing your horror show down here. You hear me? No more."

Why am I getting a feeling of déjà vu?

"Did someone say horror show?" Python cries theatrically, jumping out from his hiding place. He lugs a rock, but it falls short by several metres. In his free hand, he's *still* holding the diary cam.

The Puckered Maiden picks up her lantern and raises it high, trying to get a better look at him. The meat cleaver dangles half-forgotten from her hand. I grab a pebble and toss it into the water near to Veronica. She startles and looks in my direction. I gesture for her to join me. She hesitates, then stands up slowly.

"Come and get me then," Python says uncertainly. "I'll be delicious. Don't you want to, I don't know, chase me or something?"

The Puckered Maiden inclines her head. "Why would I want to chase you?"

"Um, isn't that what you do? You've been stalking us through the caves since we got here."

"To scare you off," she snaps. "So you'll leave and never come back."

"Oh. Well. We are actually trying to leave? So if you'll let us have our friend back . . ."

"Her?" She turns back to Veronica. "She's your friend, is she? You have no idea what kind of friend this one is."

Veronica needs to run. Instead, she stands there, frozen to the spot, staring from behind tendrils of hair that have fallen in front of her face.

"We know what happened when Veronica was trapped here last time and it doesn't matter to us," Python says. "We're still here to rescue her."

The Puckered Maiden looks back at Python. "You keep saying we. Where are the rest of you, then?"

The moment the woman looks away, Veronica moves. But not towards safety. With a shriek, she grabs the Puckered Maiden's arm. The two of them wrestle for possession of the meat cleaver, but the Puckered Maiden is strong. The cleaver inches closer and closer to Veronica's face. Veronica grits her teeth and twists the woman's arm, forcing the weapon towards her throat.

Veronica sobs with chest-shaking hiccups. "Why won't you leave me alone? Please."

The woman laughs like it's the funniest thing in the world. It's a demented cackle of a laugh, rough around the edges with a wet centre. There's something so familiar about that cackle . . .

"Every time I close my eyes, you're there," Veronica continues. "I can't do this. Just leave me alone!"

She finds a burst of strength and yanks the cleaver from the woman's grip. The two of them lose their balance and splash into the water, Veronica landing astride the woman. With a desperate howl, she brings the cleaver back to strike.

"No, wait!" I stumble out of my hiding place and catch Veronica's arm.

We can't just *kill* someone, especially not the someone I think it is hiding under that costume. But Veronica's amped up on adrenaline and she fights me, still trying to bring the cleaver down. Then Liam's there too, dragging Veronica back with his hands under her arms. She kicks and screams like she doesn't know where she even is. Then finally, gasping and sobbing, she falls still.

"She'll never stop," she whispers. "She'll never let me go."

"But that's not the Puckered Maiden," Liam says, laughing with disbelief. "That's Sally-Ann from Umber town."

FORTY-FOUR

The veil has fallen away from the Puckered Maiden's face. Underneath, there's no peeling skin and sharp teeth, just wrinkles and bright, wicked eyes. Sally-Ann, the old woman who threw blood on me while protesting the opening of the caves. She shuffles back to sit up against a rock and glares daggers at Veronica.

"What's going on?" Liam says. "I don't understand."

That makes two of us.

"You killed three people," Python says.

"And you hit me on the head with a rock," I grumble. "All because you didn't want us in these caves?"

"These caves aren't a tourist attraction, or a stupid game show," she says, sniffing.

"Jesus, Sally-Ann! What were you thinking? *Murder?*" Liam yanks the cleaver from Veronica's hand and hurls it across the cave. Veronica falls to the floor, crying silent tears.

Sally-Ann grins at us. "I wanted you out of the caves, but everything else? Nothing to do with me."

Her eyes dart over to the doorway. We all spin around. Jackie limps into the cave, terrifying in the black governess's dress that rustles like the crackle of flames.

My throbbing head picks out disjointed memories and tries to make them fit together. Sally-Ann dressed as the Puckered Maiden, showing me the way back to the others when I got lost. Sally-Ann dressed as the Puckered Maiden, throwing stones at me and Liam, right before a rock fell and almost crushed us. Almost as if she wasn't the one who pushed that rock. Almost as if she was trying to save us.

I never saw who hit me on the head. It could have been anyone. It could have been Jackie.

I think it's *all* been Jackie.

"What a lovely reunion." Jackie stoops down to pick up the meat cleaver and runs a finger along the sharp edge. She fixes me with a tight smile. "And where have you all been?"

I back away. We were right about her. She really has snapped. "Why are you doing this?" I say.

"To prove a point. I grew up in this awful town, would you believe?"

"What?" Liam says. "You're a local."

She shudders at the accusation. "God, no. Not any more.

I've worked on myself since I left. I'm unrecognizable these days."

"Ha. You're still the same," Sally-Ann gripes. "Still a big fat loser."

"Could a *loser* have become a producer of an award-winning show?"

Sally-Ann snorts. "Look at you, in your fancy clothes, with your fancy make-up, trying to convince yourself that you're *something*."

"I am something, and this episode is going to put me on the map."

Sally-Ann waves dismissively. "I couldn't care less."

"I bet you will when *everyone* wants to visit these caves. That's right. I'm going to make Umber Caves *the* haunted destination. Three murders will have the visitors flocking to this place."

Sally-Ann's smirk fails her. "I'll chase them off like I always do."

So that's what she was trying to do, dressed up as the Puckered Maiden – scare us away. And when that didn't work, she kidnapped Veronica and threatened her. It's not entirely rational, but it fits with everything I know about Sally-Ann. I'm guessing she's been playing this game for decades: impersonating her distant Kingston relative to keep outsiders away from the caves.

"The world's changed," Jackie says. "Your costumes and tricks worked thirty years ago, but nowadays every arsehole has a video camera and a hunger for fame."

Python concedes this is true with a shrug.

"You wouldn't dare," Sally-Ann says.

Jackie looks pleased with herself. "If you won't support my dreams, then I'll destroy the only thing you care about. Ha! Who's the loser now?"

It hits me. I know something about the dysfunctional bonds that holds families together while also tearing them apart. There have been times I've both loved and hated my mum; craved her attention and wanted to scream at her in equal measure.

"Wait, are you two related?" I ask.

Both women sneer at me. "That primped-up fool over there is my granddaughter," Sally-Ann says.

"All of this — you were trying to get back at your grandmother?"

"She's been putting me down my whole life," Jackie cries. "Laughing at my ambitions, telling me I'll never make it. But I proved her wrong. I did it!"

"Except your show is being cancelled," Sally-Ann sniggers. "No one watches it."

"Millions of people watch it. And it's not being cancelled. This episode is going to make everything better again. You'll see. You'll all see."

Sally-Ann blows a raspberry. "Oh please. No amount of make-up can hide the truth about you. You were a failure when you lived here, and you're a failure now."

"Wow. You're so mean," Python says. "No wonder Jackie went all murdery."

"Call me a failure again," Jackie whispers.

"Faily, faily, failure," Sally-Ann sings.

Jackie howls and runs at her grandmother, the cleaver glinting in the lantern light.

I grab Veronica by the arm. "Run," I shout.

Liam half-hops, half-trips towards the tunnel. I stagger into walls while a drum in my head throws me off course with noisy thumps of pain. Python's hyperventilating and Veronica's crying, so neither does much running. We're a useless bunch and I'm pretty sure that, if this was a horror – and it's rapidly turning out to be one – then none of us would survive.

There are screams and shrieks in the cave behind us. Splashing as the two women tussle in the water. We move along the tunnel as fast as we can, trying to put as much space between us and cleavered-up Jackie as possible.

"Where's Ben?" says Liam.

"I don't know," I pant.

Behind us, the screaming stops. I don't want to think what that means. And then comes the clicking of Jackie's one heel on stone, and the whisper of her hem as it drags on the ground.

"Where are you, little shitheads?" her voice calls, echoing through the tunnel. "I'm going to make you all wish you'd never been born."

"Quick, in here," Liam says, shoving us into a cave off to the side.

"No, not this way," Veronica says.

But there's no time to plan our route. Jackie's getting closer. It really is a horror. It sounds like she's walking at a leisurely pace, only she's catching up with us so fast. We hide behind a large rock. A thought hits me. Jackie's a Kingston. *She's* the last living relative of the Puckered Maiden.

"You need me. Or do you all want to die?" she taunts, pacing past the tunnel.

"Oh my god," Python hisses.

Her footsteps stop. "I can hear you in there, Python," Jackie says. "Come out and I'll make sure the whole world knows what you did."

"Um, doesn't she mean *or*?" he says.

"Like the world is going to listen to you," I yell. "Your grandmother is right. Your show's failing and even killing us on camera can't save it."

"Don't tempt me, Lex."

"Can we stop taunting the murderous reality TV producer?" Liam says.

Jackie steps into the cave, lit up by her head torch, holding the meat cleaver aloft like a BAFTA award. "This show is going to make me famous," she says. "No one cancels Jackie Stone."

Python closes his eyes and takes a deep breath. Then he steps out from behind the rock. I reach out to grab him, but I'm too slow. The rest of us peer out as he moves forwards to face Jackie. She stops. Folds her arms.

"You've decided to listen to sense, have you?" she snaps.

317

Python raises the diary cam above his head. "I'll throw it into the lake. I will. And you can say goodbye to your show."

Jackie pales. "Let's calm down," she purrs. "I can make you famous."

"I just want you to let my friends go."

He gestures for us to move, jerking his head towards the opposite side of the cave, where there's a tunnel leading who knows where. "Go," he says. "Get out of here."

I edge past him, keeping my eyes firmly on Jackie. Liam drags a stunned and still-crying Veronica.

"Come on," Liam says, pulling at her arm. "She's not going to hurt you."

Jackie frowns and glances at the cleaver in her hand like she's only just noticing it. "I'm not the baddie here," she says.

"Shut up or I'll throw it," Python says. "And kick that knife towards me."

She does what she's told, never looking away from the camera. "Now pass me the camera, Python, and we'll talk it out."

But we're done listening to her. I splash my way through shallow water towards a tunnel at the back of the cave. Python picks up the cleaver and backs away from Jackie, still holding the camera aloft. I don't take my eyes off her, but she doesn't budge.

We're nearly at the tunnel. It feels like everything is moving in slow motion, which it kind of is. One foot in front of the other. Liam helping Veronica. Python slowly edging away from Jackie. My brain churning around in my skull. And then I trip on something in the water.

FORTY-FIVE

Veronica lets out a brief, anguished cry and squeezes her eyes closed. I wish I'd looked away, too. The thing I tripped on was a boot. And that boot's attached to a leg protruding from behind a rock. The water around it swirls with blood.

"No," Liam gasps. "Please, no."

Ben is lying in the shallows, his arms above his head like someone hastily dragged him out of sight. In the light from Liam's head torch, his skin is bluish-white. He doesn't look real.

Python reaches us. He's still holding up the diary cam like he might throw it, his arm shaking. Jackie limps to the edge of the water and watches us with narrowed eyes.

"Why Ben?" Liam cries. "What did he do to you?"

"Go," I say, pulling Liam away from Ben's body. "We need to get out of here."

We stagger into the tunnel. My heart thunders far too fast, and the blood rushing through my head makes my thoughts spin.

Jackie's picking us off, one by one. Marla, Abbie, Ben. She tried to kill me, too. Did Veronica's tussle with Sally-Ann scare her off before she could finish the job, or was it sheer luck that I survived? Mum always said I have a thick skull.

Only ... something doesn't add up, and I can't get my thoughts to stay still long enough to work it out. The memories are swimming around in my head and I can't make sense of them.

Unless ... I stagger and have to steady myself on the wall.

"Lex?" Veronica says. Her eyes are terrified and full of tears.

"We need to keep moving," Liam says. He loops an arm around me, despite the fact he needs the support far more than I do. Because it's not my headache that made me stop. The pain is easing off and I'm starting to get this sneaking suspicion we have it all wrong.

"This way," Python says, calling back to us. "Quick, before she catches up."

I glance back over my shoulder. Jackie appears at the mouth of the tunnel, weighed down by her wet dress.

"The lake's this way," Veronica whispers. "The way out of the caves."

"What direction do we go?" Liam says.

Veronica doesn't answer straight away. It's like she's torn between wanting to escape and her fear of returning to the place that's haunted her nightmares for all this time.

"You can do this," Python says. "You're stronger than you think."

She wipes tears from her eyes. "You're right. I have to."

Liam pulls off his head torch and passes it to her. "Go. Show us the way."

Veronica swallows and nods. She leads us through a narrow crack and out into a low tunnel. She trails her fingers along the walls like she's feeling her way in the dark. It feels like atonement to me. Veronica leading us to safety when she couldn't save Laurie.

Only something's wrong. I stop again. What am I missing?

I go back to the beginning. Jackie set the whole show up around Laurie's death – Liam's determination to find his sister's final resting place and Abbie's desperation to prove that her father's conspiracy theories were something worth abandoning his family for. The plan was for the whole sordid story to play out on film and save her series.

She faked the safety surveys, all because she wanted to bring the show to her grandmother's doorstep. If she couldn't win Sally-Ann's respect, then she'd have her revenge by turning the caves into a supernatural tourist destination. But something went wrong.

The generator either malfunctioned or was sabotaged by

someone who wanted to stop the show. It gave Jackie the perfect opportunity to drag a reluctant Ben and Veronica into play, under the guise of a rescue mission that never was. Then, instead of getting us out, Jackie desperately tried to push the show forwards, even after the cave-in left us trapped.

All of that I'm clear on. What remains hazy is why Jackie decided to start murdering us. The only explanations I can come up with are the victims saw her using the secret tunnels or overheard her arguing with her grandmother, and realized she was up to something. Or perhaps she simply thought it would boost ratings if someone actually died.

But . . .

"Lex, come on," Liam says.

I give up trying to understand Jackie's motivations and catch up with Liam. Together, we stagger down the tunnel. Veronica picks up speed as we near our destination while Liam and I grow slower and slower. Python hurries at Veronica's heels as the tunnel twists and turns. When we lose sight of them, I take out my mostly-dead key-ring torch to light our way.

We reach a fork in the path. Everything has gone quiet.

"Veronica? Python?" I call.

For a second, I think we've lost them. My torch flickers off.

Then Veronica appears beneath an arch of rock. "Down here," she says.

We follow her into a high-ceilinged cavern. We're

standing on a raised walkway that looks down on a lake from which jagged rocks protrude like obelisks. There's a stony beach area to one side, reached by steplike formations on the other side of the cave.

The water is so dark. I can't imagine diving in like Veronica did and expecting it to lead me out to safety. It feels like the lake could only lead you deeper into the heart of the caves, right down into the centre of the Earth.

"Where's Python?" Liam asks.

"Over there," Veronica says, pointing ahead along a narrow walkway. "He's waiting for us."

Liam heads down the path. I hesitate. That nagging feeling again. Something doesn't add up.

I rewind the past hour in my head. A strike to the back of the head. The Puckered Maiden who wasn't. Jackie stalking us through the caves, cleaver in hand. Ben, lying dead. Following Veronica deeper into darkness. No, too far. I rewind again. I find the memory I'm looking for. Ben, lying dead. Jackie watching from the shore, her dress stiff and dry.

Her dress wasn't wet.

And there it is. Jackie couldn't have killed Ben and dragged his body into that shallow lake. And if she didn't kill Ben, then who did?

I look up at Veronica, noticing for the first time that she's holding the cleaver that Python took from Jackie. No way. Shy, sweet, strange Veronica. The girl I thought was my friend.

"This isn't the way out of the caves, is it?" I whisper.

Veronica's mouth twitches into a bitter smile. "No, Lex, it isn't. This is where she is. This is where Laurie died."

And then she flicks off her torch and everything goes dark.

FORTY-SIX

Extract from the transcript of local source telephone interview with Veronica Sanderson [VS], pre-show research for *It's Behind You: Season 3, Episode 10 (Umber Gorge Caves)*. Interviewed by Jackie Stone [JS], producer of *It's Behind You*.

JS: Veronica? Hi. My name's Jackie. I'm a producer with *It's Behind You*. Have you seen the show?

VS: Um. The odd episode, I guess.

JS: I wanted to let you know that we're going to be recording an episode of *It's Behind You* in the Umber Gorge caves and —

VS: What? No. Those caves are closed off. And for a good reason.

JS: The accident two years ago, you mean? I gather you were involved. That must have been hard for you. And hard for poor Liam, too. Laurie Cox's brother?

VS: How do you know Liam? Is he ... does he have something to do with the show?

JS: Why would you think that? I mean, I can't imagine he'd want to return to the caves where his sister died. He'd need a very good reason, don't you think? [Laughing] One of our contestants is called Liam, actually. But he's Liam West, not Cox.

VS: What? No, that's –

JS: Anyhoo, the reason I was calling is to find out if you'd be interested in working with my team when we come to Umber. After all, you must know those caves better than most. A friend of yours – Ben Brennan – has already agreed to help out.

VS: Ben's going to work for you?

JS: Between you and me, I suspect he wants to keep an eye on us TV people and make sure we don't send our poor, unsuspecting contestants into the unstable section of the caves where you were trapped.

VS: No one can go into that part of the caves. It's ... it's too dangerous!

JS: Don't worry. I wouldn't dream of digging up any bad memories for the town, even if it would make exceptional television. Exceptional.

VS: I've got to go.

JS: Of course, Veronica. Do give my love to Ben, won't you? And Liam.

FORTY-SEVEN

Liam cries out, then immediately falls silent. A second later, I'm shoved off balance. I skitter at the edge of the walkway. I grab out for something to hold on to and find gauzy petticoats. Veronica. If I'm going down, then she's coming with me. I give her dress a hard yank as I fall.

The drop is less than a metre. All the same, the rocks at the bottom knock the wind out of me. I roll over and over, skidding down a slope that must lead to the water. Veronica lands half a second after me. My foot connects with her as we tumble downward, and she cries out in pain. Good.

I slump to a halt with my arm in the cold lake. "Seriously?" I gasp. "You?"

It's hard to take it all in. I feel like I've been punched in the heart. How can Veronica be a killer? She's so . . . nice.

"No one can know what happened. It would ruin everything." She turns on her head torch, but only to the red light that bathes just a few metres of the cave in a faint glow.

She throws herself at me and I barely duck aside in time. The cleaver chinks off the stones close to where my head was. I kick her hard in the belly. She grunts and lands heavily on her back.

"It was you all along. You killed all those people," I say, clutching my ribs. Talking makes it hard to breathe, but saying it out loud makes the truth feel more real. Veronica's been behind everything. I got her so, so wrong.

"I never wanted to hurt anyone, Lex. Laurie's death was an accident, I swear. I'm a good person!"

She's pleading for me to believe she's not a murderer, while trying to murder me. Unbelievable.

I fumble in my pocket for my key-ring torch. It comes on but there's hardly any power left. I scrabble back up the rocky slope down which we rolled. Pebbles skitter under my feet. I jump and cling on to the edge of the raised path, but searing pain slices through my side and I have to let go. Instead, I stagger around the edge of the lake.

I nearly trip over Python. He's lying at the foot of the raised walkway, clutching his leg. It's clearly broken.

"Python, oh my god!" I kneel beside him. My torch has faded to a watery beam that makes him look like he's fading out of existence.

"Get out of here," he gasps.

I glance over my shoulder. Veronica is chasing me, but she's skidding on the slope.

"Go," he repeats, gritting his teeth against the pain.

I nod. At best, I can lead her away from him.

"There's no point running. I know these caves and your torch is failing," Veronica says, her voice cracking with tears. She makes it to the top of the slope and stalks towards me at an unhurried pace. She drags the cleaver along the wall with an awful screeching noise.

"How could you do this?" Python says. "We're your friends. Ben was your friend."

"I loved him and I know he loved me, but he couldn't see past Laurie," she replies.

"Is that why you killed her? So he'd be with you instead?" I say, struggling to catch my breath as I crawl over the uneven rocks.

"It wasn't like that! After the cave-in, Laurie was still so angry. She came in here and when I tried to tell her it was the wrong way, she called me a freak and I ... I pushed her down those steps over there. She didn't get up. I was so scared I'd be found out, so I weighed her body down with rocks and I rolled her into the water. It's fifty feet deep down there."

"If it really was an accident, you wouldn't have lied." I glance around, desperately scanning for a tunnel or alcove. My torch is barely lighting more than half a metre now. It won't be long until I'm completely in the dark.

"I couldn't let the truth come out, don't you understand? Ben would never have forgiven me," she says. "And can you imagine what people would have said? Poor Veronica. Pathetic, desperate Veronica."

"And you're not?"

"Shut up, you don't know me."

"Clearly not," I laugh painfully. "Of everyone here, I never had you pegged as a cold-blooded murderer."

"But I'm not! I gave you all so many chances to turn back. But Jackie kept finding a way to keep the show alive. She'd built the whole episode around Liam wanting to find his sister's body."

"And you needed to stop him." I duck into a low tunnel, but it's a dead end and I have to back out. I slip behind a cluster of stone columns and hide from Veronica's red beam.

"I tried to warn him against coming here," Veronica says. "He refused to listen. So I sabotaged the generators hoping the show would be cancelled. But even with half the power out and the electromagnetic lock on the door jammed, Jackie still refused to pull the plug. That's when I realized I'd have to come into the caves myself and make sure Liam didn't discover the truth."

Wow. The girl is cold. She came here fully intending to resort to murder if she couldn't stop the show. Suddenly, all the strange mishaps that befell us make sense.

"You were trying to kill Liam all along," I say. "Python's accident! You switched off your torch and tried to push Liam off that cliff along the Bone Road."

Python gasps. "And you pushed me by mistake!"

"And then you tried to crush me and Liam with that rock," I continue, "but Sally-Ann managed to warn us away by throwing pebbles at us."

"Sally-Ann has always suspected that there was more to what happened to Laurie. But she gets confused a lot, these days. Besides, she couldn't tell without admitting that she's been living down here in the caves and moving around using all her secret passageways."

I spot a tunnel across the cave. I don't think I can reach it, though. Not without Veronica and her cleaver catching up. Shit, my ribs and head hurt. My vision's getting hazy around the edges and all I want to do is lie down and sleep. I check Veronica's looking the other way, then run behind another rock to rest for a moment.

"Why did you kill the others?" Python shouts. I think he's trying to buy me time.

Veronica's torch turns towards Python. "When I first snuck into the caves, that cameraman caught me. He started asking all these questions and I just panicked. I picked up a rock and I hit him when his back was turned. He tried to get away from me, but I followed him and hit him again. And again. Then I had to wait until all of you were trapped in that locked room to get rid of his body."

Poor Cameraman Carl. My heart sags slightly. I'd hoped we were wrong about his disappearance.

"Marla was an accident, too," Veronica continues. "There's a secret passageway running from inside the boat ride tunnel that comes out near the laboratory cave. I knew that Laurie's stupid hat was going to give me away – I could remember her throwing it at Ben after the cave-in. I was going to sneak through to look for it, but Marla caught me. She started saying how an actress recognizes an actress, and that she knew I was up to something. So I had to stop her."

"And Abbie?" Python says.

I make myself move. I scuttle behind another rock and duck down. My torch fades. I bash it against my palm but it dies completely.

Veronica's red light bobs closer. "She kept asking me all these questions about Laurie and the Puckered Maiden. I couldn't keep track of my answers, but she was writing everything down. She made this comment about how proving the existence of the supernatural means disproving any possible human explanation, and then she asked where I was when Marla died."

"So you murdered her too, and then you murdered the boy you supposedly loved," Python says.

"I did love him! But he remembered how I'd not brought a torch with me the night Laurie died. He worked out that I couldn't have gone off by myself like I said."

That's it, then. Veronica killed Carl, then Marla, then Abbie, then Ben, and she tried to kill me, too. Maybe she thought I'd seen something that would link her to Ben's murder. Maybe she'd decided that we'd all have to die if she was going to keep her secret.

Maybe she's come to enjoy killing people and just can't stop.

She must realize where I'm hiding because her footsteps speed up. She taps the cleaver on every rock as she passes.

"You won't get away with this," Python shouts.

"Sure I will. Once you're dead, I'll go back for Jackie and Sally-Ann. I'll say you were all killed in the cave-in, and they'll believe me. Just like last time."

I grope my way across to another rock, digging my fingers into its cracked surface to keep me from collapsing. The tunnel out of the cave is ten metres away through the darkness, if I remember correctly. I'm so close.

Veronica chuckles softly and her footsteps approach. "Although I think I'll tell a different story with you, Lex," she says. "I'll say you survived the cave-in but you fell to your death as we tried to escape."

The clumsy sidekick. It's one thing to try to kill me, but besmirching my good name? This means war. *I'm* the star of this show, not Veronica. If I'm going out then it will be doing something awesome and memorable, even if there's going to be no one left to remember it.

I face the red glow that surrounds Veronica. Pulling on my last reserves of strength, I charge out of the darkness, screaming my own name. Is this a step too far? Who cares.

Veronica squeals in shock and jumps aside. I go down hard. I literally fly through the air, praying I land somewhere that doesn't hurt too much. Nope, it hurts. I

335

skid to a halt and lie there with my cheek pressed against the cold ground.

Veronica laughs in disbelief. "Jackie would be so proud," she sneers.

She paces towards me. Closer, closer. The red light finds me.

"Lex!" Python yells. "Lex, get up."

But it's too late for that.

Out of the corner of my eye, I see Veronica bend down and pull the cleaver back to strike.

"Veronica?" I say.

She hesitates. "Huh?"

"Who's the sidekick now?" I roll on to my back and kick her in the chest. She topples backwards down the rocky staircase – the same staircase where Laurie fell to her death.

There's a horrible crunch as she bounces off one of the rocks, followed by the clatter of metal. The torch beam flips over and over, then falls still. I can just make out Veronica's unmoving shape. She reminds me of the little puppet earring, dropped on the ground with its limbs splayed out in unnatural directions.

I lie back and this time when I pass out, I'm not faking.

FORTY-EIGHT

I wake up to a bright light flashing into my eyes. "Lex? Lex, wake up," says a voice. Liam's voice.

"Shall I try mouth-to-mouth?" Python says.

"Don't even think about it," I slur. I open one eye.

Liam looks terrible. He's clutching a heavily bleeding gash on his jaw that narrowly missed his neck. But he's not dead. Unless I'm dead too. And I'm fairly sure I wouldn't be in this much pain if I was dead.

I sit up carefully. My head throbs with every tiny movement; my side cries out with every breath. But all in all, I'm doing better than the others.

Python is competition with Liam for the person who looks closest to death. His leg injury is horrific, and he's hideously pale. He won't be swimming out of here, not that there's anyone left who knows where the lake is. I laugh and, after a few moments, Liam and Python join in. We're so screwed.

Python picks up the diary cam and presses record. "Hey, folks, it's Python here, reporting back from Umber Gorge caves and the set of *It's Behind You*. I never thought I'd say this, but I think I'm done with this show." He drops the camera and leans back against the wall.

A clicking-dragging noise approaches. Jackie, with Sally-Ann scurrying at her heels. She peers down at Veronica's broken body lying in the dark and wrinkles her nose. "I don't suppose you got any of it on film, did you?"

"I tried to warn you," Sally-Ann grumbles. "And you didn't listen."

"Because your warnings were the most cryptic bullshit I've ever heard! What is wrong with you people?" I say.

"The family's always been eccentric," Jackie admits. "My great-great-great-whatever-aunt became the Puckered Maiden, after all."

"You know what, I don't care any more," Liam says. "Please tell me one of you knows a way out of here."

"We're cut off," Sally-Ann says. "The only way out is through the lake your friend swam through last time. I'll show you."

We leave Python in the cave with Jackie to wait. Once the outside world knows there are survivors, they'll have to send in rescuers. As we follow Sally-Ann out of the cave, Jackie picks up the diary cam.

"So, Python, tell me how you feel," I hear her say.

"Well, Jackie, I'm not sure where to start . . ."

I shake my head and leave them to it. Liam hesitates at the edge of the cave. He stares down at the water. Not at Veronica, lying broken and bleeding, but at the final resting place of his sister.

"I thought I'd feel more," he says. "I thought discovering the truth would be like a weight lifting off me, but it isn't."

"What does it feel like?"

"Like I'm tired and hungry and I want to go home?"

I take his hand. "I'm sorry you can't take Laurie home with you."

He stares down at the water, then he smiles weakly. "Sure I can. All of this has made me realize maybe ghosts are real, after all. They're stories that have been told so many times, they've taken on a life of their own. They stay with you for ever, no matter where you go. Do you know what I mean?"

"I think I do," I say, and we turn our backs on the water and walk away. I imagine Laurie's ghost walking on his other side, made up of a thousand memories that gleam with a light of their own.

We're quiet for the short walk to the lake. Liam's broken ankle makes him grimace with every step. Sally-Ann finally leads us into a wide cavern. It looks a lot like the Echo Chamber. Half is bare mud and the other half is a shining expanse of water. It's peaceful, on the surface. But I know it hides underwater caves and passageways, one of which leads out to the real world. One of dozens.

Veronica was lucky to find it. Or maybe lucky isn't the right word. She came out the other side as someone else; someone who'd resort to murder to keep her secrets from being discovered. I'm not sure if she was always like that and it just took the caves to bring it out in her, or if this place changed her. Maybe it will change me, too.

"I'm a good swimmer," Liam says, noticing my worried expression. "I'll get out and I'll get help. The rescue team will be here within hours."

I nod slowly. "Yeah. Sure."

He unlaces his boots, gasping with pain as he releases his injured ankle. He reminds me of my mum, pretending to be brave because she thinks others need her to be. She's always the strong one. So when I hear her crying in her room after I'm in bed, I don't know what to do.

The truth is, the thought of losing my mum is the worst thing in the world. All this time, I believed I was scared of ending up like her, living a life that isn't perfect, potentially cut short. Instead, I'm scared I will have to live my own life without her in it, never measuring up to the person she is.

I'm not selfless, I'm not caring; I'm a terrible friend. I don't think I've ever done something for another person unless it benefitted me. Until now.

Now? I suddenly get it. When Mum cries, it's not because she's scared of dying and scared of what she hasn't achieved in her life. She's scared for me, and a little bit for Dad, too. Scared to leave us alone without her there to be the one who holds us all together and gets shit done.

I smile at the realization. I'm scared, but not for myself. For everyone who's relying on me.

I stand on tiptoes and kiss Liam on the lips. He's surprised enough that the head torch drops from his hand. Then he tentatively puts an arm around my waist and pulls me closer.

A long second later, I grin and step away. "You make me want to be a better person," I say, snatching up the torch before he can.

Liam stares at me in confusion. He gets it too late. By then, I'm already running for the water. I dive in as he shouts at me to stop. But this is our best chance of not dying. For the first time ever, I'm not doing something for attention or because it makes me look good. I'm a freaking hero and I don't even care if anyone else knows it.

The water swallows me up and it is so icy and so, so dark, even with the torch. My heart thunders at a million beats per minute. My muscles scream in pain. But if Veronica could do this – murderous little Veronica – then so can I. I kick hard with my legs as my lungs cry out for air.

There are a dozen narrow passageways down here and who knows where they lead. I take a few seconds to shine the torch down each, then I pick one. I can hold my breath for a minute, I reckon. Maybe longer if I have to. And there might be air pockets along the way. Who knows?

I kick harder, using my free hand to pull myself along on the rough walls of the tunnel. The torch is failing, and then the light is gone. I keep swimming as darkness swallows me up. It reminds me of something Mum said after the chemo left her so weak that I flinched when I held her hand, with its papery skin and sharp bones.

"This is all part of the adventure that's life," she said, kissing my hair and squashing my quiff. "And sometimes we have to find our way through the darkness to reach the light."

EPILOGUE

Extract from the transcript of live video stream hosted by Python42 [P]. ME, ME, ME!!!!!! Review of *It's Behind You: Season 3, Episode 10. ARRGHHHH!*

P: BABES! I am sooo HAPPY you're here with me. Today is the day you've been waiting for. The reason you're all here. The event of the CENTURY. Yes, I am finally ready to speak about the last EVER *It's Behind You* episode. The one where people DIED.

[Recorded cheering]

P: But first, ten seconds of dancing for our fallen friends.

[Music, shuffling sounds]

P: OK, enough of that. We'll be revisiting some of their best ever moments later and finding out more of their STORIES. But first, let's take a few questions from all you lovely people out there and then we'll watch a NEVER-before-seen clip from the episode.

P: Let me scroll through the questions. All right, here's one. Tom's asking if I think it's exploitative that the TV company made an episode even though real people died. Yes. Yes, I do. And yet here we all are. Here YOU are, Tom, driving by the car crash and craning your head to look. Next!

[Sound of screeching brakes]

P: Casey would like to know why Jackie isn't in prison. It's a good question. It turns out the law is sketchy when it comes to TV producers provoking contestants into killing each other. It's hard to prove and she covered her tracks well. I mean, she *deserves* to be in prison …

[Clanging sound of a door being closed]

P: Next up, Laura is asking how Sally-Ann escaped the caves, what with being ancient. Same way the rest of us did. A team of experienced rescue divers, breathing apparatus and a whole lot of guide ropes. She had it easy – unlike yours truly, whose

ENTIRE LEG was hanging by a thread. No, not really. But I do have metal pins holding me together so I'm basically half-robot.

[Beeping sound effects]

P: Lots of you are asking about the lovely Liam. What's his skincare routine, what music does he listen to, what's his favourite pizza topping. I can't answer any of those questions, but I *can* tell you that Liam is fine. He's gone off to university to study MATHS. I know, you'd never have guessed – but then none of you were paying attention to his personality, were you? PERVERTS.

[Wolf-whistling]

P: Next question. Martyn wants to know if I believe in ghosts. Nope, not any more. Like Abbie once told me, people are the scariest thing in this world.

[Spooky sound effects]

P: Amelie wants to know if my experience on the show changed me. Nope. No lessons have been learned, other than always carry a torch. And if it *had* changed me, I wouldn't be telling you lot. Because we don't watch reality TV for the truth, do we? Sex, humiliation and death, that's what you vultures want.

[Recorded laughter]

P: So what's next for me? As you know, I'm moving

on from this channel and I'll be hosting my own show on ACTUAL TELEVISION. I know, it's amazing. I'm going to be reviewing reality shows from around the globe. Baking competitions! Rich bitchy women arguing! People giving birth. Not sure about that one as I'm not great with blood, but the things I do for my FANS.

[Recorded applause]

P: All right, one more question and then I'll play a clip. I've saved this one for last. What happened to Lex Hazelton? Obviously the show left it up in the air whether she lived or died. So what do you think, people? Answer below in the comments. Did Lex's hubris finally see her DESTROYED – or is she out there somewhere, strutting around in a sharp suit and causing trouble?

[Jaunty music, cut off abruptly]

P: Oh, hang on, this new comment's a good one. SophiaK says: "What kind of stupid question is that?" And on that note, this is Python, signing off.

Acknowledgements

I'm proud of this book for reasons other than the words on the pages. At the start of 2020, I was looking forward to the release of my debut, preparing to have my second baby, and attempting to write the scary book two dreaded by many an author. And then came the … well, everyone knows what came next. This book proved to be my doorway into another world, through which I could briefly hide from the tough bits of 2020. I hope that it finds a few readers who enjoy escaping into its pages as much as I enjoyed writing it.

None of it could have happened without my partner Phill and his unwavering support. From taking the two small humans out for long walks so I could write, to being this story's biggest cheerleader. Phill, Eliza and Max are the best family I could ever hope for, and this book is dedicated to you all.

Huge thanks also go to my agent, Chloe Seager, and

my editor, Lauren Fortune, who saw the potential in this book and gave it a shove in the right direction. Thanks also to Genevieve Herr, Jamie Gregory, Jessica White, Pete Matthews, Rebecca Gillies, Ella Probert, Rachel Phillipps and everyone else at Scholastic who kept on being amazing as 2020 made everything so much more challenging.

A final thanks goes to all the people who probably don't know what a huge part they've played in making this book happen. The semi-strangers who've chatted to me online and helped keep me sane; the readers who've reached out to say that they loved *Good Girls Die First*; the other writers who've become my friends during what was a strange debut year. I can't wait to meet you in person one of these days.

THE NIGHT BEGAN WITH BLACKMAIL:
Eight o'clock. Portgrave Pier. Can you keep a secret?

Ten teenagers lured to a derelict carnival. Each one with a
dark past they are determined to keep hidden. As they start to
die, is it an unknown killer they need to fear ... or each other?

Mind games. Murder. *Mayhem.*

HOW FAR WOULD YOU GO
TO SURVIVE THE NIGHT?